FROM LIGHTNING TO LOVE

EVERNIGHT PUBLISHING ®

www.evernightpublishing.com

Copyright© 2019

Kory Steed

Editor: JC Chute

Cover Art: Jay Aheer

ISBN: 978-0-3695-0035-9

FROM LIGHTNING TO LOVE

DEDICATION

For Mark who was the first to love me for who I am and who continues to love me and believe in me. For his unwavering support and inspiration, for his insight into the written, spiritual, emotional, and physical language of love, and for his gentle guidance during the honing of this novel, I am forever grateful.

ACKNOWLEDGEMENTS

Before anyone else, I thank my partner, Mark, for his keen editorial eye and suggestions during the writing of my manuscript.

I owe special thanks to Erin Leaf, my beta reader, for her pointers on head hopping, her suggestions on the sequencing of scenes, and for her assistance in identifying the weaknesses in the first draft. Also, thank you, Erin, for allowing me to vent my frustrations about the writing process and for permitting me to challenge your suggestions which only allowed me to realize that you were right so many times.

To the many, many people and animals I have known over the course of my lifetime who have allowed me to love and care for them, who I have worked with professionally, or whom I have treated during my career, you have each touched my heart, left an indelible mark on my mind, or my soul. I have learned from you how to live my life, just as often as I have learned how not to, for you have inspired me to be a better person, a better friend, or a better healer. I hope this story does you and your memories justice.

To the Evernight Publishing family of authors and readers, who through their Facebook groups have been so welcoming and encouraging during the editing of my manuscript. Your words and stories have enlightened me, delighted me, and made me laugh, and I will never forget your support.

My heartfelt gratitude also goes out to my copy editor, Jane Chute, for all her hard work on my behalf, including her attention to detail and suggestions for dialogue.

Finally, to Evernight Publishing for believing in my story enough to take a chance on an unknown author.

I love you all,

Kory Steed

FROM LIGHTNING TO LOVE

The Lightning Series, 1

Kory Steed

Copyright © 2017

Prologue

Friday, September 4, 2009, 8:00 PM local time
        News crawl on television screens in Hinnen Valley, Idaho

"A small commuter plane has disappeared from radar over the Wasatch Range of the Rocky Mountains in southeastern Idaho. The last transmission from the pilot reported he was experiencing engine and electrical problems after being struck by lightning from a quickly developing thunderstorm. Tune in at 11:00 for more on this developing story."

Section One
Sky Fallen

Chapter One
Down to Ground

Sunday, September 6, 2009, 8:20 AM
Day Two

Jason was jarred awake, wincing against the bright spear of a cruel sunbeam that struck his eyes. Now high enough in the sky to penetrate the thickness of the forest canopy, the bright morning sun pierced the upper branches of the tall evergreens at just the right angle to enter the quiet darkness of his well-appointed, but disheveled, modern cabin through a thin slit between haphazardly pulled heavy drapes. It was well into morning, well past his normal rising time, but for very good reason.

Jason's head rested in his crossed arms on the handmade table he'd fashioned from timber he'd logged himself from the surrounding forest. It seemed that only moments had passed since he'd laid his head down, but that had been hours ago. Even before taking in his surroundings, Jason realized he was shaking, still rattled by his memories of the day and night before. Then he realized yesterday had been his thirty-seventh birthday.

"Oh, God, it's morning already," he whispered, remembering at the last moment the broken and battered form that slept in his comfortable king-sized bed behind the makeshift curtain not ten feet away. He'd had just enough strength left to stretch a rope between two of the cabin's vertical supporting posts and sling a blanket over it before exhaustion overtook him. He'd have to be careful not to make any noise—so accustomed to living by himself for the past eleven years, he rarely thought of another person at all. Any noise he had made in the past was only his noise, for there was no one else around to hear, not for miles and miles.

He blinked against the sun, looking for the hands of the antique grandfather clock that stood against the wall across the room. It was one of the few things he'd brought with him from his past, but it was so large, he had to have it airlifted to his remote, well-fortified home by helicopter. Set deep within the confines of the end of the Wasatch Range in the Bear River Mountains of Idaho, he lived quite alone—or he had, until yesterday.

Fortunately, he'd silenced the clock's deep, resonating chimes within a few hours after he first set it up. At the time, the last thing he needed was to be reminded on the quarter-hour of the time as it passed. Though he had disconnected the chimes, he'd come to appreciate the slow, soft tick-tock, tick-tock, tick-tock of the clock's internal mechanisms, as they paced the heavy brass pendulum to sway to and fro. It was doubtful, though, that even the chimes could have woken the cabin's other occupant. Not after yesterday.

Though he was briefly annoyed with himself for having slept so late, Jason realized after all he'd done the day before, he really needed the sleep. If the clock had chimed, he wouldn't have slept at all, and little did he know, those past few hours were the last real sleep he'd get for a long, long time.

His stomach grumbled. *Did I even eat yesterday?* he thought. It grumbled again. *When did I eat last?* His belly squealed in protest. *Now I remember: I had a full breakfast of flapjacks, fried eggs, and smoked longhorn before heading out the front door.*

He looked around the common area of the cabin. His trauma kit lay open next to a bucket of cold, bloody water and wrappers from dressings and bandages formed one of several piles of debris. Next to it was another pile of shorn off, bloodied and sap-covered, tattered clothing and a pair of high-top sneakers bearing the name of what he assumed was some celebrity athlete he'd never heard of. Between them were pieces of pine branches and needles.

It didn't look like his home at all. It was more akin to the trauma bay of a MASH unit at the edge of a war zone in the moments right after shuttling off the latest wave of casualties to the OR. That was a better description.

****

Saturday, September 5, 2009, 6:40 AM
Day One

Jason left the security of his cabin to assess what damage the storm from the night before had ravaged on the peacefulness of his mountain home. Sitting high atop an incline, the cabin was set far enough from the base of the eastern ridge of high mountains to avoid the rock slides that thundered down its face on occasion. The heavily fortified, twenty foot, razor-wire-topped and electrified stockade that surrounded his cabin protected him from bears, cougars, and wolves, but not Mother Nature. He checked the barn: everything was fine. Nellie and Sarah, his donkeys. Heather, the nanny goat, and her mate, Jasper were all standing at the gates to their stalls waiting to be fed, and the chickens were pecking peacefully around the small, coarsely manicured lawn that lay just beyond the barn's main door. The smokehouse, root cellar, and water well also checked out fine and what remained of his cabbages in his vegetable garden had fared pretty well, too. He was sure the potatoes and carrots had been well protected under the ground by the tall-grass mulch he'd piled there, but he checked them anyway. The yard's grass had grown to above mid-thigh level, so he made a mental note to let Nellie, Sarah, Heather, and Jasper out to graze so they could work it down to a manageable height.

Before he inspected the roof, Jason quickly fed and watered the animals, collected five eggs, and milked Heather. He left the stall gates and barn door open and carried the milk and the eggs to the kitchen, then washed the eggs and poured the milk into a bottle and then put them in the fridge. With the eggs and milk taken care of, he went back out to the side of the cabin to get his ladder to check the satellite dish, windmill, and solar panels on the roof. He'd be without Internet and phone service if the dish was damaged, and his large bank of batteries that supplied most of his electricity wouldn't last more than a few days if they weren't kept constantly charged. He'd never used even a fraction of the heating oil from the underground tank for his backup furnace and diesel generator, but he didn't want to have to put them into service.

It wasn't likely anyone would think of him or even know of his troubles, but that was his own fault. He'd distanced himself so far from society, only his attorney, financial manager, and the company he'd contracted with to helicopter in supplies twice a year even knew where he was. It wouldn't be for another two months or so before he received his next shipment or any contact with the outside world.

Jason began to climb the ladder, but was stopped short just below the roof's edge by a glint that caught the corner of his eye. That's when he saw it: a limp human form hanging from parachute cords that were tangled in a tall evergreen just outside the stockade, some twenty feet off the ground. Forgetting his reason for going to the roof, he hurried up the last four rungs to get a better look. From his vantage point he couldn't tell if it was breathing, but it certainly wasn't moving on its own, just swaying in the gentle breeze with the sun reflecting off the links between the cords and risers. There was only one way to find out.

As he turned around to head back down the ladder, he noticed that only the mount for the satellite dish was attached to the roof. When he ran over to it, he saw that the dish had been completely ripped off its housing and was left partially hanging by its cable over the far edge of the roof. The impact caused half of the dish's bowl to cave in on itself and the receiver module was in pieces on the ground.

"Fuck!"

Then he remembered the solar panels and windmill. He ran up and over the roof's peak to check them on the southern exposure. They were all intact, but the panels were partially covered by debris. He quickly threw off the broken evergreen branches and used his hands to brush away the needles and leaves that had accumulated. At least he'd have lights and electricity, but there was no way to contact the outside world.

Jason hit the ground running and headed to the barn where he pulled out the eight-foot wagon he'd built. He fitted Nellie and Sarah with their collars and harnesses and hooked them to the wagon. Built to haul supplies and the logs he'd felled from the forest into the confines of the stockade, he hoped it wouldn't be hauling a corpse this morning.

Nellie was a rare donkey indeed. She was gentle, and she loved Jason. She'd known him from the day she was born. He'd raised her all alone since she was orphaned at seven months, after her mother had been killed by a large male cougar some nine years ago while she tried to protect her daughter. While Nellie's physical scars from the attack had faded, she still carried emotional ones, but they weren't strong enough to dim her dedication to Jason. She'd do anything for him, and she always enjoyed pulling the wagon.

Sarah, her daughter, had been born in the spring three years ago. She'd been sired by artificial insemination from a specimen Jason had purchased through the veterinarian who choppered in to see the animals twice a year. Though she also loved Jason, Sarah had a mind of her own and during her early years, balked at his requests to do any kind of work. She'd tested the limits of Nellie's patience until she reached the age of three. It was Jason's diligence and even-tempered manner with her that eventually won out. Since then, she'd calmed down quite a bit.

Once they were hitched, Jason led Nellie and Sarah to the cabin where he loaded two blocks and tackle, extra ropes, carabiners, ascenders, his helmet, gloves, climbing spikes, and his climbing harness into the wagon. He also loaded his emergency medical kit, some heavy corrugated splints, and the canvas army stretcher he'd procured before he left the army, from the cabin's storage room. If the body in the tree was alive, it would need first aid at the very least.

By the time Jason had led the girls out around the stockade and over to the tree below what he could now see was a male figure, a good thirty-five minutes had passed, and he still wasn't moving. Jason tied Nellie and Sarah to the trunk of the tree to the right and put on all his climbing gear. He tied one end of a two-hundred-foot coil of climbing rope to a tree trunk to the left, just below a protruding limb stump that was close to the ground. He threaded the other end through the pulleys of the blocks and then tied it off to himself. He attached the blocks to a carabiner on the right side of his harness and his medical kit and another fifty-foot rope coil to a carabiner on his left. Once he had all his gear, he began to climb the tree.

Jason tied off his safety line to the tree trunk once he reached the guy. Now he could see that he was breathing, but he realized the medical kit would be of no use. There was no way he could have done anything for him so far above the ground and so precariously suspended from frayed parachute cords.

The guy was hanging in the air with his head just below a branch about four feet out from the trunk. The parachute's cords were tangled through some of the branches on the same limb, and they were snagged and tangled through higher limbs until they reached what remained of the shredded parachute about twenty more feet up. Many of the cords had snapped, probably from a combination of the stress of the impact and fraying by the sharp ends of branches that had broken. He estimated the guy had a good fifty pounds on him, so he considered his next move carefully.

Jason examined the limb to determine whether it was sound. Slowly he shifted his entire weight to the limb and gently bounced up and down to test it. There was no reaction at all from the guy. Although the limb itself felt and appeared to be solid, Jason thought better of climbing out on it unsecured, so he attached one of the blocks to the trunk above his head before looping a length through his chest carabiner and let out enough of his safety line to stop him and the guy short of the ground should they fall. After retying the rope to himself, he planted his feet against the trunk and carefully lowered himself down with the safety line so he was hanging horizontally right in front of the guy.

He reached out and threaded the tackle's remaining length of rope at his chest carabiner through the parachute's cord links and tied the rope off between them. Then he added the guy to his safety line through his carabiner. If the guy fell, Jason would fall right along with him, but there was no other way to get him down.

He lifted the guy's helmet visor so he could see his face. "Hey buddy, you in there?" There was no response, but Jason was momentarily taken aback by the stunningly handsome face that had been concealed by the visor. The guy was breathtaking. He had a chiseled chin, a cosmopolitan nose, high cheek bones, and dirty blond, short-cropped hair. *What a looker!* he thought to himself. No sooner had the words crossed his mind, then he remembered why he was there and got back to work.

He checked the guy's harness. It was secure and intact with no evidence of damage to the hardware or straps that looped between and around his thighs and butt. Jason transferred his weight to the tackle line and, while bracing himself with his safety line, took up the tackle line's slack between himself and the guy and refastened the line to himself. While holding on tight to the ground line with his left hand, Jason took out his ten-inch Bowie knife from the sheath in his harness and cut what remained of the parachute's cords.

Together, they dropped six feet while the rope pulled through the pulleys. When he felt the sharp tug of the rope as it pulled taught, Jason tried to let out the tackle's ground line at a rate that allowed him and the guy to slowly glide down. Though he did his best to slow their descent, the guy hit the ground with more of a thud than the gentle stop he'd intended, but at least he was down.

Jason quickly dropped to his feet, unhooked himself from the lines, and removed his harness, gloves, and helmet. He opened his medical kit and untied the ropes that were fastened to the guy's harness before he began to examine him. He was fairly certain the guy didn't have a cervical spine injury because he could still hear him breathing, but he checked his reflexes anyway––thankfully, they were intact. If the guy had snapped his neck, it would have happened from his crash landing through the tree and the sudden stop. There was no way Jason could have stabilized him all by himself while at the same time winching him down the twenty feet to the ground. If he didn't have a fractured spine after all that, he likely didn't have one at all.

When he carefully removed the guy's helmet, he found a thick clot of blood inside the padded back lining that came from a deep, long laceration at the back of his scalp. Jason opened a sterile dressing and pressed it against the laceration and secured it with a roll of gauze. Then he immobilized the guy's neck with towels and cravats. He also found a fracture of his right forearm and left lower leg, and his left ankle was twisted outward at a gruesome angle, but the foot had a good, strong pulse. There were lacerations all over his body with twigs and small pine branches imbedded in more places than he could count, and he was cold, very cold. It was likely that he was hypothermic as a result of hanging while wet from the rain in the wind high above the ground.

"This guy's fucked."

Jason ran to the wagon and hoisted the canvas stretcher over the side and then grabbed the splints. Quick and dirty, he immobilized the guy's arm and leg with the splints and wrapped them with the attached cloth straps to keep his limbs from falling out when he moved him to the stretcher. He opened the stretcher next to the guy and rolled him away while bracing the stretcher against his back. Then he rolled him back and shimmied his body to its center.

With three canvas straps, Jason secured him to the stretcher and then led Nellie and Sarah to back the wagon up close to the guy's head. He released the latch that secured the wagon's bed and tilted it down to the ground. He then shifted and lifted the stretcher onto the tailgate. As he climbed up into the wagon's bed, Jason braced one boot on each side and hoisted the stretcher up, slowly making his way further up and back. He repeated brace, pull, brace, pull, brace, pull until the stretcher was nearly up to the headboard. Then he secured the stretcher to the bed with a length of rope and tilted it down until the latch snapped closed. He'd return for the block and tackle and ropes later.

After leading Nellie and Sarah through the stockade's great door, he locked it, then led them up to the cabin where they backed the wagon up to the porch before he chocked the wheels. Fortunately, he'd built the wagon bed to the same height as the porch floor to make it easier to unload supplies. While he unhitched the girls, and removed their collars and harnesses, he was already running down a checklist in his mind of what might need to be done for the guy—but he knew, with trauma, you can never know for sure what you'll find. While he tended to the guy, the girls could roam free within the confines of the stockade until he had time to get back to them.

In view of his head injury, Jason didn't want to do anything that could increase the guy's intracranial pressure, so he lifted the foot of the stretcher just high enough to get a good grip and pulled it off the wagon and onto the porch. After bracing the front door open, he lifted and dragged the stretcher and its occupant, head first, into the center of the main room next to his table and got to work.

After closing the door, he went straight to the kitchen sink and turned on the faucet, adjusting the water to as hot as he could stand. Sterility was all but impossible out here, but he scrubbed his arms, hands, and fingers over and over again for all they were worth with brown soap and a brush to remove as much dirt and pine sap as possible. Then he made hot water bottles with a dozen, sealable, one-gallon freezer bags and wrapped them in hand towels.

He pulled out all his medical equipment and supplies from his well-stocked storage room including gloves and suturing materials, syringes, bactericidal ointments, medications, dressing and bandages, a heavy cotton blanket, and all his wooden and metal splinting hardware and set them up on the table. Over the eleven years he'd lived alone, he'd acquired quite a hoard, with nearly as varied a supply as that of a rural medical clinic. Being wealthy certainly had its advantages, as did having an old army doctor friend who could order whatever he needed or wanted.

First things first. As he leaned down to pack the guy's body with the homemade hot water bottles and cover him with the blanket to keep him warm, Jason smelled urine and feces. That would have to be the last thing he'd take care of. He worked quickly and efficiently, his training from years before kicking in, and examined the guy from head to foot, being careful to just uncover the parts he was evaluating and then immediately cover them back up to keep in the heat. Jason listened to his lungs with his stethoscope. They were clear, so at least for now, pneumonia wasn't setting in.

The triage complete, Jason prioritized his care and, moving from injury to injury, treated each to the best of his ability and within the limits of his supplies.

He had to cut away clothing and shave away many areas of hair that were clumped with blood or tree sap to expose each wound as he moved carefully over his body.

By the time Jason had finished, the guy didn't have a stitch of clothing left and many of his heavily haired areas were bald. The guy never moved a muscle or let out a single moan of pain while Jason cleaned, debrided, and sutured his numerous wounds, several of which also required drains. Nor did he cry out when Jason set his bones.

He had no idea whether the guy would make it, but he'd done everything in his power to save him. After he turned him over to clean where he'd soiled himself, Jason took a chance and injected all two million units of penicillin he had on hand into his butt, but it was, in his opinion, worth the risk. The guy wasn't wearing a medical alert bracelet, and there were simply too many sources of infection. To delay treatment with antibiotics could prove fatal.

Once finished, Jason briefly uncovered him to expose his body. He looked him up and down, top to bottom, and front to back to be sure he hadn't missed anything. Then it hit him. Up until that moment, other than seeing his face in the tree, he'd never looked at the guy as an entire person. He was really just a kid, no older than his early twenties, Jason estimated, and he was in shape. *God, like a brick shit house, he's in shape.*

"Good God, and he's sculpted!" he exclaimed aloud, noting the perfect contouring and trim job that had been done on what remained of his barely half-inch pubes. He sported the full athletic sculpting style but with a slightly smaller wedge.

Whoever created this masterpiece really highlighted his exquisite package to its maximum. Even his shaft is clean shaven. And look at those balls! They're

*like huge, hairless globes. And his chest and belly hair …
It's been trimmed to a quarter-inch. This kid certainly
knows how to manicure and display his assets to their
best, that's for sure.*

Then he came to his senses. *Jesus Christ, Jason,
shut up! Shut the fuck up! Don't even think it! That's
totally inappropriate.*

At least the kid had youth on his side. Jason
hadn't seen a body this well-developed since the GIs
he'd treated back during the Gulf War. But this kid was
fortunate in one way: he lacked the hardened face that
only came with battle. As breathtaking as he was, his
face was soft, beautiful really, in an All-American-Boy
kind of way, but his body, his body was the epitome of
masculinity, and he was lying there right in front of
Jason.

Jason's loins began to surge. He could easily
reach out and … *Fuck! Fuck! Fuck! Knock it off! He's
just a kid, Jason. He's just a kid, and he's completely
dependent on you for his survival. He's your patient now,
and he'll remain so, until he either dies or survives and
makes it back to civilization. There can never be
anything between you. Never.*

He had no idea who the kid was, where he came
from, or what he did, but that wasn't important right
now. If it was meant for Jason to learn his identity, he
would, in time. Right now, the kid was fighting for his
life.

After dragging him across the floor on the
stretcher, Jason grabbed several large plastic trash bags
from the supply room and laid them out on the bed. Then
he covered them with bath towels to catch any wound
drainage. He hung his stethoscope above the headboard
and then lifted the stretcher into his own king-sized bed,
slid the kid off it, and covered him up with a sheet and

blanket. Then he took the water bags and refilled them with fresh hot water, rewrapped them in extra pillowcases from the closet, and stuck them along the kid's entire body, under his armpits, on his groin, and between his legs just under his scrotum.

Jason hadn't used the wood stove in the center of the cabin since the spring, but it was closer to the bed and it would help to keep the kid warm. He took some coals from the kitchen stove and started a fire in it, adding some thin log splinters for kindling. They caught almost immediately, so he added a split log and then two more a few minutes later.

Finally finished with all he could do, Jason looked at the hands on the clock. It was half past two in the morning. The last thing he remembered was lying his head down on the table, convinced that he just needed to rest his eyes for a minute.

Chapter Two
The Smell Of Pine

Sunday, September 6, 2009, 8:22 AM
Day Two

"God, do I have to pee!" Jason's prostate was throbbing, and his dick was so hard there was no way he could bend it to piss in the toilet. His bladder felt like it was going to explode, but before he took care of that, he had to check on the kid.

He peeked around the makeshift curtain and found him asleep with the bedsheet and blanket tangled up into a ball by his right foot and the water bags scattered around the bed. He reached down and collected the now cold bags and then straightened the sheet and blanket and covered him up. He put the bags in the sink and quickly tiptoed out through the kitchen, gently closing the screen door and headed to the side of the porch.

As soon as they heard the screen door creak, Nellie and Sarah began to bray and Jasper started bleating for their breakfast, but Heather, Heather's bleating was shrill. "Oh, God. The poor girl! She's gonna bust if I don't get her milked, and like now."

Jason quickly pulled his thickly-veined eight inches from his fly and let it rip. His golden stream moved pebbles as it rushed down the hill beside the cabin. By the time he'd completely emptied himself, it had traveled some twenty feet away. While his bladder emptied, his erection subsided as the blood eased from the shaft. He tucked it back into his pants and hurried back into the kitchen to wash his hands, then he ran to the barn.

Though Jason knew he had let Nellie and Sarah roam free, from the looks of things there was no evidence any of the animals had ever left the barn. Nellie, Sarah, and Jasper stood in their stalls, but Heather was pacing next to the milking table, shaking, and there was milk streaming from both udders. He didn't even have to bribe her with oats. As soon as she saw him, she jumped up onto the table. By the time he'd finished, she'd given up just shy of three quarts. She hopped down and gave him a good, strong butt in his rump as if to say, "What took you so long?" and "Don't do it again!"

He scratched Heather's head and apologized for the delay, then tossed some sweet grass and extra feed into the trough. Nellie, Sarah, and Jasper pitched in and helped her finish it. With the milk and six new eggs in tow, he made his way back to the cabin, wondering where the day would lead.

As he reentered the cabin, Jason was struck by the strong smell of pine. No, not pine, pine sap. Pine was a normal smell—it was everywhere up here in the mountains, but it was subtle, and even less so inside his cabin. The kid's body and clothing had been covered in the thick gooey stuff from all the branches he'd broken as he fell through the tree.

Jason was sure, there was still some sap remaining in several deep lacerations and the through-and-through penetrating wounds he'd suffered from branches that superficially pierced his limbs and had imbedded themselves in his torso. But that wasn't all. He also had bleeding from his broken bones and all his wounds, and that could do him in. Infections in his wounds could, also… Infections that traveled to his fractures could do him in. Or any combination of them could do him in. The worst of all though was the jagged, deep gash on the back of his head. There was no puncture through the kid's helmet so it could only have come from the sheer force of the impact, like dropping a watermelon onto the sidewalk. Jason had cleaned it out, put in a drain, and sutured it closed—but it was the possibility of an internal brain injury that really had him worried. Minimally, he had a concussion and a bad one at that, because he still hadn't regained consciousness.

Jason didn't know when the kid would wake up or even be able to eat, but he realized he'd have to eat himself in order to keep up his own strength while he cared for him. If the kid survived and woke up no less, Jason wouldn't have time to prepare his normal three meals a day. This kid was going to require a lot of care and around the clock including small, frequent meals, and Jason was the only one who could provide that.

Before he started on food, Jason emptied and refilled the bags with hot water and rewrapped them. Then he quietly returned to the kid and found him again completely naked with the sheet and blanket on the floor to the left of the bed. This was going to pose a challenge if he was ever going to not only get the kid warmed back up, but also keep him warm. Either the kid was a restless sleeper, or something was going on in his head that was making him restless. He picked up the linens and again replace the hot water bags around, on, and under his body and covered him. Then he added another two split logs to the central wood stove and went back to the kitchen.

He stoked the kitchen stove's coals and added some firewood to the glowing embers. While the embers caught the wood, he grabbed his big, sixteen-quart stock pot and threw in two whole frozen chickens, three bags of mixed vegetables, and a bag of frozen cut green beans from his garden. Then he added a dozen quickly washed and diced, unpeeled potatoes, a pound of fine dried egg noodles, a handful each of dried parsley and seasoned salt, a dozen chicken bouillon cubes, and a good number of turns from the pepper grinder. He filled the pot with hot water up to two inches from the rim, covered it, and set it atop the back burner of the stove.

While he was putting the soup together, he cut two slices of sourdough bread and smeared on peanut butter and jelly and then downed the sandwich in a few bites, washing it down with a glass of Heather's milk.

He could easily live on chicken soup and leftover sourdough bread for a couple of days. In addition, there was always plenty of smoked longhorn and venison, and eggs could be scrambled and cooked in less than three minutes. Besides that, if the kid woke up, he could start him on broth from the soup, that is, if he didn't have internal injuries. Time would tell.

With his food now taken care of and his belly temporarily satisfied, Jason scrubbed his hands and forearms in the big kitchen sink and then stealthily approached the bed. He pulled the curtain back to check on him. He was still out cold. *Such an angelic face. God damn it, Jason. Knock it the fuck off!*

He put on a pair of gloves, like he'd been trained to do, and sat down in a chair next to the bed. He checked the kid's pulse at his left wrist. It was 110, high for an athletic young male, but strong and steady. With all the kid had been through, no wonder it was elevated. He reached over and pulled down the kid's lower eyelid to check the color. It was still pink, but barely so, an indication that he was at least a little anemic, probably from the blood loss from his wounds and fractures, and possibly from internal bleeding.

He lifted his stethoscope from the headboard and gently pressed it against the kid's chest on both sides, pausing to listen to each lung segment from top to bottom and side to side for problem noises. His breathing was nice and steady, and his lungs were still clear, a sign there was still no pneumonia or atelectasis present. He moved on to the kid's belly, listening for the gurgle of bowel sounds. They were present and very active in all four quadrants. There was no tympany on percussion, which suggested there was no paralysis of his intestines. "So far, so good."

Next Jason checked the skin on his left forearm for tenting, a late sign of dehydration. It was mild, remaining standing for four seconds, which suggested the kid was somewhat volume-depleted, not only from dehydration, but also from the blood and plasma he'd lost. In a young, healthy male like this, it should be well under three seconds. He hoped the kid would wake up soon and that he'd be able to begin to take in fluids. If he didn't, he'd likely begin to go downhill fast.

Moving from his torso to his limbs, Jason checked on his wounds and fractures. He found no signs of infection, but many of the dressings were moderately saturated with blood and serum. Of the wounds he'd inserted drains in, all were completely saturated, another likely cause of his volume loss. In view of the fact that he hadn't taken in anything for at least twenty-four hours, this was turning into a real nightmare.

There was no way to know how much blood the kid had lost while he hung from the tree because the rain would have washed it away. In addition, his mid-right forearm and left lower leg at the mid tibia level were more than a bit swollen, more so than they were after he'd reset the bones, another indication that blood and serum had seeped into the muscles and tissues when the bone ends cut their way through. Fortunately, the kid hadn't moved those limbs so the splints were holding up well. His left ankle dislocation was also swollen, but not much more than it had been after he reduced and splinted it the night before.

All the pulses below those injuries were strong which was a good sign. If he lost the pulses, it meant that either the bones themselves or the swelling had pressed the blood vessels shut, and no blood supply would mean tissue death. Not only would he lose the limbs, the toxins from the dead tissue seeping into his blood stream would eventually kill him. Jason had performed limb amputations before, but here, out in the middle of nowhere, he didn't have the equipment he'd need. If push came to shove, he'd be forced to use his carpentry tools.

Damn it, what the hell am I going to do if I can't control all these possible sources of blood loss?

A pungent, one-of-a-kind odor reached Jason's nose. *Urine!*

The kid must have just peed himself. Jason lifted the sheet to expose and check his groin area. The urine was dark. The stain began where the tip of the kid's penis ended at the top of his left thigh and ran down both the outside and inside beneath his scrotum, disappearing into the towels. Luckily there wasn't a whole lot of it and the bath towels soaked it up. The last thing the kid needed was to be jostled around because Jason had to change the bed. The stream of urine was so concentrated it had a visible thickness to it. No wonder the smell was so strong. *Shit, there's no doubt about it now, the kid is definitely dehydrated.*

Jason went into the bathroom and half-filled two small buckets with clear, hot water. He added soap to one and grabbed a washcloth and hand towel and then returned to clean him up.

No sooner had Jason begun to lather up his thigh, groin area, penis, and scrotum to remove the urine, then the kid began to moan. Startled, Jason looked up at his face to see if he was coming to. They had been the first sounds he'd made since Jason had found him.

"This shouldn't be hurting him," he whispered, "I haven't even touched his abrasions yet."

Suddenly, Jason recognized that those weren't the moans of pain. The kid's head turned slowly from side to side while he continued to moan from deep within his chest. Then the kid's heavy, thick, seven-inch flaccid penis began to grow, and quickly. Jason's pulse began to thud in his ears and his breathing quickened. He felt his own cock beginning to fill with blood. Jason began to tremble, and he froze.

In less than a minute the kid's cock reached its fully erect, ten-inch length. The shaft was a good two and a half inches wide, and it was covered with bulging veins that ran up and down its length, completely encircling it. Then it began to move on its own.

"Damn, it's huge!" Jason said aloud.

A bead of clear, thick fluid began to pearl at the slit of the thick, bulbous head. It was as thick as honey. At first Jason made himself believe it was just urine, but there was no denying what it really was. The bead of clear liquid grew and grew until it began to slowly ooze down the now darkening, pulsating, swollen helmet.

"Christ, it's pre-cum!"

Jason's own cock was now fully erect. It throbbed that painful throb than only one thing could take care of.

More and more of the thick fluid oozed from the kid's slit, until it slowly slid beyond the head and down the shaft. The flow increased slightly, and it split into two streams that slowly dripped over Jason's gloved hands. He'd never seen pre-cum so thick before.

Jason quickly let go of the kid, but his penis was so hard it remained standing at a forty-five-degree angle above his belly. Jason threw the hand towel over it as he leapt from the chair, but the weight of the towel had no effect. The kid's cock continued to jump, lifting the towel with each pulsating and quickening beat.

When the kid began to moan again, Jason backed away. "No! No! Please no! No! Please!" The kid's voice was ragged and rough.

"Oh, God. What have I done? What have I done to this kid? God, forgive me. Not again. Not again!"

Jason's cock went limp. He ran from the bed, out the door, and down the steps. Hearing the creak of the screen door, Nellie and Sarah brayed and Heather and Jasper bleated, but Jason didn't notice them. He continued to run across the eighty yards of thigh-high grass to the stockade's gate. He unhooked the heavy timber slide latch, opened the great, gated door, and ran. He ran down to the bottom of the hill and up the path to the top of the next hill to the clearing that held the helipad. He dropped to his knees, wrapping his arms tightly around his chest, and hugged himself. With tears streaming down his face, he began to weep.

"Not again! Please, God, not again!"

Chapter Three
Flashback

Sunday, September 6, 2009, 10:00 AM
Day Two

"No. No. Please, no. Please. Don't stop. Please. Please, Nathan, don't stop," he mumbled.

Slowly, Aaron opened his eyes, but he couldn't get his vision to focus. He thought he'd heard a sound like a door banging shut, but it was quiet all around him now. Then, in the distance he thought he heard birds chirping and what sounded like donkeys, but that couldn't be. His mouth was thick and dry. He tried to swallow and began to cough. His head started to pound like no headache he'd ever had. Everything hurt.

Is this a hangover? I don't remember drinking last night. What was last night?

Aaron smelled chicken soup, but even the smell couldn't stimulate his saliva. He tried to call out, "Hello," but it sounded more like a croak.

His belly, chest, arms, and legs burned like they were on fire and his right butt cheek ached like a motherfucker. He made a move to sit up but was immediately overcome by shooting and searing pains from his right arm and left leg. He squeezed his eyes closed against the pain. There were flashes of light behind them. His head exploded. He returned to darkness.

****

Friday, September 4, 2009, 5:47 PM

The moment the lightning struck, the left engine

began to flame and sputter. The pilot immediately reached over to the control to shut down its fuel supply while increasing power to the engine on the right. Aaron grabbed Nathan's hand. They both were shaking.

"Oh, my God!" Aaron yelled.

Nathan tried to reassure him. "It'll be okay, Aaron. We're gonna be okay."

"Hang on, boys, it's going to get rough!" the pilot called back. "You better put those parachutes on, just to be safe!"

With the small plane bouncing around in the violent wind, it took all of Nathan's strength to hold on to his seat while reaching back to grab a chute off the floor behind them. He began to help Aaron put it on.

The pilot tried to restart the engine, but it was dead. Smoke poured from the engine and began to come into the cabin. He picked up the radio's mic. "Mayday! Mayday! Mayday! Two Tango Whiskey Seven Niner. At 12,000 feet and descending rapidly. Heavy winds. Struck by lightning. One engine out. Smoke in cabin."

The cabin was cramped, but with a lot of effort, Nathan finally got the parachute on Aaron.

"This is ATC Salt Lake. We've got you, Two Tango Whiskey Seven Niner. You're breaking up. Repeat your emergency."

"I say, Two Tango Whiskey Seven Niner. Struck by lightning. Violent storm. One engine out. Can't get it restarted. Heavy winds. Losing altitude fast and there's smoke in the cabin. Now at 11,000 feet. Don't know if I can make it into Hinnen Valley Regional."

Nathan reached back for another chute and a helmet. "Put this on, Aaron," he said as he passed the helmet to him and then he put on his own chute. Flames began to come from the instrument panel.

"Two Tango Whiskey Seven Niner. What's your

present altitude? Over."

The airplane's radio began to spark.

"Now at 10,500 feet and descending. Heavy winds. Losing altitude!" the pilot shouted into the microphone,

Another thirty seconds went by. There was no response from air traffic control.

"ATC Salt Lake, come in!"

"ATC Salt Lake, come in! This is Two Tango Whiskey Seven Niner. 8,000 feet now and descending. Heavy winds. Losing altitude."

After putting on his own helmet, Nathan reached back for the third chute and helmet and passed them up to the pilot. The flames coming from the instrument panel were growing.

"Repeat. Two Tango Whiskey Seven Niner. What's your present altitude? Over," said the air traffic controller into his headset. He repeated, "Two Tango Whiskey Seven Niner. Come in. Over."

Two Tango Whiskey Seven Niner's radio was dead.

The pilot yelled back, "Okay boys, the radio's out. I can't let go of the yoke, so you're gonna have to open the door yourselves and jump for it! Wait ten seconds, and then pull the ripcord, here!" The pilot grabbed the ripcord's handle on the parachute by his side to show them.

"You two first, and then I'll follow right behind you," the pilot yelled. "Try to find an open patch of ground, and avoid trees at all cost. When you get close to the ground, pull down on the two steering toggles to slow your descent. When you hit the ground, roll! God's speed. Now jump!"

Nathan reached across Aaron and opened the door. Wind rushed through the cabin, immediately clearing the smoke, but it fed the flames, and they began to shoot out of the instrument panel into the pilot's face. The pilot screamed. In seconds, his head was consumed in an inferno.

"I'll be right behind you, Aaron!"

Nathan pushed Aaron out of the cabin with so much force he was thrown into the wing strut causing him to tumble over and over as he fell.

Remembering how he'd seen jumpers open their arms and legs, Aaron was able to right himself on his back ten seconds after hitting the air. He looked up for any sign of Nathan, but he was nowhere to be seen. In the next moment, the plane exploded into a ball of fire. He was gone.

"Nathan!"

****

Sunday, September 6, 2009, 10:15 AM

As Jason pulled himself together, he realized he had done nothing wrong. Regardless of his inner thoughts and his own physical reaction to the kid's hard-on, he knew he was caring for the kid appropriately. He just hadn't realized that he still carried mental scars from eighteen years ago.

Jason knew that being gay was not the same as being a sexual predator, regardless of what some people thought, or said, or even preached, and he certainly wasn't one. Cleaning the kid up was the right thing to do, and his moaning and erection were completely understandable considering the stimulation he'd created with the soapy washcloth. It was impossible to know what trauma or abuse the kid had suffered in the past. His moaned words could certainly be explained by just such an event, and in view of his head injury, who could know what was really going on in his mind?

Jason realized that he had run away from the kid because of that incident in his past. Back then, he'd also done nothing wrong. As a corpsman and while he was training to be an army medic, he was bathing a trauma patient who was in skeletal traction behind a closed curtain on the surgical ward of the army hospital where he was based.

Those memories came flooding back.

****

9:15 AM, January 17, 1991

"Okay, buddy, we're almost finished," Jason said as he began to wash Corporal Calvin Garrison's penis and scrotum. The corporal's penis was thick and heavy in Jason's hands, more so than any other patient he'd bathed so far, but it figured, the corporal was stocky. Jason had no idea the corporal was also a sexual predator.

The next thing Jason knew, Garrison's penis became a throbbing, nine-inch erection. Garrison began to contract his PC muscles, making the glans of his penis swell and the shaft jump.

"Oh, baby," Garrison barely whispered, "you do that so well." He raised his eyebrows and shifted his glance back and forth between Jason and his penis then made a tube with his left hand, barely moving it up and down, but it was enough to show that he wanted a hand job. Then he mouthed the words, "Suck it, baby … suck it," as clear fluid began to ooze from the opening.

Jason froze. He didn't know what to do, particularly once he realized what the corporal's gestures meant. It had never happened to him before, and he was just a kid himself, a skinny, five-foot-ten, eighteen-year-old, still a virgin with peach fuzz on his face, and more importantly, unsure of his own sexuality. Just then the charge nurse pulled the curtains open, and the corporal began to scream.

"He's jerking me off! The faggot's jerking me off! Jesus, get him off me!"

At an imposing, broad-shouldered, six feet tall, Captain Gwendolyn Turner had no difficulty lifting Jason off his feet when she grabbed him by the collar and pulled him away from the bedside and out into the hall, finally shoving him hard against the wall.

"Just what the hell do you think you're doing, Mister? No, don't answer that! Into my office right now!"

Jason was shaking so hard he could barely walk down the fifty feet of corridor that led to her office. She slammed the door behind them, and with her hands on her hips laid into him. "Mister, you better level with me. I want the truth, and I want it now!"

"Ma'am, I didn't do anything. I didn't do anything wrong. I was just giving him a bed bath like I've done dozens of times before. Nothing like that has ever happened, I swear it. I don't understand why it happened."

"Then what the hell was that I saw?"

Jason began to cry. "I don't know. Ma'am, I swear I didn't do anything wrong. I didn't."

She looked him up and down. "I'm sorry, Corpsman, but I'm going to have to file an incident report based on what I witnessed and Corporal Garrison's accusations. An inquiry will be opened. As of right now, you're off patient duty until this matter has been settled.

"You're confined to barracks until further notice. You'll be notified when the inquiry is scheduled and you'll report to testify as ordered. You're to head straight to your barracks. Make no detours, and speak to no one.

Except for meals, you're to stay there. I'll be calling your commanding officer to inform him immediately. Now pull yourself together, and get out of my office!"

That night, January 17, 1991, America went to war with Iraq. Three days later, Jason was ordered to report to his hearing.

Chapter Four
A trial like no other

10:00 hours, January 20, 1991

"This court is now called to order," the lead judging officer stated. "Let the record show, present are myself, Major Timothy Black, Major Raymond Constantine, and Captain Claudia Sellers. For the prosecution is Major Robert Scottsdale. For the defense is Captain Anthony Matthews with the accused, Corpsman Jason Ackerman."

"Corpsman Ackerman, you are being charged with the deviant sexual assault of a male patient under your care. Do you understand the charges that have been filed against you?" Major Black asked.

"No, sir. I didn't do anything wrong."

"I didn't ask whether you were guilty, Corpsman. I asked whether you understand the charges."

Jason looked at his attorney. "Say yes," Captain Matthews whispered to him.

"Yes, sir. I understand them."

"Good, then we can proceed. How do you plead?"

"Not guilty, sir."

"You may be seated, Corpsman. Council, call your first witness," Major Black directed to Major Scottsdale.

"First, Your Honors, I'd like to submit into the record this deposition from Corporal Calvin Garrison, the victim in this crime, who could not be present because he is still in skeletal traction on the hospital ward."

"Accepted into the record. Call your first

37

witness."

"Before I do that, Your Honor, I would like to add that Corpsman Ackerman will never find redemption for committing this heinous crime. He sexually assaulted an invalid patient, a fellow soldier who is a hero I might add, while in his care, and I am certain he will be found guilty!"

Jason shrunk in his chair.

"Major Scottsdale, you are out of order, sir," Major Black bellowed. "Strike that last comment from the record," he directed to the stenographer. "There is no jury here for you to try to impress, Major. We deal only in facts in my courtroom, and I caution you to stick to them! Now call your first witness!"

Major Scottsdale knew he wouldn't get away with his opening statement, but he felt all the better for having made it. He was on a mission to weed out every faggot who had infiltrated his army. "The prosecution calls Captain Gwendolyn Turner."

Captain Turner was called in from the hallway and sworn in.

"Captain Turner," Major Scottsdale began, "on the seventeenth of January of this year, you witnessed a sexual assault on Corporal Calvin Garrison, an invalid patient under your care, by the defendant. Is that correct?"

Jason was shocked that his attorney didn't object. He knew he didn't sexually assault the corporal.

"No, sir, that is not correct. I witnessed the defendant holding Corporal Garrison's erect penis in his hands."

"Ha! So you say the penis was erect!"

"Yes, sir, it was erect."

"So he was sexually assaulting the Corporal, then."

"I can't say that I witnessed that, sir."

"Why not?"

"Because, sir, to know whether an assault was taking place..."

"Objection!" shouted Major Scottsdale.

"Major," warned Major Black, "you cannot object to your own witness' testimony. The witness will continue."

"Yes, Your Honor. I cannot know whether an assault was taking place. In order to know that, I would have to know the assailant's thoughts, or he would have had to share his intentions with me either prior to, during, or after the contact."

"But you say the corporal's penis was erect."

"Yes, sir, it was very erect."

"Very erect, you say!"

"Yes ... sir." Captain Turner rolled her eyes, but only Jason and Captain Matthews noticed it.

Maybe she's on my side after all, Jason thought to himself.

"So then, Captain Turner, why does that not prove an assault was taking place?"

"Because, Major Scottsdale, and I'm surprised you don't know this yourself, men get erections all the time."

"They do? Explain, please."

"I don't know how to answer that." Captain Turner looked to the three judging officers, an expression of frustration on her face.

"Captain Turner, can you offer any more information?" Major Black asked.

"Well, yes, sir. An erection is a normal physiological response to physical stimulation. That's all, sir."

"Move on, Major Scottsdale," Major Black

ordered.

"Captain Turner, how did you come to witness the defendant holding Corporal Garrison's very erect penis?"

"I entered the patient's room and slid the curtain aside to check on Corpsman Ackerman's progress."

"So he was hiding behind the curtain."

"No, sir, he had the curtain drawn. All patients are provided privacy while they're being bathed."

"Isn't that unnatural?"

"Unnatural, sir?"

"Yes, unnatural."

"Do you mean uncommon or unusual?"

"Same difference, isn't it?" Major Scottsdale suggested.

"No, sir, it isn't and no, it wasn't unnatural, unusual, or uncommon. Patients should always be provided privacy whenever possible when they might be exposed."

"Very good. Captain Turner, did Corporal Garrison say anything at the time of the incident?"

"Yes, sir. He said, 'He's jerking me off. The faggot's jerking me off. Jesus, get him off me,'" Captain Turner answered in a dispassionate voice.

"Is that a direct quote?"

"Yes, sir. Those were the corporal's exact words."

"And he said those words exactly as you just stated them?"

"No, sir, he was screaming them."

"He was screaming them, you say! Well, that's understandable, don't you think?"

Captain Turner remained silent.

"I asked you a question, Captain Turner."

"I don't know how to answer that. Yes, he was

screaming."

"Well, you do believe him, don't you?" Major Scottsdale asked.

"No, sir, I don't necessarily believe him."

"Why not?"

"Because, sir, I questioned all the staff under my command about Corporal Garrison. I received many reports that would refute his claims."

"I object! Your Honor, hearsay."

"She's your witness, Major Scottsdale," Major Black stated, "Again, I remind you, you cannot object to your own witness' testimony."

"What did you do then, Captain Turner?"

"I escorted Corpsman Ackerman to my office where I questioned him."

"And what did he tell you?"

"He denied the incident."

"He denied the fact that he was holding Corporal Garrison's, and I quote you now, very erect penis in his hands?"

"No, sir."

"So he admitted it then?"

"No, sir. There is no question that Corporal Garrison's penis was erect and that Corpsman Ackerman was holding it. Corpsman Ackerman denied that he had done anything wrong."

"Did you believe him?"

"Not at the time, necessarily, but I put much more credence in his statement now."

"Objection ... withdrawn," Major Scottsdale said angrily, but he regained his composure quickly.

"Did you witness anything else, Captain Turner?"

"I'm not sure that it's relevant, sir."

"I'll be the judge of what is and is not relevant, Captain Turner!"

Major Black cleared his throat. "No, Major Scottsdale! I'll be the judge of what is and is not relevant! Proceed, Captain Turner."

"Well, sir, there was Cowper's fluid coming from his meatus."

"I beg your pardon? Cowper's fluid? Meatus? What are those?" Major Scottsdale asked with interest.

"Your Honor," Captain Turner asked, "may I speak frankly? I think it would be helpful if I explained a few anatomical structures using layman's terms."

"Yes. Please do, Captain Turner," Major Black directed.

"Thank you, Your Honor. The Cowper's gland produces Cowper's fluid. It's also known as pre-seminal fluid, pre-ejaculate, or pre-ejaculatory fluid. The layman's term is pre-cum. It serves as a lubricant, and it neutralizes the acidity present in the male urethra from urine. It coats the urethra and is exuded from the meatus at the glans during sexual arousal and prior to ejaculation. The urethra is the tube that connects the bladder to the meatus. The meatus is the opening or the slit at the tip of the penis. The glans is the thickest end or head of the penis."

While Captain Turner spoke, Major Scottsdale furiously scribbled down each word she said on a legal pad.

"And why is all of this relevant, Captain Turner?"

"Well, sir, I don't believe it is?"

"Then why did you just give us an anatomy lesson, Captain Turner?"

"Because, sir, you asked. I believe your exact words were, 'Did you witness anything else, Captain Turner?' So I told you what the other thing was that I witnessed. I did offer that I did not think it was relevant."

"I have no further use for this witness!" Major

Scottsdale said while slamming down his legal pad.

"Your witness, Captain Matthews?" Major Black directed.

"Thank you, Your Honor," Captain Matthews said as he stood up.

"Captain Turner, have you formed any kind of opinion on this case?"

"Objection, Your Honor!" Major Scottsdale shouted.

"I'll allow it," Major Black directed. "Go on, Captain Turner."

"Yes, sir, I have. Corpsman Ackerman has been exemplary in the conduction of his duties while caring for surgical patients on my ward. He is thoughtful, courteous, and efficient. I've never known him to lollygag or waste time in any way. It is obvious to me, as I believe it will soon become to everyone present here today, that he is innocent of the charges."

"Objection, Your Honor," Major Scottsdale said angrily.

"So noted," Major Black answered.

"I have no more questions, Your Honor," Captain Matthews said as he sat down. "Thank you, Captain Turner."

"The witness is excused," Major Black directed. "You may step down, Captain Turner."

Captain Turner left the witness chair, but instead of leaving the courtroom, she took a seat along the wall near the doorway.

"Call your next witness, Major Scottsdale."

"I have no further witnesses, Your Honor."

"You may call your first witness, Captain Matthews," Major Black directed.

Captain Matthews stood. "The defense calls Corpsman Logan Edwards."

Corpsman Edwards was called in from the hallway. He walked to the witness stand and was sworn in.

"Good morning, Corpsman Edwards. Do you know the defendant, Corpsman Ackerman?"

"Not really, sir. I've seen him around."

"Have you discussed this case with Corpsman Ackerman at any time, in any way?"

"No, sir. I haven't seen him around in a few days."

"Very good. Corpsman Edwards, will you please tell the court about the times you've taken care of Corporal Calvin Garrison, particularly when you were bathing him."

"Yes, sir. I took care of the corporal on three separate occasions."

"What did that care entail?"

"Well, sir, I helped the surgeons with his dressing changes and did some of them myself."

"Did you ever have the occasion to bathe Corporal Garrison?"

"Yes, sir."

"How many times?"

"Um, as I said, three, sir."

"Did anything out of the ordinary happen during any of those three bed baths?"

"What do you mean, sir?"

"Did Corporal Garrison's penis ever become erect during his baths?"

"Um, yes, sir. During his first bed bath, he got a hard-on, um, sorry, an erection."

"Did anything else happen at that time, Corpsman Edwards?"

"What do you mean, sir?"

"Did anything come out of Corporal Garrison's

penis when it was erect?"

"Um..."

"Please answer the question, Corpsman."

"Well ... yes, sir. Um..."

"Go on, Corpsman. Answer the question. What came out of Corporal Garrison's penis when it was erect?"

"Oh, man. Sir, I ... um..."

"Answer the question, please."

"Sir, it was oozing pre-cum like a motherfu ... Oh, man! Sorry, sir, I mean fluid. It was oozing fluid!"

"It's okay, Corpsman. You can say pre-cum. We just had an anatomy lesson in here before you took the stand." Captain Matthews said as he looked toward Captain Turner with a smile. "So what did you do?"

"Nothing I could do, he was out cold, or at least I thought so. His eyes were closed, and he wasn't moving anything else."

"And that's all that happened then?"

"Yes, sir. I finished his bath and left."

"Did you report the incident to anyone?"

"Incident?"

"His erection?"

"No, sir, we were taught that it happens sometimes."

"And the second time you gave him a bed bath? Was he unconscious then?"

"No, sir. He was wide awake."

"Tell the court what happened."

"Well, sir." Corpsman Edwards hesitated.

"Go on, Corpsman, you're not in any trouble here."

"Well, sir, I gave him his bath and when I started to wash his penis, it got really hard, and he started to moan and his eyes rolled back in his head. Then it started to twitch."

"It?"

"Yes, sir, his penis."

"Did anything else happen that second time, Corpsman Edwards?"

"Oh, sir!"

"Did anything come out of Corporal Garrison's penis when it was erect the second time you bathed him?"

"Yes, sir, it was oozing a lot of pre-cum. Damn! Oh, sorry, sir!"

"What did you do?"

"I told him to knock it off, sir. I rinsed it off real quick and then I left."

"Did you tell anyone what happened?"

"No, sir, I didn't. Nothing like that had ever happened to me before, sir."

"Weren't you disturbed by what happened?"

"Yes, sir, to tell the truth, I was," Corpsman Edwards began to squirm in the witness chair as he continued, "but I told myself what I was taught in my training, that it happens sometimes."

"It's okay, corpsman. You're not in trouble."

"Yes, sir. Thank you, sir."

"Tell us about the last time you bathed Corporal Garrison."

Corpsman Edwards got red in the face.

"It's okay, Corpsman. Tell the court what happened."

"Okay, here goes. It was a week ago. He was awake when I went into his room. I told him I was going to give him his bath, real loud, so the other guys, um, patients in the room could hear me."

"Other patients?"

"Yes, sir, he was in a ward room."

"How many other patients?"

"Five, sir, it was a six-bed ward room."

"Go on, Corpsman."

"So then I filled a basin with hot water and pulled the curtain closed around his bed."

"And then what happened?"

"He was real cool until I pulled the curtain. Then he smiled this weird smile at me. First, I put on a pair of gloves, and then I bathed him with a washcloth and soap and water just like I've bathed every other patient I've ever bathed, but before I got to his groin, I stopped."

"Did you wear gloves each time you bathed Corporal Garrison?"

"Yes, sir."

"Why?"

"'Cuz that's what we were taught, sir."

"Go on. Why did you stop?"

"'Cuz then I whispered, 'Don't start,' to him."

"Why didn't you give him the washcloth to finish himself?"

"He's got two broken arms. He couldn't."

"Go on."

"So, he nodded his head like he understood me, but when I uncovered him, his penis, man his penis was already partly hard. I tried to go real quick, but then he started to lick his lips, and his penis got full-blown hard again. Yes, sir, I know you're gonna ask, so yes. Yes, sir, it was really oozing pre-cum. Then he mouthed the words, 'Suck me. Please suck me,' to me, and then he started to thrust his hips towards me."

"What did you do then?"

"I hightailed it out of there. Just left him there."

"And...?"

"I told a nurse that I felt sick and asked her if she could finish his bath for me. Then I ran to the bathroom.

By then I really was sick, and puked my guts out into the toilet."

"What was the nurse's name?"

"Lieutenant Sorensen, sir."

"Thank you, Corpsman Edwards. No further questions, Your Honor."

Major Black looked at the prosecutor. "Your witness, Major Scottsdale."

"No questions, Your Honor."

"Corpsman Edwards, you are excused. You may call your next witness, Captain Matthews."

"The defense calls Lieutenant Amanda Sorensen to the stand," Captain Matthews said as Corpsman Edwards left the courtroom.

Lieutenant Sorensen was called in from the hallway. She walked to the witness stand and was sworn in.

"Good morning, Lieutenant Sorensen. Can you please tell the court whether you know the defendant, Corpsman Ackerman?"

"Yes, sir, I do."

"How do you know the corpsman?"

"He's assigned to my ward."

"Have you discussed this case at all with Corpsman Ackerman?"

"No, sir. I have not. He hasn't been on the ward these last few days."

"Very good, Lieutenant. Will you please tell the court about your care of Corporal Garrison?"

"Corporal Garrison is an orthopedic patient on my ward. He has multiple fractures of both arms and his right leg, which is in skeletal traction."

"Lieutenant, please tell the court about an incident involving Corporal Garrison and Corpsman Edwards that took place one week ago, on January fifteenth of this year."

"Yes, sir. Corpsman Edwards was assigned to bathe Corporal Garrison. During the bath, he came to me, the corpsman I mean, and told me that he felt sick and asked if I would finish the bath. Then he disappeared into the bathroom."

"Then what happened?"

"I entered the patient's room and found the curtain pulled around his bed. When I moved behind the curtain, Corporal Garrison was sleeping, or so I thought."

"Was he covered with a sheet?"

"All but his groin area was covered."

"Why?"

"Well, I assumed that was as far as Corpsman Edwards had gotten."

"Go on."

"I found the bath basin's water was cold, so I emptied it and refilled it with hot water. When I returned, Corporal Garrison was awake. I asked him how far the corpsman had gotten with his bath. He told me the only thing he hadn't finished was, as he put it, his 'private parts.' He seemed embarrassed to say it. So I put on a pair of gloves and began to wash his penis and scrotum."

"Then what happened?"

"He started to lick his lips, and then he developed an erection. He started to thrust his hips towards me while he mouthed the words, 'Suck me, baby, suck me real good.'"

"How could he thrust his hips if his right leg was in skeletal traction?"

"He still had one good leg, sir."

"What happened next?"

"I grasped his penis firmly and pushed his hips back down on the bed."

"How firmly did you grasp his penis?"

"Firm enough to make it become flaccid again, sir."

"And then?"

"I finished his bath and left."

"Did you report the incident to anyone?"

"Yes, sir, sort of."

"Sort of how?"

"I passed it on in my report to the next shift."

"Thank you, Lieutenant. No further questions. Your witness, Major Scottsdale."

Major Scottsdale stood and said, "I have no questions for this witness. Sidebar, Your Honor?"

"Lieutenant Sorensen, you are excused," Major Black ordered. The Lieutenant got up from the witness chair and then took a seat next to Captain Turner at the back of the courtroom.

"I want to see how this turns out," Captain Turner whispered to Lieutenant Sorensen.

"Me too," Lieutenant Sorensen whispered back.

"I was really hard on the kid," Captain Turner whispered.

"You didn't know, Captain," Lieutenant Sorensen whispered as she rested here hand on the Captain's arm.

The two attorneys met in front of the three judging officers.

"Do you have any more witnesses who are going to have similar testimony?" Major Scottsdale asked Captain Matthews.

"Yes, one corpsman who is going to give corroborating testimony."

"Your move, Major Scottsdale," Major Black said.

"Your Honor, I've heard enough. I had no idea. I'd like to drop all charges and expunge this from Corpsman Ackerman's record."

Major Black directed the attorneys back to their seats and then conferred with the other two judging officers in whispers before speaking.

"Corpsman Ackerman, please rise," Major Black announced in a loud voice.

Jason stood with Captain Matthews.

"Corpsman Ackerman, all charges against you have been dismissed. This incident will be expunged from your military record. The Court and Major Scottsdale would like to offer you our sincerest apologies for any distress this matter may have caused you. You are free to go and resume your duties. I understand you have nearly completed your training to become an army medic. I wish you all the luck in the world, son. Godspeed."

Captain Turner and Lieutenant Sorensen rose to congratulate Jason.

"Congratulations, Corpsman," Lieutenant Sorensen said shaking his hand.

"Congratulations, Corpsman. I'll be happy to have you back on my ward where you belong," Captain Turner said as she placed her left hand on his shoulder and then shook his hand.

Captain Turner and Lieutenant Sorensen exchanged smiles as they followed Jason out of the courtroom.

Chapter Five
We interrupt our regularly scheduled
programming

Sunday, September 6, 2009, 11:25 AM

Jason realized he'd been walking in circles around the helipad for what must have been over an hour. When he saw he still wore latex gloves, he remembered what had happened. He peeled the gloves off and shoved them in his pocket as he headed back toward the stockade. After locking the stockade's great door behind him, he returned to the cabin to check on the kid.

On the way he considered whether the kid was as volume depleted as he had initially thought, considering the size of the erection he'd developed. Though he would never know for sure, it was possible that his body had kicked in some compensatory mechanisms, the renin-angiotensin system came to mind, which radically conserves the loss of fluids through urine and raises the blood pressure. *Yeah, he's gotta be dehydrated to some degree coz he hasn't had anything to drink in at least twenty-four hours, but the amount of blood he's actually lost, I'll never know for sure.*

As Jason opened the screen door, the cabin was quiet. He couldn't even hear the kid breathing. He hurried to the bed and found the kid was still out cold, but he wasn't as Jason had left him.

"What the fuck?"

Jason could see that he was breathing just fine, albeit quietly, but he was disheveled and appeared to have been moved. The bedsheet and blanket were tangled up, the water bags were scattered across the bed and on the floor, his right leg was dangling over the side of the bed, and the towel he'd thrown over the kid's erection was bunched up in his hand. He straightened the kid out, removed the water bags, and covered him with the blanket.

Jason went back to the kitchen and washed his hands and then returned and took the kid's pulse. It was between 110 and 120, a little higher than just an hour before. He pulled down the kid's left eyelid to check the color of his conjunctiva. It was about the same. The dressings he'd never gotten around to changing that morning appeared to have even more drainage. The kid was slowly deteriorating by the hour in front of his eyes, regardless of how much blood he had actually lost.

Jason placed his right hand on the kid's left shoulder and gently began to rock him. "Hey, buddy. I need you to try to wake up. Come on now, open your eyes for me."

The kid stirred. "Nathan! No!" The sounds he made were barely intelligible, more like rushing air.

"Come on, buddy. Now open your eyes for me." Jason continued to gently rock his shoulder.

"Nathan! Nathan!" The kid's voice was a hoarse whisper. He buried his right cheek into the pillow. "Nathan! Nathan! No!"

Jason continued. "You're okay, buddy. You're okay. Come on now, wake up for me. Open your eyes for me and wake up."

The kid's eyelids fluttered.

"That's it, buddy. Open your eyes. You can do it."

Slowly, Aaron opened his eyes. He tried to turn his head, but the back of it burned like hell. He turned his eyes toward the sound of a voice to his left, but they still wouldn't focus properly.

"There you are," Jason said encouragingly. "How are you feeling?"

"What happened," Aaron croaked. He tried to speak again, but his voice failed. He scraped his tongue against his teeth. It was so dry it sounded like sandpaper in his head.

Jason ran to the bathroom and returned with a cup of cool water and a washcloth. He pressed the center of the cloth with his finger to make a point, then he dipped the point into the water and placed it against the kid's lips. The kid immediately began to suck greedily on the cloth. Jason dipped it in again and returned it to his mouth. He dipped it again and again, more than a dozen times. The kid couldn't get enough of it.

"Thirsty," Aaron said with still much of a croak.

"Okay, let me get you a straw."

When he returned from the kitchen, Jason dipped the straw to the bottom of the cup and trapped the water with his fingertip. Placing the straw in the corner of the kid's mouth, he released his finger, allowing a few milliliters to drain inside his cheek. The kid swallowed, choking a little.

"More," he asked.

Over the next several minutes, Jason had given the kid nearly all of the cup.

"Better," the kid said.

"What's your name?" Jason asked.

"Aaron. My name is Aaron."

"Hello, Aaron. I'm Jason."

"Where am I? What happened? Why can't I see right?"

"You're in a cabin in the mountains," Jason answered while wiping his eyes with the washcloth.

"What?"

"You're in my cabin in the mountains. We're in

southeastern Idaho."

"How'd I get here?"

"I don't know what happened, but I found you hanging from a parachute in a tree on my property."

"Oh, my God! Nathan!" Aaron started to sob, but there were few tears.

Jason patted his shoulder and let him cry. As his sobbing softened, Aaron fell back to sleep. Jason sat quietly at his side for the next hour.

****

When Jason realized Aaron wasn't going to wake up for a while, he cleaned up the piles of debris in the common area and put his trauma kit and Aaron's sneakers away in the storage room. He knew Aaron would tell him what happened in his own good time. What was important right now was getting him turned around from dehydration.

He cleaned out the bath buckets and refilled them. Then he returned and gave Aaron a quick bed bath, taking care of those areas around the dressings that needed the most attention, but he avoided his groin.

Sunday, September 6, 2009, 11:30 AM
Local Breaking News, Hinnen Valley, Idaho

"Good morning, ladies and gentlemen. We interrupt our regularly scheduled programming to bring you the following breaking news. We've just learned that the small commuter plane that disappeared from radar at approximately 5:52 PM on Friday, September 4 over the Wasatch Range of the Rocky Mountains in southern Idaho was carrying Aaron Jaeger, the newly signed CFL quarterback for the Nevada Bighorns.

"The plane is reported to have been carrying only Jaeger and one pilot. The last transmission from the pilot reported he was experiencing engine and electrical problems after being struck by lightning from a quickly developing thunderstorm. Jaeger recently signed a three year, fifteen-million-dollar contract with the Bighorns that included an initial signing bonus of four million. Jaeger is scheduled to start as quarterback in the Bighorns first game of the season, next Sunday.

"It is reported that Jaeger was headed to a remote, private lodge and spa for a week of R & R before beginning the season.

"Jaeger was last reported to be in the company of his trainer, Nathan Taggart, however, Taggart is not listed on the plane's manifest. As of this broadcast, Taggart could not be reached for comment. We will continue to keep you apprised of any new developments in the story as they arise. We now return you to our regular programming."

Within minutes, this story was rebroadcast by every major network.

Sunday, September 6, 2009, 2:00 PM

When Aaron woke up, tears immediately formed in the corners of his eyes. Jason reached up with a tissue and wiped them away.

"Okay, Aaron. It's okay. Close your eyes for a minute. They're all crusted. I'm going to rinse them out."

Jason went into the bathroom and took out a clean washcloth and hand towel. He saturated the washcloth with hot water and partially rung it out. When he returned, he slowly and gently wiped the cloth across Aaron's eyes several times and then dried them.

"Thanks," Aaron whispered.

"You're welcome. Here, have some more water. Do you think you can handle a straw?"

Aaron nodded his head so Jason held the straw to his lips. "Now take it slowly," Jason whispered reassuringly.

After he'd taken half a cup, Aaron let go of the straw. "Thank you."

"You're welcome."

"Tell me what happened to me. Please." Aaron whispered.

Jason slowly explained all that he knew, how he'd found Aaron, how he lowered him from the tree, what his injuries were, how he treated them, and how he got him into the cabin and finally into his bed. He left out the part about his raging hard-on. While Jason spoke, Aaron steeled himself against the news he was given. His career was over, that he knew for sure, and Nathan was gone.

When Jason finished speaking, Aaron whispered, "Thank you for saving me. Did you find Nathan?"

"No, I'm sorry. I didn't find anyone else."

"He's dead."

"What do you mean?"

"Nathan's dead, I know it. I watched the plane explode."

Again, tears fell down Aaron's cheeks. Jason wiped his eyes and sat quietly until he finished crying.

"I'm sorry about your friend."

"He was more than a friend. He was my ..." Aaron couldn't bring himself to say the word.

"That's okay, Aaron. It's okay."

"No, it's not okay. He was more than a friend."

"I think I understand, Aaron. I'm sorry. I'm so, so sorry."

"Do you understand? Can you really?"

"I think so," Jason whispered.

"Nathan was my life. I hoped we would be ... one

57

day, we'd be..."

Though he was afraid by his implied admission and shocked that he'd said it out loud and to a stranger no less, Aaron turned his head towards Jason. His gaze was returned by the gentlest, kindest smile Aaron had ever seen. Jason took Aaron's left hand in both of his and gently patted and stroked it. Though he was very weak, Aaron squeezed back with all the strength he could muster. Then his arm went limp, but Jason held on. Minutes passed as they remained like that, Jason holding Aaron's hand, in silence.

"Aaron, you need to start taking in nourishment. You've lost a lot of blood."

Aaron nodded. "I'll try."

Jason went to the kitchen and removed the chickens from the pot to a cutting board and skinned and boned them, then diced the meat into bite-sized pieces. He returned the meat to the pot, stirred it up, and then ladled some soup without broth into a bowl until it was one-third full. The soup had been simmering for several hours, so everything was melt-in-your-mouth soft. He mashed the soup into a paste with a fork and then stirred in extra broth to thin it out. By the time he'd finished, the soup had cooled enough to eat. He also made Aaron a large mug of bouillon. He carried it all to Aaron on a bed tray and then reached to the bedside table and pressed a button. Slowly the head of Aaron's side of the bed began to rise. "I'm impressed," Aaron whispered in surprise.

Slowly Jason spooned the soup into Aaron's mouth and wiped his chin whenever some of it leaked out until he'd finished the bowl. Aaron didn't realize how hungry he was. The soup tasted better than anything he'd ever eaten before in his life.

"Is there any more?"

"We'd better stop there, Aaron. I don't know for

sure what kind of shape your belly's in. You've been through a violent trauma, and I don't want you to develop any more complications than you've already got."

"What do you mean?" Aaron asked.

"I don't have any indication that you have any internal organ damage, but I don't have any way to know for sure and there isn't a hospital for miles and miles around."

"When do you think they'll come for me?"

"Aaron, I don't know. We're deep in the mountains of Idaho. There's no road access at all, and it's rare to ever see a plane fly overhead. I had this place built here for just that reason."

"So no one's coming?"

"I'm sorry, but I don't think so. No. At least not for a while."

"I see." Aaron closed his eyes. "Well then my career's really over, isn't it?"

"What do you mean?"

"I'm Aaron Jaeger. I'm the new quarterback for the Continental Football League's Nevada Bighorns. What day is it?"

"It's Sunday, September sixth."

"I'm supposed to start in the opening game next Sunday. I am so fucked."

"I'm sorry, Aaron, I don't follow football, and way out here I don't get a paper or television."

"How did you know what to do for me?"

"I was a medic in the army. I did two tours in Iraq, but I left fifteen years ago, last month. Medical discharge. PTSD. I'm okay now, but it was hard-going there for a while."

"Well then how'd you get all the stuff you used on me?"

"Aaron, I'm very comfortable, financially. I have a friend, a doctor I used to work with after I was discharged from the army. Anything I want he orders for me, and I have it drop-shipped here by helicopter twice a year. I can get just about anything I need."

"Wow! You rich or something?"

"I'm very comfortable, that's all."

"Then you can get in touch with him? Your doctor friend?"

"I could, that was until yesterday. The storm took out my satellite dish. I'm not due for another supplies delivery for another two, two and a half months."

"So what are you going to do?"

"There's nothing I really can do. I haven't had any major problems since I've been here. This place is fitted with all the latest technology and comforts of home, and it was built with the weather in mind. As technology has advanced, I've added whatever became available, but the one thing I never considered was a satellite phone. I regret that now.

"I depend on solar panels and a small windmill for my electricity. I have a thousand-gallon underground oil fuel tank that feeds a generator and furnace, but I had them put in only for emergencies. I've used them just a couple of times so far, but that's it. The solar panels and windmill have supplied all the power I need."

He paused, then went on.

"My hot water comes from a four-panel solar heater on the roof that feeds two tanks, a ten-gallon in the kitchen and a thirty in the bathroom. Both run through supplemental, point-of-use propane water heaters that I can turn on if I want really hot water. Because I'm alone here I cook with wood, and I heat this place in the winter with a couple of wood stoves since I've got plenty of timber all around me."

"And my arm and my leg. How are those going to get fixed?"

"Aaron, please understand, I'm completely off the grid up here. Completely. I've never been without the ability to communicate with the outside world whenever I wanted to, even though that wasn't that often. I've been trying to think of a way that I can get you back to civilization. At best, it's at least a two-day trek out of here by foot, coz of the mountainous terrain, but it'd likely be more like three, and you wouldn't survive that long if I left you by yourself. Not with your present injuries.

"You've lost a lot of blood, and you've got a lot of lacerations and several puncture wounds, some of which I've put drains in, and your broken bones are very unstable. I've done my best to set them and your dislocated ankle, and I'm hopeful that they'll heal properly, but movement of any kind over the next month, possibly longer, could be catastrophic. With the exception of lidocaine as a local anesthetic, I have no medications here for pain other than aspirin, ibuprofen, and acetaminophen, and right now you can't even have them because of their side effects.

"In a hospital, you'd be in an ICU right now, and you would have had plates and screws inserted in your bones by an orthopedic surgeon. Simply put, you'll be bed-bound for the foreseeable future. There's simply no way I could transport you out of here right now."

Aaron was silent. He closed his eyes and turned his head away from Jason. Eventually he fell asleep.

****

While Aaron slept, Jason formulated many plans for Aaron's rescue, but they each fell apart the further he took them. There was just no way he could get Aaron off the mountain any time soon. It was early evening before

Aaron woke again.

Sunday, September 6, 2009, 5:45 PM

"Hello," Aaron called, "Jason?" There was no answer. He couldn't see past a blanket that was strung over a length of rope below the foot of the bed.

"Hello? Jason?" he called out again.

Jason sat bolt upright from the army stretcher he'd placed on the floor next to the bed. He blinked his eyes.

"There you are," Aaron said with a quizzical look. "What're you doing down there?"

"Sorry, I must have fallen asleep," he said as he stood up. "I put the stretcher down there so I'd be close by if you needed me."

"I didn't mean to startle you."

"That's okay. It's just that I'm not used to hearing someone call my name."

Aaron was completely uncovered again, and he had a full-blown erection that stood at half-staff over his belly. It bounced gently in time with his pulse. Jason stared at it.

"Impressive, isn't it!" Aaron said jokingly.

"Oh, sorry," Jason said, averting his eyes.

"No problem. I'm used to it. Guys are always staring at my dick."

"Hey, aren't you cold?" Jason asked, trying to change the subject, "I packed you with hot water bags when I first got you into the bed. You were really cold and it was the only thing I could think of to warm you up quickly. Should I bring them back to help keep you warm?"

"Thanks for doing that for me. I'm a little cold, but I'm used to waking up this way. And no, I don't need them anymore. I seem to push the sheets off me when I sleep. I wake up cold all the time."

Jason shook out the blanket and sheet and covered Aaron's body. "Let me get you another mug of bouillon. I'll be right back."

"Hey man, I gotta pee," Aaron called behind him. "How's that gonna work?"

"Hold on a minute," Jason called back. When he returned, Jason sat the mug down and went to the supply closet where he found an old white porcelain coated metal urinal he'd picked up at a garage sale while he was staying in his parents' home before they died. He'd only ever used it as a vase for wildflowers.

"Here you go," Jason said as he handed the urinal to Aaron. "Can you manage?"

"I'm not sure. What do I do with it?"

"You stick your penis in it and pee."

Aaron took the urinal and tried to position it, but no matter what he did, the opening of the urinal pointed downward.

"Well that's not going to work," he said. "It'll dump right back out all over me."

"Haven't you ever been in the hospital before?" Jason asked.

"No. Never. Can you help me?"

"Are you sure?" Jason asked.

"Yeah, man. It's okay."

"Okay." Jason put on a pair of gloves, took the urinal from Aaron, and slid it over his erection. "Now just pee," he said as he tipped the bottom of the urinal downward to keep the urine from spilling.

"What, man, you think you're gonna catch something from me?" Aaron asked a little bitingly as his stream started to flow.

"Not at all. It's just habit," Jason answered. "In

the hospital, we always wore gloves whenever handling bodily fluids. It's just standard protocol. Universal precautions, it's called."

"What for?"

"For any communicable diseases that can be transmitted through body fluids."

"You mean like AIDS and STDs?"

"Exactly. Also hepatitis, and a whole slew of other things like MRSA, VRE, Candidiasis, C. diff, the flu, shingles. The list goes on and on. There's a whole bunch of things."

"Well, Jason. I don't have AIDS, if that's what you're worried about. I get tested. Regularly."

"As I said, there's a whole bunch of things, and it's just a force of habit."

Aaron nodded his understanding. "Okay, I'm done."

Jason tapped the tip of Aaron's penis with the lip of the urinal to dislodge a drop that remained at the end of his urethra.

"Shake twice, tuck once," Aaron said, reflexively, "Hey, sorry 'bout what I said a minute ago. I don't know what came over me. Sorry, man. Really, I'm sorry."

"Aaron, it's okay. No harm done. Feeling better?" Jason asked with a smile.

"Not really."

"Really, Aaron, it's okay. I'll be right back. In the meantime, drink this."

Jason tested the mug of bouillon. It had cooled enough to drink so he handed it to Aaron with a straw.

"It's chicken bouillon. It has lots of salt in it, and you need to replace that."

Aaron drank the entire mug in less than half a minute. When Jason returned, Aaron was red in the face.

"What's wrong, Aaron? Are you in pain?"

Aaron didn't answer. He just got redder in the face and turned his head away. Jason leaned forward and placed his hand on Aaron's shoulder. Aaron jumped.

"Man!" Aaron exclaimed, "What am I gonna do when I have to take a shit?"

"You'll go on a pan. A bed pan, or in your case, probably a fracture pan."

Jason walked back to the storage closet and pulled down the bed pan and fracture pan that he'd bought at the same time as the urinal. He returned with them and placed them on the bed next to Aaron. Aaron looked at them with an expression of disgust.

"Man, you gotta be kiddin' me!"

"You got a better idea, Aaron?"

"Well how the hell am I gonna wipe my ass?"

"You won't be able to. I'll do that for you."

Aaron became silent again.

"Aaron, I've already cleaned you up once, when you were out cold, after I got you down from the tree."

Aaron looked back at Jason, red in the face. "I can't, Jason. I just can't."

"Okay, Aaron, we better get this all out in the open right now."

"What do you mean all out in the open?"

"Do you want to live?"

"Yeah."

"Really?"

"Yeah, man. I want to live," Aaron answered with defiance in his voice.

"Well, there's no easy way around this. Can I be straight with you?"

Aaron nodded his head.

Over the next fifteen minutes, Jason went through all the ugly, gory, and disgusting details of what the next few months would entail. From dressing changes and wound care, to suture removal and fracture care, as well as feeding and meals, and all the ins and outs of personal hygiene including use the of a bedpan.

In addition, Jason explained the chores he would be doing on a daily basis while caring for Aaron so that he could keep the place running, as well as the necessary care the animals required, because they would be supplying them with all the eggs and milk they'd be consuming.

"And you're going to be able to do all this for me, along with all that other stuff?" Aaron asked with a look of astonishment on his face when Jason had finished.

"Well, Aaron, there's no one else here to do it. Who did you think would care for you?"

"Sorry, Jason. I didn't. Think, that is. I just didn't think at all. Why would you do this for me, a stranger?"

Jason sat down in the chair next to the bed. "Because you're a human being, and I'm a human being." They didn't talk for several long minutes. Finally, Jason broke the silence.

"You hungry?"

****

Jason removed the stock pot from the stove and ladled another full bowl of soup for Aaron. It had broken down so much that it was now almost the consistency of mush. He also made him another large mug of bouillon, beef this time. No sooner had Aaron finished the soup and bouillon, then he fell asleep.

Jason washed out his bowl and his spoon in the sink and placed them in the dish rack. Then he ladled himself a bowl and cut off two thick slices of sourdough bread and slathered them with Heather's butter. He filled the sink with cold water and put the pot in it to cool it down before he put it in the fridge. When he finished eating, he washed his bowl and spoon and added them to the dish rack. The soup pot had cooled enough, so he put it away.

Jason carried a mug of vegetable bouillon for Aaron and sat it down on a wooden card table he'd set up next to the bed where Aaron could reach it, then he began to examine his dressings.

Chapter Six
Stirrings

Sunday, September 6, 2009, 7:40 PM

The sensation of someone touching him caused Aaron to stir. He woke to find Jason examining his body. Silently he watched him. He was impressed by the degree of concentration Jason projected, and he was humbled by the genuine concern and gentleness with which Jason checked his dressings.

"How do they look?"

Jason jumped just the slightest bit. "Sorry, Aaron. I didn't realize you were awake."

"Sorry I startled you."

"They look like they need changing. All of them, and they can't wait 'til morning. You also really need a bath. Okay?"

Aaron turned his head to his left and smelled his armpit. "Phew, I stink. Sorry, man, I didn't realize just how bad I smelled."

"It's all part of being sick or injured in your case, Aaron. Don't worry about it."

"So how's that gonna work? Who's gonna do it?"

"I am."

"You?"

"Yes, Aaron, it's like I said before. There's nobody else here, is there?"

"Oh, man! I don't even know you. Oh, sorry, man. I mean, Jason. Sorry. That was real shitty of me, after all you've done for me."

"Aaron, before I was a medic, I was a corpsman."

"What's that?"

"It's army lingo for orderly. Bathing soldiers was part of my job while I was in training to become a medic."

"All right. I guess it's okay. So what do I have to do?"

"You don't have to do anything but lie there. Please let me know if I hurt you. Oh, and there's another mug of bouillon, vegetable this time." Jason pointed to the mug. "Drink as much of it as you can. I want to be sure we're replacing your fluids as quickly as possible."

****

Over the next hour, Jason removed Aaron's dressings, cleaned his wounds, redressed them, and bathed as much of him as he could. He had to change the water and replace the washcloths and towels several times from all the blood and drainage that came off Aaron's body.

More often than not, Jason would nod his head and murmur a positive, "Hmmm," or click his tongue, or raise his eyebrows and stare, wide-eyed with a slight smile as he worked from would to wound. He moved very slowly when he examined, cleaned, and redressed the wounds on Aaron's fracture limbs.

"So, doc, how do they look?" Aaron asked while sipping the bouillon.

Jason smiled. "Not bad. Not bad at all. Much better than I expected. There's no sign of infection, and the seepage from your wounds has slowed down tremendously. I'm amazed and very pleased. I guess that's what happens when you're young and healthy."

Aaron let out an exaggerated breath. "Phew! That's a relief."

"Thing is, Aaron. You can't move a muscle, really. I have no way of stabilizing those fractures beyond the splints I've put on them. If you move they could come out of alignment, and I have no way of knocking you out to reset them. That was the only good thing about you being unconscious for as long as you were."

When Jason got to his groin and began to lift the sheet, Aaron stopped him.

"That too?" Aaron asked.

"It's part of your body, isn't it? You've used the urinal, right?"

"Yeah, I guess."

"Well, how many times do you normally bathe or shower?"

"At least once a day, two or three times when I'm at practice or playing."

"And why's that?"

"I get all hot and sweaty."

"Do you wash your junk whenever you shower?"

"Of course, they get all hot and sweaty too!"

"Well there you go. It's been days!"

"Yeah, I guess you're right."

"Don't worry. It'll be over before you know it."

Jason emptied the buckets and refilled them with clean water. When he returned, he started by lathering up Aaron's upper thighs and groin, but when he moved to his scrotum, Aaron got a far-away look in his eyes. As he lifted Aaron's sizable penis with both hands, Aaron closed his eyes and let out a gentle sigh. When Jason began to lathered the soap into it, it began to change, becoming slightly heavier and slightly longer. And Aaron's smile grew right along with it.

Jason worked as quickly as he could. As he drew the washcloth along the underside of the penis' shaft, he inadvertently milked the urethra, causing a brief stream of pre-cum to pour out of the tip.

Thank God that's over, Jason thought.

As he dried everything off, Aaron's penis grew a good one and a half inches more. While he was rubbing it dry, another larger stream of pre-cum spilled from it, but it was immediately absorbed into the towel.

"That's enough for tonight. I'll wash your back tomorrow when I bathe you again."

"That wasn't so bad," Aaron said as he opened his eyes and smiled a huge smile. "Thanks, Jason. Really, not bad at all!"

"I'll give you a better bath tomorrow."

"Understood, now back to that dirty detail. How am I gonna take a shit and not move? I can't even pull myself up with this bum arm."

"We'll move very slowly and cautiously, and take it one step at a time."

"Okay, I trust you know what you're doing. Thanks again." Aaron yawned. "Sorry, Jason, but I'm dead tired. I gotta go to sleep."

"Me too, Aaron. It's gotta be close to eleven by now."

"You got a watch or clock or something I can keep here with me? I always like to know what time it is."

"Sorry, Aaron, no. The only clock is the grandfather clock over in the corner, and there's one on the microwave, but I put that away years ago. I haven't had any need for it."

Jason pulled the curtain back. "That's the grandfather clock over there," he said, pointing.

"I can't really see the face or the hands, only the side of the clock. I guess it doesn't chime, huh? I haven't heard it."

"No, I disabled the chimes the day it arrived. Tell you what. Tomorrow, I'll turn it so you can see its face, but it'll take some time. I'll have to re-level it. How would that work for you?"

"Thanks, man, that'd be great!" Aaron yawned again. "Sorry, Jason, I'm fading fast."

"Don't even think about it. I'll be right down here on the floor. Just call me if you need me. If I'm not here when you wake in the morning, it's because I'm outside taking care of the animals. It doesn't take long, only about fifteen to twenty minutes. I'll leave you a note on the bed if I go out, but you can be sure that I'll be coming right back. One more thing, I'm going to mix you up another mug of bouillon. I want you to take some before you fall asleep, and it'll be here on this card table if you wake in the middle of the night. Keep drinking it. I have chicken, beef, and vegetable. Which do you prefer?"

"Okay, Jason. Thanks. I like them all. It doesn't matter."

Jason returned with a mug of chicken bouillon and then laid down on the stretcher.

"Thanks."

"You're welcome, and if you need help with the urinal, wake me. Okay. Good night, then."

"Night," Aaron answered and then swallowed several mouthfuls of the bullion.

As Jason drifted off, he thought it curious that although Aaron's penis had grown, it hadn't become erect in the slightest. It made him wonder just how much blood the thing held and how much was required to bring it to full staff. Then he was asleep and dreaming.

****

Jason woke up several times through the night which was rare for him. He realized it was because of the sound of someone else's breathing. He wasn't accustomed to it. Each time he woke, he sat up for a few minutes to watch Aaron sleep. He was so peaceful when he slept. As Jason drifted back to his dreams, the words,

"So beautiful," echoed through his mind.

****

Monday, September 7, 2009, 6:50 AM

Jason woke to the sound of Big John, the rooster, crowing. The sun was just breaking over the horizon. He stood up from the stretcher and looked down at Aaron. He was sound asleep, and he must have pushed the sheet and blanket off himself again, because it was tangled up around his right leg. Jason pulled them back up over him and then used the bathroom and shaved his neck in record time.

He threw a load of laundry into the washing machine. With two of them there it was piling up, and he'd need to get ahead of it. While the washing machine ran, he returned to check on Aaron. He was still asleep, so Jason left a note and headed for the barn.

Before leaving the cabin, he added two split logs to the central wood stove and the kitchen stove and removed the trays beneath them, dumping their ashes into the ashcan to cool.

****

Aaron woke with a start. He remembered dreaming of Nathan and blow jobs, lots and lots of blow jobs. Then he remembered waking more than a few times during the night. Several times it had taken him a few moments to realize that he was in a strange place, but the pain he felt when he tried to move helped him to remember where he was and what had happened. Then he remembered Nathan's death, and he cried himself back to sleep.

****

Nellie, Sarah, Heather, and Jasper greeted Jason at the barn door. Everyone was hungry. Even the chickens let him know they were looking for feed by clucking and cooing as they marched around his feet, pecking at his boots. Having not been milked again the night before, Heather was dripping milk again. While he poured feed into the trough, she let him know she was overdue a second day in a row by butting him again before she hopped right up onto her milking table.

****

When Aaron woke again, he remembered seeing Jason watching him twice. He realized that Jason couldn't tell that he was watching him back. Jason was so handsome. Even with everything that had happened to him, all the physical and emotional pain he felt, Aaron realized just how lucky he was to have Jason there. Then he fell back to sleep.

****

Jason made quick work of the milking, but he had to use his spare, one gallon stainless steel milk pail. He chided himself for forgetting to milk Heather in the evening a second day in a row and promised himself to not let it happen again. Once finished, the pail held nearly three quarts again. He took a moment to pet each of the animals, then he filled their water trough and left the stall doors stand open again. It would take more than a few weeks for them to graze down the yard's tall grass.

Jason tossed out more feed and scratch for the chickens on his way back to the house. He poured the milk into a second bottle and put it in the refrigerator beside the bottle from the day before. Then he washed out the pail and returned it and the pail from yesterday back to the barn, remembering along the way that he had forgotten to gather the eggs.

Jason returned to the house with five eggs and after washing them and the six from the day before, he put them in a new bowl in the fridge, and took out five older eggs for breakfast. Then he had an idea. He went to the kitchen closet, took out the microwave, and then carried it to the dresser at the side of his bed when he went to check on Aaron. Aaron was still sound asleep, and there were tear stains down his cheeks. Seeing that the bedsheet and blanket were jumbled up again, he straightened them out and covered him up.

When he returned to the kitchen, he sat his twelve-inch cast iron frying pan on the front burner and dropped in a spoonful of Heather's butter and one of bacon fat. He used one egg for a slightly thin batter and cooked up twenty small pancakes, stacking them on a plate as they came out of the pan, and held them in the proof box over the oven to keep warm. Figuring that Aaron would probably be very hungry, he scrambled the remaining eggs, cut slices of smoked bacon from a slab and mixed up a pitcher of orange juice from frozen concentrate.

When he returned to check on Aaron again, he found him wide awake.

"I used it all by myself," Aaron said with a smile, pointing to the urinal.

Jason plugged in the microwave and set the time. "Now you have a clock. I thought this might be easier for you to see, but I'll be happy to turn the grandfather clock for you as well if you still want it."

"Thanks, Jason. This is great and no, I don't need another clock."

"Why didn't you let me know you were up?"

"I could smell that you were cooking, and I didn't want to disturb you."

"Aaron, you wouldn't have disturbed me. Are you hungry?"

"Starving," he said, rubbing his belly with his left hand. "What's for breakfast?"

"I made pancakes, and I've got scrambled eggs

and smoked bacon ready to put in the pan. I also made a pitcher of orange juice. Interested?"

"Yes, sir."

Jason reached across Aaron's abdomen and picked up the urinal.

"Better! Much better! There's a lot more in here," he said weighing the urinal in his hand. "Obviously, we're getting your fluids replaced. Now, how are you feeling?"

"Thirsty as all get out."

"How about a real tall glass of orange juice?"

"Sounds great, but then again I'd drink just about anything right now."

Jason went to the kitchen and poured the orange juice for Aaron. "This should hold you for a bit," he said when he returned. "Breakfast will be ready in just a few more minutes. I have honey, but no pancake syrup. Is that okay?"

"Sure!"

Jason emptied and rinsed out the urinal in the bathroom, washed his hands and then returned it to Aaron on his way back to the kitchen. Ten minutes later, he carried a full plate of scrambled eggs, pancakes, and bacon on the bed tray along with the pitcher of orange juice, a tall glass of Heather's milk, and salt, pepper, honey, and ketchup on the side. He set the tray over Aaron's lap and then raised the head of Aaron's side of the bed.

"I think it's so cool that you have an electric bed all the way out here," Aaron said as he drank down half the juice.

"An electric, king-sized bed with separate controls for each side."

"Wow, man, all the comforts of home!"

"I told you this place was decked out."

"You weren't kidding!"

Jason cut up Aaron's pancakes and bacon into bite-sized pieces and poured honey all over the pancakes, adding it over the bacon at Aaron's direction. Then he seasoned the eggs and added ketchup until Aaron indicated for him to stop.

"You up to feeding yourself?" he asked as he placed the tray over Aaron's waist.

"Yeah, I'd like to give it a try."

"Try to drink all the milk and some more juice, okay?"

"That shouldn't be a problem."

Jason sat down and watched Aaron get started. He seemed to be doing pretty well on his own, so he went back to the kitchen and returned with his own plate of food. Aaron ate ravenously so there was no conversation. By the time Jason was halfway through his food, Aaron had started to slow down.

"You finished, or do you need some help?" Jason asked.

"Sorry, you're still eating. I'll wait. Just getting a little tired, that's all."

"Oh, no. I'm happy to help." Jason put his plate on the card table and then helped Aaron with his breakfast. Once Aaron had gotten through about three-quarters of his plate and half his milk, he held up his hand.

"I'm stuffed, Jason, and my arm and leg are really aching. Isn't there anything you can give me for the pain?"

"Sorry, Aaron … like I said, all I've got is aspirin, ibuprofen, and acetaminophen, and you can't have any of them right now."

"You got any booze? I'm really hurting."

"At this hour?"

"Yeah. Please."

"I've got scotch."

"That'll do."

Jason took Aaron's plate to the kitchen and returned with the liquor and a tumbler. He poured about an ounce.

"Give me half a glass," Aaron said.

When he saw Jason raise his eyebrows, he added, "That's nothing for me. Look how big I am. I can handle it."

"Okay, if you say so."

Jason began to pour again, and as he did, Aaron reached up and tilted up the bottom of the bottle. The tumbler was three-quarters full when Aaron stopped. Jason frowned. "I'll be fine, really, Jason."

After Aaron had drunk down the scotch, Jason picked up his plate and sat down to finish his breakfast. While he ate, Aaron drifted off to sleep.

When he finished eating, Jason folded up the bed tray and took his plate to the kitchen. He put Aaron's milk in the fridge and then carried his plate out into the yard and scraped it off for the chickens to finish.

Chapter Seven
I am too

After washing the dishes, Jason returned to find Aaron was still asleep.

He'd pushed most of the blanket and sheet off himself again, so Jason pulled them back up before emptying the washer. He hung the laundry on two lines that ran between hooks that were bolted around several of the cabin's vertical supporting posts in the common area and then he returned to Aaron.

"Hey, Aaron," Jason said while tapping his shoulder, "How about you let me start getting you washed up?"

"Huh, what? What?" Aaron said as he opened his eyes.

"How about you let me start getting you washed up?" Jason repeated.

Feeling the effects of the scotch, Aaron looked up at him sheepishly, but nodded his head and averted his eyes in embarrassment. He remembered how his dick responded the night before.

"It's okay, Aaron. You'll get through this. Would you like to get started yourself? You can do as much as you feel up to. Or, if you prefer, you can drift back to sleep, and I'll bathe you."

"Okay," Aaron answered, "Deal. I'll start, but I don't know how far I'll get or how good I'll do."

Jason soon returned with the two buckets of water and two washcloths and towels. He placed the tray back over Aaron's waist and sat both buckets on it, then dropped one washcloth into each. "I don't know what to do?" Aaron said.

"Squeeze out the soapy washcloth and start with your eyes and face, but keep your eyes closed," Jason said encouragingly. "Then squeeze out the other washcloth and wipe the soapy water away. You do that alternately on each area you wash. Once you've rinsed, dry yourself with the towel. Don't worry, I've got plenty of bath linens."

Aaron began, a bit clumsy at first, but he soon got the hang of it. "Sorry, I'm right-handed. I'm clumsy with my left."

"You're doing just fine," Jason encouraged. "Keep going."

Jason lowered the sheet down to Aaron's waist. As he started on his chest, Aaron became frustrated when he dripped water on some of the dressings.

"I can't do this right, and I'm getting tired," Aaron said as he threw the washcloth into the bucket. "Can you help me, please?"

"Sure. Just lie back, and I'll finish up for you, but first I'm going to get some fresh dressings and bandages."

Aaron closed his eyes, intending to drift off to sleep. He was well under the effects of the booze by the time Jason returned. Jason put on a pair of gloves and began with Aaron's chest. Each time the washcloth passed over his pecs, Aaron sighed quietly. His large nipples were becoming erect. Unconsciously, Aaron attempted to move his right hand to his groin but winced immediately at the pain.

"Relax, Aaron, and try to hold still."

Jason moved to his abdomen. Aaron began to slowly lick his lips. Soft growls began to rise from his chest.

"Uh, Aaron, you okay?"

"Yeah, Jason, I'm great. Booze is helping.

Thanks."

"Aaron, please try to relax."

"Oh, I'm relaxed. Real, real relaxed. Feels good, really, really good, Jason," Aaron said quietly. Then he turned his head and looked deeply into Jason's eyes.

Jason moved on to Aaron's left arm and hand, then his right upper arm and hand, avoiding his forearm. When he moved to the lower half of his body, Aaron let out a deep sigh. His body went limp. A serene smile appeared on his face while Jason massaged the soapy washcloth up and down his thighs.

Aaron slowly reached his left hand under the sheet and began to gently stroke his penis. As he slid his hand up and down the shaft, the sheet slowly moved up to his abdomen, revealing what was happening.

"Uh, Aaron, what are you doing?" Jason asked, in a higher than normal voice.

"Sorry, Jason. It just feels so good. I'm feeling more relaxed now." Aaron's words began to slur. His penis was nearly fully engorged, and his testicles had pulled up tight in his scrotum.

"Aaron, I don't know what to say."

All embarrassment gone, Aaron answered in a thick voice, "Jason, I feel wonderful. So, so good. I haven't come in a week. Nathan and I ... Oh, Nathan! Oh, Nathan, I'm so, so sorry!"

Tears began to flow from Aaron's closed eyes. He released his penis, and his erection began to subside as he wept. Jason patted Aaron on the shoulder and then sat down in the chair in silence.

****

A few minutes later, Aaron opened his eyes and looked at Jason. "I'm better now, Jason, and I'm so, so sorry. I couldn't help it. Really. I haven't come in over a week. Nathan and I," his voice caught for a moment, but he continued, "Nathan and I hadn't seen each other in seven days. That's why we were on the plane." His voice caught again.

"We were going on a retreat where we could be ourselves and to celebrate my birthday, my twenty-third, but it was a secret. No one knew Nathan was with me."

Jason was stunned. *His birthday? His birthday was when? Saturday?*

"It's okay, Aaron," Jason said encouragingly, but he was freaking out inside. "This kind of thing can happen. It's a normal physiological reaction to physical stimulation, but please believe me. I'm not trying to cause it."

"Oh, I know it's not you, Jason, believe me, it's me. I can get hard at the drop of a hat. It's embarrassing. I'll get a hard-on on the field from just the friction from my jockstrap, and I've always gotten one in the showers. All I have to do is start to soap myself up, and I'm rock hard and twitching in just a few seconds. It's a curse. I'm so sorry."

"It's okay, Aaron. Really it's okay."

"Thanks for understanding, Jason, but still ..."

Jason gave a quick nod and smiled. "You okay to go on? This bath really needs to get finished."

"Okay," Aaron nodded, and closed his eyes. He drew in a breath and tensed his mouth.

"Try not to hold your breath. You could pass out. And don't tense your body. Remember your fractures. Relax. Whatever happens, happens."

Jason finished washing and rinsing Aaron's thighs. He moved on to his right lower leg and right foot. Over the course of the bath, he removed each dressing one by one and washed, rinsed, and dried as close as he could to each wound before redressing them, including the fracture sites of his left leg and right arm. Then he helped Aaron turn on his side so he could wash as much of his back and buttocks as he could reach. When he finished, he wrapped both washcloths in a towel.

When he turned back, Aaron said, "My right butt cheek is really sore."

"That's from the penicillin injection I gave you while you were out. I didn't find a medical alert bracelet on you. Do you have any allergies?"

"No, none."

"Good 'cuz I took a big chance giving that to you. You have a lot of sources of infection. If I hadn't and you developed an infection, it could have been fatal."

"I'm glad you did. It was the right thing to do."

Jason nodded, "I'll be right back."

He tossed the washcloths into the hamper and dumped the buckets into the toilet. After scrubbing and rinsing the buckets out in the shower, he froze. *Fuck, I didn't do his junk!* He walked back to Aaron with a distressed look on his face.

Aaron looked up at him. "What's wrong?" he asked.

"Aaron, I'm sorry. I forgot to wash your groin area before I did your back, but it really needs to be done. Once I'd washed your butt, the washcloth was too soiled to finish up."

Aaron nodded, "I'm sorry you had to do that, Jason."

"It's okay, Aaron. Do you think you're up to me finishing?"

Aaron sighed, resolved at what was to come. "Yeah, go ahead, Jason. Just do it."

Jason went back to the bathroom and refilled the buckets. He took out two clean washcloths from the bathroom closet and dropped one in each bucket. When he returned, Aaron had his eyes closed. "It'll be okay,

Aaron."

Aaron opened his eyes and looked at him.

Jason went on, "This is going to need to be done every day. You've got abrasions and pine sap on the inside of your thighs."

"That's my fault," Aaron said. "I forgot to pull the steering toggles after Nathan pushed me out of the plane. I watched it explode and come down in pieces. All I could think of was losing him. I couldn't stop crying. It wasn't until I actually saw branches on the trees that I realized I was still falling fast. I must have pulled them at the last minute."

"That explains a lot about your injuries," Jason said. The abrasions are right in the creases between where your thighs meet your abdomen, next to your scrotum, and besides, your penis and scrotum really do need to get washed every day, anyway. You've been sweating between your legs, and that's an area that's really prone to skin breakdown, particularly when you're bed-bound, because it's always moist and it's dark. That can lead to infection."

Aaron nodded his head. "Thank you, Jason. Really, thank you. I know this can't be easy on you. I'll do my best."

"Again, don't hold your breath. Don't tense your body. Try to remain relaxed. We'll get through this. I promise." Jason put on a new pair of gloves and lifted the sheet to expose Aaron's groin.

Wringing out the soapy washcloth, he lifted it from the bucket and lifted Aaron's penis into his hands. As he began to lather it up, Aaron's eyelids fluttered, and he gently moaned. Then his lips tightened.

Oh, Jesus, here we go again! Jason thought.

Aaron grunted as his flaccid penis began to swell. Immediately, Jason lowered it to Aaron's abdomen and let go of it. It continued to grow in length and girth and rise up off Aaron's belly. "Jason, I'm sorry. I can't help it," Aaron said with a whimper in his voice.

"It's okay, Aaron, but I'm going to finish this. Ready?"

Aaron nodded his head but kept his eyes closed, and drew in a breath.

Jason picked up Aaron's now fully erect, ten-inch, throbbing penis and finished lathering it. Aaron's breathing quickened, and he began to pant.

"Relax, Aaron."

The engorged glans was now pulsating with each of Aaron's heartbeats. The moment he finished, Jason released it, but it hovered over Aaron's abdomen bouncing up and down.

"I'm okay. I'm okay," Aaron said between clenched teeth.

"Relax, Aaron. You're tensing up. Remember your fractures." Jason moved on to the scrotum, lathering the soap deep into the skin folds. Aaron moaned more and more and began to roll his head from side to side.

"Relax. Relax," Jason said in a calm, soothing voice. He continued down to the perineum being very gentle, as well as where the inner thighs met the abdomen in the creases of the groin. Aaron winced and his erection began to subside.

"There are some ugly abrasions here from when the parachute's harness straps dug into your skin when you came to a sudden stop in the tree, Aaron."

"It's okay, Jason. At least my hard-on is going away."

Jason dropped the soapy washcloth into the bucket and picked up and rung out the other washcloth. As he wiped the shaft to remove the soap, Aaron's penis began to stiffen again.

"Aaron, can you look at me for a moment?"

Aaron opened his eyes.

"It seems there isn't any way I can do this that won't give you pleasure, I mean stimulate a physical response, and it has to be done. We can't not have your genitals washed daily, so..."

Aaron raised his eyebrows, "So? What?"

"Aaron, this is difficult for me to say, especially with your fully erect penis bouncing over your abdomen, but how would you feel if something did happen?"

"What do you mean?"

"I mean if when I'm rinsing your penis and scrotum, you become so aroused that you ... I mean too aroused that you can't ... I mean..."

"You mean if I come?"

"Yes, ejaculate."

"You said it yourself just a minute ago, if something happens, it happens."

"That isn't exactly what I meant at the time. What I meant was that you might become aroused, but if that did happen, I mean, if you did ... um ... ejaculate, you'd be okay with it?"

"Jason, like I said, I can't control it. It's embarrassing, but there's nothing I can do about it."

"Okay, but I'm going to try to do this with as little stimulation as I can."

"Okay, go ahead and finish." Aaron closed his eyes.

Jason picked up a bath towel and folded it lengthwise. Then he slid it under Aaron's scrotum and wrapped it around the base of his penis to make a dam. He picked up the clean washcloth, partially wringing it out over the bucket, then began to squeeze the water over Aaron's penis and scrotum. As soon as the water began to drizzle over the glans, it swelled even more. In just a few seconds, Aaron's penis was fully erect again. His moaning became louder.

Even though Jason had just said to Aaron what he said, he was beside himself. "What if I am less gentle, Aaron? Would that be better?"

"I don't know, Jason. Really, I don't know, but it's not your fault, whatever happens. I want you to know that. It's not your fault. But know this too, I can't help but think about my cock right now."

I can't believe this is happening again, Jason thought, but aloud he said, "You're going to be okay, Aaron. It's going to be okay. I'm going to stop using the washcloth and just pour some water over it to rinse it off." Just like the day before, a bead of pre-cum began to form at the opening of the urethra, but it was thinner, now that Aaron was better hydrated.

Jason hurried. He gently trickled just enough water down the shaft and over the scrotum to rinse them. The towel absorbed the water as it fell. As he poured, Aaron's moans turned to groans.

"Am I hurting you?"

"No, Jason, this is not pain. Definitely not pain!" Aaron began to grunt rhythmically.

Jason continued to pour more water, and was just about finished when Aaron began to pant again.

"Please, help me, Jason! Help me!" Aaron begged, "Please!" Like a faucet that had been turned on, pre-cum began to flow from the pulsating, swelling head.

"We're finished, Aaron. All done," Jason said with a sigh of relief.

"Oh, my God, I need to come! I've got to come!" Aaron began to reach for his throbbing, leaking penis with his left hand. "Just a few strokes..." Aaron's thighs contracted.

"Aaron, no! If you move, it'll destabilize your

fractures."

Aaron had a hold of his spasming penis and was stroking it fiercely. "Oh God! Please Jason! Please!"

"No, Aaron, please stop!"

Aaron's hand moved up to the swollen glans as he closed his hand and rubbed his palm over and around it quicker and quicker as it grew redder and redder. "Yes! Yes! I'm almost there! Almost there!"

"Aaron!"

"Here it comes!" Aaron yelled.

"Aaron, do you want to be a cripple for the rest of your life? Do you ever want to walk again?"

"Fuck!" Aaron yelled at the top of his lungs. He released his hand. "Oh, Jason. I'm sorry! Fuck! Fuck! Fuck!" Aaron's cock continued to throb and bounce. His stream of pre-cum had formed a pool in his bellybutton until it overflowed, eventually reaching the towel where it was absorbed by the thick, hungry, looping threads, but it was too late.

A huge, thick stream of white cum was ejected from his slit, just reaching his chin. A second stream spewed onto his upper chest, then another less forcefully landed at the top of his belly and his lower chest, and then a fourth into his navel, and then a fifth slid down his shaft, until eventually the cum oozed out less and less, covering Aaron's glans like the vanilla dip coating on a soft-serve strawberry cone. Then it was over.

Jason plopped himself into the chair and watched Aaron's cock as it continued to throb and bounce. More cum oozed over and down the swollen head and slid down the slowly receding shaft.

Jason's heart was pounding, and his breathing quickened. His cock was rock hard and straining to break free from the restriction of his jeans. He realized that he was looking at the most beautiful cock he'd ever seen.

He was completely unaware that he was licking his lips, or aware of the longing look on his face.

Jason quickly stood up and picked up the buckets. He turned to carry them into the bathroom just in time so that when Aaron opened his eyes to look over at him, he didn't see the longing on Jason's face.

When Jason returned, Aaron looked up at him. He had covered himself so that the sheet now extended from below his groin all the way up to his neck. The cum that had struck his chin was gone, but there was still a large wet area over his chest and abdomen.

"I just have to take the towel away."

Without waiting for an answer, Jason lifted the sheet. Aaron's penis lay flaccid on the saturated bath towel. There was a puddle of thick cum on his chest and belly.

Jason removed the saturated towel and wiped up the cum with a dry hand towel and folded it into another towel. Then he grabbed a new one and gently moved it down between Aaron's thighs to wipe up what remained of the rinse water. Aaron winced as the towel passed across the abrasions, but he didn't make a sound. Then Jason took a clean sheet out of the linen closet and replaced the wet sheet with it.

"Jason, I don't know what to say. I'm so embarrassed, and I feel so ashamed. I mean, Nathan died just three days ago, and here I am jerking off."

Jason struggled to clear his head. It was so filled with images of Aaron naked and the things he imagined they could do together, but he pulled himself away from that. He realized he had to, for Aaron's sake.

"Would you like to talk about Nathan?"

"What's wrong with me, Jason? I mean, Nathan's dead. How could I possibly think about sex?"

"You're a healthy young man, Aaron. Sex and

orgasms are normal things, particularly for someone as young as you are. They're a part of life, and when people are stressed, like you are now, and have faced death, like you just did, they have a need to reaffirm life—and the most basic way to do that is to procreate. That's why they turn to sex. Often it's mindless, but nevertheless, it happens."

"But, Jason, I wasn't trying to make a baby!" Aaron paused. He was frustrated.

"Aaron, sex is sex."

"Jason, do you not get it? I've never had sex with a woman."

"So."

Aaron just stared at him, dumbfounded.

"Aaron, we don't need to talk about this."

"Do I have to spell it out for you, Jason?"

"You don't have to say anything. I don't want you to feel uncomfortable."

Aaron blurted out, "Jason, I'm gay!"

"Do you think that matters to me, Aaron?"

"Well yeah! You're taking care of a gay guy, and I just came all over your bed!"

"Aaron, it doesn't matter."

"It doesn't matter? What, that I'm gay, or that I just started to shoot the biggest load of my life? God, if I hadn't stopped it probably would've hit the wall!"

"None of that matters ... to me."

"You're not making any sense, Jason."

"What do you mean?"

"Don't try to be so nice about it, so understanding." Aaron rolled his eyes and made air quotes with his left hand when he said, understanding.

"I'm not, Aaron. I am too. I'm gay."

"Oh."

Aaron was silent for a long moment. Jason

waited.

"But then why didn't you jerk me off or try to suck me off or take advantage of me in some way?"

"Aaron, you do me a disservice. Being gay doesn't mean that you want to suck every dick you see." *Oh, but God, what a cock he has. What a body. Fuck! Fuck, Jason. Stop this.*

"No? Well hell, I have, every chance I've ever had, and Jason, I've gotten off with a lot of dudes. That was, until Nathan."

"Well you're young. The two things that young men think about the most are having orgasms and their next meal. The older you get, the more you'll find out there are other things that are more important than sexual conquests."

"Well, the older guys I've done didn't care about anything but sex."

"Perhaps that was only when you were with them, when they were looking for a sexual encounter. Not everyone matures at the same rate. Did you know any of them long-term, in a nonsexual way?"

"Uh ... no, not really."

"Then you only knew them for just that reason, sex. Aaron, I've seen a lot of death. It makes you put things into perspective."

"How old are you, Jason?"

"I'm thirty-seven."

"Hell! You sure don't look it. I wouldn't have put you past twenty-eight to thirty. Hell, you look damn good for someone that old."

Jason blushed. "That old?" he said mockingly, as if he'd been insulted.

"Just pullin' your leg. So, when's your birthday?"

Jason paused for a moment, not sure how or whether to even answer.

"Oh, come on, Jason. It's not like it's some kinda state secret or anything. Or is it?"

Jason shook his head no. "No, it's no secret."

"So when is it? Come on, tell me!"

"It was two days ago, on September fifth."

Aaron's eyes grew wide. "No way! You're shitting me! That's my birthday!"

"No, I realized we had birthdays close together when you told me about yours, but I didn't know the exact date."

"How about some lunch?" Jason said, trying to deflect the conversation, "It's gotta be close to that time. Do you want something to eat or did your bath tire you out? Maybe you'd like to sleep for a bit?"

"Sleep? No! I'm hungry as all hell. Maybe, coming has recharged my batteries. Let's eat!"

"And drink. You've got to keep drinking fluids. You want juice or bouillon or both? Oh, is chicken soup okay again? I'll get it out, and I can heat it right up in the microwave, thanks to you."

"Sounds great. Bouillon and juice and soup. And then we can talk some more. You're a fascinating guy, Jason. I've never met anyone like you."

****

While Jason was preparing lunch, Aaron got to thinking. *I can't believe it. Was Jason just making it up about his birthday? Did he say it to make me feel better? Is he going to use it later on to try to take advantage of me? Aaron's head began to spin. Then he remembered the look on Jason's face.* "No," he realized, *"he'd never do that. He's one of the good guys. He'd never take advantage of me, but what if he wanted me, really wanted me, in the right way? That would be okay, wouldn't it? For us to be together?"*

Chapter Eight
Wreckage

Monday, September 7, 2009, 10:15 AM
Local Breaking News, Hinnen Valley, Idaho

"Good morning, ladies and gentlemen. Some very disturbing developments are just in concerning the Aaron Jaeger story. We've just learned that the transponder from the plane identified as carrying quarterback, Aaron Jaeger, that disappeared last Friday evening from radar over the Wasatch Range of the Rocky Mountains has been located, among wreckage that was spotted in rugged, mountainous terrain from a rescue plane searching the Bear River Mountains.

"The Bear River Mountains are in the northern most section of The Wasatch Range in Idaho, which is part of the western Rocky Mountains.

"It is reported that the debris field does not appear to contain an entire airplane. Based on these findings, it is feared that the plane must have broken apart in mid-flight, and that parts of it may be scattered over a greater area than has already been searched.

"Because of the steep, mountainous terrain, it's unclear whether rescue crews will be able to reach the wreckage any time soon, due to thick forestation. Plans for a ground search and rescue are currently being formulated. We can only hope that Jaeger and the pilot survived the crash, and that rescue crews can reach the wreckage in time. Temperatures in the region are known to dip into the lower forties over night at this time of year.

"It has been confirmed that Jaeger never checked

in to the lodge where he had planned a one-week vacation before starting the Nevada Bighorns' 2009 – 2010 football season as their new quarterback. In addition, Jaeger's trainer, Nathan Taggart, has not yet been located. Stay tuned. We will continue to keep you updated on this breaking news story. We now return you to our regularly scheduled programming."

****

Tuesday, September 8, 2009, 6:45 AM

Jason woke up suddenly with an idea that just wouldn't let go. He realized he could use his blocks and tackle to make a sling of sorts to winch Aaron up when he had to use the bedpan. While he showered, he came up with a design for the contraption in his mind.

He put on his climbing gear and checked on Aaron before he left the cabin. Again, Aaron had pushed off the sheet and blanket and needed to be covered up. It was a good thing that Aaron was fast asleep because he knew it would take some time to recover his ropes and gear. He jotted a note and left it on the chair and then moved the chair right next to the bed so that Aaron couldn't possibly miss it.

Jason quickly took care of the animals and left them at their feed trough, then went out of the stockade and climbed the tree where he'd found Aaron.

After untying the block and tackle and unfastening all the ropes, he climbed down and carried everything to the cabin, picking up the pail of Heather's milk and five eggs from the barn on the way. As he approached the cabin, he could hear Aaron yelling his name. He dropped the block and tackle on the porch and ran inside.

****

When Jason found Aaron, he was disheveled,

sweating, and in a state of panic.

"Aaron, did you try to get out of bed?"

"Jason, I was so worried. What if you fell?"

"Aaron, I'm fine."

"Yeah, but what if you were killed? What would have happened to me? I'm sorry. I know that sounds selfish, but I was so worried."

"Aaron, I wasn't killed. I'm a skilled climber."

"You're my lifesaver, Jason. What would I have done? What would I have done without you?" As Aaron continued to speak, tears began to flow down his cheeks. "I'm all alone. Nathan's gone." His tears turned to sobs. "I'm all alone. I'm all alone now, Jason. I'm so alone."

Jason put the milk pail and eggs on the kitchen counter and washed his hands before returning to Aaron. He sat down on the edge of the bed and patted Aaron's arm while he sobbed. Aaron clutched at Jason's arm, then his back, and then the back of his neck with his good arm, pulling him in, all the while calling Nathan's name. As the minutes ticked by, Jason moved in closer and held him tight. Soon, he was stroking the top of Aaron's head, then his face, and then brushing his forehead with his thumb, while he whispered comforting words. They stayed like that for ten minutes.

Finally, Aaron let him go and began to wipe his eyes. Jason reached for a tissue and handed it to him.

"Please, Jason, please don't ever leave me alone like that again. I woke up, and you were gone. I was scared. Then I found your note, and I was really scared."

"I'm sorry, Aaron. I won't ever be gone that long again, but remember I have to care for the animals in the mornings and in the evenings."

"Why did you have to get that stuff out of the tree anyway?"

"Because I came up with an idea to make it easy

for you to use the bedpan without jeopardizing your fractured leg."

"Oh, Jason, I should have known! I should have known! You always put others before yourself. You were only thinking of me. I'm so, sorry Jason. I'm so, so sorry. There I was thinking only of myself, but I didn't have to. You were thinking of me. You! You're here to take care of me. I'm such a fool."

"It's okay, Aaron. It's going to be okay." Are you in pain? Did you try to move?"

Aaron nodded his head.

"Okay, I better check you over."

For the next several minutes, Jason tested Aaron's splints and checked his dressings.

"You were lucky, Aaron. Your bones don't appear to be out of alignment, and your dressings weren't disturbed. I'm sorry you were scared, but you have to remember that there's nothing holding your bones together. I'll say it again. If those bones come out of alignment, I have nothing to knock you out with before resetting them. There's no way you could take that amount of pain. So please, don't try to get out of bed. Don't move. and please, please try to not upset yourself. You'll only pay for it in the long run."

"Yes, Jason. I'll do what you say."

Jason walked away and returned in a moment with the bottle of scotch and a tumbler, and an old brass school bell with a wooden handle he'd brought from his parents' home. Then he poured Aaron half a glass of the amber liquor.

"Here, drink this. It'll help with the pain, and I'm going to give you two of these," Jason said. He reached into his pocket and pulled out a pill bottle.

"What are they?"

"Aspirin."

"I thought you said I couldn't take aspirin because of the side effects."

"That was only for the first few days. I had to be sure you didn't have internal bleeding. If you had, it would have shown up by now. Now take them too. They'll help with your inflammation which will help with your pain."

"Thanks, Jason. What's the bell for?"

"It's for you to ring if I'm ever outside and you need me. I can't believe I didn't think of that before. Will that work for you?"

"Yeah, thanks, Jason. It's great, and sorry. I was acting like a hysterical little school girl there for a minute."

"It's okay, Aaron."

Jason was shocked by Aaron's reaction, but he hoped that he hadn't revealed that. He told himself that it was due to fatigue, the physical and emotional trauma he'd suffered, and the loss of his lover, but still, the way he reacted seemed more like a child.

Once Aaron fell asleep, Jason started another load of laundry. While the washing machine ran, he went to his library and read up on the psychological effects of trauma and loss. He found a section on regression and learned that it's not uncommon for patients to revert to an emotional level consistent with a much younger person, particularly those who are physically dependent on others to care for them. The book also warned that caregivers must be careful not to allow the dependence to go on for an extended period of time. To do so would only make the patient's dependence more difficult to break and could lead to long-term psychological deterioration.

As he read on, Jason found references to PTSD. He was reminded that he too had suffered many of the same symptoms when he was battling the condition himself. All the more, he felt not only sympathy for Aaron but also empathy, but he warned himself not to become invested emotionally in Aaron's dependence. Otherwise, he could wind up battling the return of his own PTSD that he'd worked so hard to put behind him.

****

Tuesday, September 8, 2009, 10:00 AM
Breaking news bulletin

"Good morning, ladies and gentlemen. This just in. There are new developments in the Aaron Jaeger story. As you may recall, Jaeger was the newly signed quarterback for the Nevada Bighorns.

"We've just learned that the partial remains of two adult individuals have been recovered from the original crash site we first reported on this past Sunday morning, as well as another debris field that was located approximately one-quarter mile away. It is reported that the remains were too damaged to make a definitive identification of the individuals. As a result, a forensic pathologist has been called in, and the remains are now being compared to dental records as well as undergoing DNA testing.

"The coroner has stated that it may be several weeks before positive identification can be made, but we fear the worst as there were only two individuals reported to have been flying in the plane, Jaeger and the pilot.

"In a related story, the whereabouts of Nathan Taggart, who was Jaeger's trainer and the last person to be with him, remains unknown. The FBI has been called in to assist with the investigation of his disappearance and to determine whether it is in any way related to the downed airplane.

"When asked for a comment, a very shaken Hank

Thompson, the coach for the Nevada Bighorns, stated, 'It doesn't look very good.'

"We will keep you advised of any updates on this tragic story as they become available. We now return you to our regularly scheduled program, already in progress."

****

Through the remainder of Tuesday and all of Wednesday, Jason continued to take care of the animals, prepare their meals, and build the sling for Aaron. As he gained strength, Aaron tested his limits but was immediately reminded by the pain that he had a long way to go and that he really was confined to the bed. Jason had to pour him several half tumblers of scotch in addition to the aspirin, and he added acetaminophen to the mix to help him manage it. He warned Aaron that he would have to lay off the booze as a medicinal remedy soon.

When the chicken soup ran out, Jason made tuna salad for lunch. He also brought in a longhorn rump from the smokehouse and three large carrots he'd dug up in the garden. He roasted them with potatoes from the root cellar and a quartered onion and served them for dinner with another quart of green beans he'd taken from his freezer.

Jason crafted the sling out of a bolt of canvas he kept in the supply room and some 2" x 4" boards. He made the sling in several independent segments and sewed seams into each segment with a leather awl and then attached canvas loops for the ropes. Aaron felt better emotionally and became invested in the project by asking questions and commenting on the progress. It was helpful for Aaron to see how Jason created the sling when he moved his table to just beyond the end of the bed creating a large flat surface to spread out on.

It became a little tense when Jason had to climb

into the rafters above the bed to rig the blocks and tackle to the open beams and string the ropes through their pulleys. Aaron repeatedly warned him to be careful and caught his breath, nervous every time Jason moved from one beam to another overhead. Once Jason had completed it all, he worked one sling under Aaron's back, one under his right leg, a third under his left leg, and a fourth under his buttocks that could be easily removed when Aaron needed the facilities.

The sling worked great, and Aaron was ecstatic. He made whooping sounds whenever Jason raised him into the air and lowered him back down to test it while he adjusted the ropes. Jason found that the slings made bathing Aaron much easier, and Aaron had no trepidations about personal hygiene from that day on.

As the days passed, Aaron had more and more difficulty 'keeping it together' as he put it, when Jason washed his groin, but he hadn't developed a full-blown erection like he had on Monday.

****

Thursday, September 10, 2009, evening

After dinner on Thursday, Jason sensed that Aaron was becoming bored or restless or both. With the sling complete, he didn't have anything to focus on anymore. "Hey, Aaron, do you like to read? I've got an extensive library."

"Sorry, Jason, I'm not much of a reader. I'm more of a TV kinda guy. Too bad you don't get TV out here."

"Well, that's true. I don't get television broadcasts, but I do have an extensive DVD movie collection. Would that interest you?"

"Hell yeah, that'd be great!"

Jason took the curtain down and moved his

flatscreen TV to the end of the bed, allowing Aaron an unobstructed view. It took Jason a few minutes to explain how his elaborate video system's remote control worked, but it wasn't long before Aaron had mastered it. The DVD player held multiple discs that could be selected at the push of a button, and Aaron busied himself watching movies. It helped with his boredom and kept his attention for the next twenty-four hours.

****

Friday, September 11, 2009, 8:00 AM

While Jason bathed Aaron, he was pleased that there hadn't been even a hint of an erection during his bath, but little did he know, Aaron had already taken care of that while Jason was out with the animals.

****

Friday, September 11, 2009, 11:00 AM
Breaking news

"Good morning, ladies and gentlemen. On this hallowed day, in the shadows of the terrorist attacks that befell our country on September 11, 2001, we're coming to you with breaking news about Aaron Jaeger's disappearance one week ago today. We're taking you now to Chuck Jackson, who is live at the coroner's office in Hinnen Valley where a news conference is just about to begin. Come in, Chuck."

"Yes, good morning. It's 11:00 AM local time here in Hinnen Valley ... Oh, here we go. The coroner has just stepped up to the podium."

"Good morning, ladies and gentlemen. We've completed our preliminary investigation on the human remains that were recovered from the Bear River Mountains crash site.

"The partial remains of two adult males were

recovered from two separate areas. Remains from both individuals were found at both sites. What this means is the bodies were blown apart in an explosion in midair before they fell to the ground and were scattered throughout the area.

"From partial dental records, we can say with certainty that the identity of one of the individuals was the pilot, Samuel Johnson, of the twin engine plane with the registration two T W seven nine that took off from Oklahoma City at approximately 5:00 PM and was headed to Hinnen Valley Regional Airport when it disappeared from radar.

"We can also say with certainty from partial dental records that the second individual has been identified as Nathan Taggart, a trainer associated with the Nevada Bighorns. I'll take your questions now."

"You said Nathan Taggart. Taggart wasn't on the plane."

"Obviously, he was."

"Was Aaron Jaeger found?"

"No, he has not yet been found alive."

"Does that mean that Aaron Jaeger is dead?"

"I did not say that," the coroner said with annoyance in his voice.

"Could any of the remains be those of Aaron Jaeger?"

"None that we've identified so far."

"Did any remains found not belong to Johnson or Taggart?"

"It's too soon to say. DNA testing has only just begun. It will be a few weeks before we get those results back."

"So Aaron Jaeger could still be alive?"

"I have no evidence to prove or disprove that."

"So where is Aaron Jaeger?"

"Listen up, people! The remains that were recovered offer no information as to Mr. Jaeger's whereabouts. Let me be clear. From all accounts, Mr. Jaeger boarded the flight. There are witnesses to confirm that, and he was also on it when the plane took off because no one got off the plane after it was boarded. Once it took off, the plane made no landings. It remained on radar from the time it took off until it disappeared from radar after making a Mayday call."

"Were there parachutes on the plane?"

"That can be surmised from parachute parts I have identified from some of the materials that were brought to me for analysis. That's all I have for now. Good day."

"Well there you have it, folks. Aaron Jaeger or his remains have not been found. Back to you in the studio."

"Thanks, Chuck. We'll keep you up to date as new information comes into us. We now return you to our program, still in progress."

Section Two
Bodies in motion

Chapter Nine
Come lie beside me

Friday, September 11, 2009, evening

All day Friday, both Aaron and Jason had been haunted by the one-week anniversary of Nathan's death. Jason was afraid to bring it up for fear it would upset Aaron, and Aaron was afraid if he said it out loud, he'd lose it.

After dinner, Aaron asked Jason if he would watch a movie with him, and he agreed. Thirty minutes into the movie, Jason began to squirm in his chair.

"What's wrong, Jason?"

"Oh, my butt's going numb. I made this wooden chair for sitting at the table while I ate, not for sitting like this. It's no big deal."

Though completely innocent, the aftermath of the next few minutes were far-reaching for both of them.

"Well, there's plenty of room next to me," Aaron indicated by reaching across with his left arm and patting the bed on his right. "Why don't you just lie down over here?"

"It wouldn't be right, Aaron."

"Why not? There's plenty of room."

"For several reasons, Aaron. First, you're injured, and I wouldn't want to cause your limbs to shift in their splints when I climbed onto the bed."

"Well, you've washed the right side of my body multiple times already and that hasn't happened, so that's one down."

"Okay, I'll give you that one. Second, and most importantly, you're my patient. It would be inappropriate for me to lie on or in a bed with you."

"Hold it right there, buddy-boy!" Aaron answered. "I'm not your patient, not really. You're not a doctor. You're not a nurse. I'm not in a hospital, and you're not a medic in the army anymore. I'm lying in your bed," Aaron emphasized the word your, "the bed of a decent, caring man who found me injured in the forest, saved my life, and is caring for me as if I was family, and besides, a few days ago I asked why you were doing all this for me, a stranger. Remember?"

Jason was becoming uncomfortable. "No, I don't remember." He was doing all he could to maintain an emotional distance from Aaron, but the feelings and physical attraction he was developing for him had become almost overpowering at times.

Keep it together, Jason, keep it together.

Thankfully, he had his chores and animals to keep him busy to the point that with all of that, and his care of Aaron, he hadn't had a moment's peace in a week. Even so, twice he had to leave the cabin to go outside to masturbate when the arousal he felt while bathing Aaron's naked body had become too much for him to bear.

For the first time, Jason was able to admit the attraction to himself. *Oh, my God, I'm falling for the guy. I've been deluding myself about it all this time.* But Jason just couldn't shake the guilt he felt about it all.

Am I taking advantage of the situation, of Aaron? Am I a pervert? Am I a sexual predator?

"And what did you say?" Aaron snapped his

fingers, jarring Jason back to the present. "Hey, Jason, I'm talking to you. What did you say to me?"

"I don't remember." But he did.

"You said, and I quote, 'Because you're a human being, and I'm a human being.' That's what you said. You're the kindest man I've ever met, so I can't enjoy watching this movie in good conscience while you're squirming in your chair with a numb butt."

Jason blushed, but tried to hide it with a smile.

"So what do you say?"

Jason caved in. He really did miss his bed. "Okay, but you'll tell me if I hurt you, right?"

"Yes, of course."

Jason was exhausted physically, mentally, and emotionally. He crawled onto the bed on top of the blanket and laid down. Once he experienced the familiarity of his own bed, he began to drift off before another fifteen minutes of the movie had played.

****

Not even midway through the movie, Aaron noticed that Jason was in a deep sleep when he realized his breathing had changed. Aaron became filled with an overwhelming sense of peace. Not wanting to wake Jason, he lowered the TV's volume to a whisper. Several times he looked over to watch the man sleeping beside him, and each time he smiled.*Such a beautiful face. Such a beautiful man. Such a strong, kind, beautiful man. If only I could find someone like him.*

Before the movie ended, Aaron had fallen asleep as well.

****

Saturday, September 12, 2009, 6:00 AM

Jason was jarred awake from a nightmare before daybreak. "What!" he shouted. He was startled so violently that he shook the bed. *The eighth anniversary of September 11th was yesterday, and I completely forgot about it.*

It took a moment for him to remember that although he was in his own bed, he shouldn't be, and that confused him. Once he got his bearings, he remembered Aaron, his rescue, his care, and the feelings he was developing for the man.

When he looked over at Aaron, it was obvious that he'd been disturbed by the shout from the unsettled look on his face, but it hadn't been enough to wake him. He also noticed that the sheet and blanket were off him again, and he had another raging erection. He was so focused on Aaron's penis, he didn't realize that by thenAaron had woken up. Instinctively, Jason began to reach for it, but withdrew his hand almost immediately.

"You can touch it," Aaron whispered.

Jason nearly jumped off the bed.

"No really, Jason, you can touch it. Please, you have my permission," he said more clearly.

"Oh God, what's happening?" Jason whispered.

"I watched you sleep last night, Jason. You're a beautiful man. I'd be lucky to find someone like you."

"Aaron, I'm sorry." Jason sat up and swung his legs over the side of the bed, turning away.

"Jason, listen to me."

Jason stood up and walked towards the window. He wanted to run away.

"Jason, look at me."

Jason turned to face him, unaware that his own erection was straining against his jeans. He focused his gaze above Aaron's head. Aaron focused on the bulge in Jason's jeans.

"Can I be honest with you, Jason?"

Jason didn't answer.

"Jason, I can't believe I'm saying this, but here goes. We have to be realistic about this. You're a man. I'm a man. You're gay. I'm gay. And for God knows how long, we're gonna be confined to this cabin. It could be months."

"Everything you've said is the truth," Jason answered quietly, lowering his eyes to meet Aaron's gaze.

"Jason, I can't pretend to know what's going on in your head, so I can only speak for myself, and please believe me when I say this. I have needs, Jason, physical needs. I always have, and I now find that I'm very attracted to you. I don't think it's just because of what you've done for me or that I think I owe you something. Well, to be honest, that may be part of it, sort of like hero worship or something, but it's only a small part, and besides, if I'd have met you on the street before I met Nathan, I would've jumped your bones in a minute."

Aaron tensed his mouth and closed his eyes momentarily. Jason noticed the look on Aaron's face at the mention of Nathan's name. When Aaron opened his eyes again, he looked directly into Jason's eyes.

"Jason, I don't think you know just how darn handsome you are. You have a powerful masculine musk, and I'm drawn to it. The first time I got a hard-on when you were washing me, it was purely physical. I couldn't help it, but over the past few days, I'm finding myself wanting you more and more. I can't believe I'm saying this, but I want you to make love to me. I'm a very good lover, Jason, though obviously," Aaron waved his arm over his broken body, "I can't back that up right now."

Jason looked blankly at Aaron. He didn't speak.

"Well, say something, Jason. What are you feeling?"

Jason forced the words out. "Aaron, it would be wrong."

"How can that be when I'm throwing myself at you right now!"

"St ... Still..." Jason stuttered.

"Jason, you're not taking advantage of me. You're not seducing me. You haven't drugged me in some way. I'm the one asking you."

"Aaron, I can't!" Jason half shouted, half cried and ran out the front door.

****

After a few minutes, Jason came back in and walked to the bed. "Jason, tell me what's wrong. What are you afraid of? What happened to you?"

Jason began to cry.

Aaron watched him for a moment and then said, "Oh, you dear man. You poor, beautiful, dear, sweet man. What is it?"

"Aaron, it's not you," Jason said through his tears.

"Tell me, Jason. Tell me what happened."

"Aaron, this is so difficult for me. I haven't spoken of it in nearly a dozen years so please bear with me and just listen, okay?"

"Yes, Jason. I promise."

"My first tour began at the start of Operation Desert Storm. It lasted a year. When I returned to the States, it was to a different base than the one I left from for a very good reason, but that's not important right now.

"I was assigned to a MASH unit. I worked with surgeons in a trauma unit and soon they recognized that I had an aptitude for trauma care. It all just seemed to make sense to me. I was given advanced training in trauma assessments and treatment prioritization, medications and suturing, and splinting and bandaging. I soon found myself working right beside them in the trauma bays.

"It wasn't long before I was assisting them in surgery, often starting to open up the guys when the surgeons were overwhelmed with other patients. Then they'd come in and take over, but dozens of times I had to do the surgeries by myself with other medics assisting me. I did so well that my chief surgeon recommended me for enrollment in the army's Physician Assistant Program. He told me to think about becoming a surgeon myself and that the PA program would help me to decide whether it was a life I'd want down the road. The base's commanding officer wrote a glowing report and that got the ball rolling for me.

"After returning to the States, early in 1992, I took and excelled in several courses over the next several months, but my formal education was interrupted when I was told I was needed for a second two-year tour that would start later that year. Once back overseas, I found myself in a different MASH unit again. My superiors and the surgeons I worked with were also impressed by my skills.

"I have to backtrack for a moment. During my first tour, I was seduced by a superior, a male medic, but soon we developed a deep, loving, physical relationship. I also found love with another medic, during my second tour, but both of those relationships ended each time I returned to the States. I've kept both of them a secret to this day. I had to.

"Unfortunately, my second tour did not go as well as the first. I began to develop symptoms of PTSD and eventually, I was returned to the States for inpatient treatment in the spring of 1993. After a month, I was discharged from treatment.

"I continued my classes while I worked in the hospital, but compared to what I had been doing in the MASH units, I found my work unfulfilling and unchallenging. The more I missed my former lovers and thought about my work in the MASH units, the more I remembered the horrors I'd witnessed. This made my PTSD symptoms all the more pronounced, until it became a vicious cycle. As a result, my academic performance suffered.

"After two more voluntary admissions for inpatient psychiatric treatment, I was given an honorable discharge from the army late in the summer of 1994. I returned to my hometown to live with my parents, but the PTSD persisted. My traumatic memories, were so deep, that I couldn't hold on to a job for more than a week at a time.

"My loneliness and continuing bouts with PTSD cost me dearly. I sought help from the V.A., but never informed them of my homosexuality. I couldn't. After returning for several months of inpatient treatment in the psychiatric unit at the V.A., my condition finally improved.

"After I was discharged from the V.A., I took a job as a technician in a civilian Emergency Department where I befriended a physician who was also ex-military. My new friend understood and was sympathetic about my PTSD and as a result, over many months, we developed a deep platonic friendship that has lasted to this day. He's the doctor who ordered all the medical supplies I've stocked up.

"I returned to the V.A. for follow-up, outpatient, group therapy for another year until I was finally discharged from care completely. Though my memories of the battle injuries I witnessed still haunt me, and probably will for the rest of my life, I've learned how to put them in perspective and manage them.

"During the time I worked in the ER, I became more sexually active. Sometimes I'd hook up with paramedics and cops I met in the ER, but mostly it was with guys I met in bars. Unfortunately, none of them ever developed into anything beyond a one-night stand.

"On one such evening, I was shaken to my core. As I left one of the bars I frequented, that time with an off-duty cop, we were confronted by an older woman who wore a placard that read, Repent your sins! It is only through God's forgiveness that you will find salvation. She handed me a pamphlet titled, "Repent! Repent criminals! You will only find redemption by confessing your sins to God the Father! Repent! Repent! Repent your sins!

"Into my second year in the ER, I became less and less satisfied with my work and my personal life. One day, on a whim, I bought a lottery ticket in the summer of 1996. I won. Instantly I became a multimillionaire. I had more money than I could ever spend over several lifetimes. I quit my job and decided I needed to get away from the hustle and bustle of society and live alone in solitude. I gave a million dollars to my parents and a million dollars to my friend, the physician. Then I disappeared from the face of the earth.

"Over the next year, I searched for secluded parcels of land and finally bought two hundred acres here in the remote mountains of Idaho. It's so remote that there aren't any paved roads for miles and miles. At the time, there were a few dirt trails and deeply rutted, narrow dirt roads the ran through my property. I wanted to prevent access so I had all of them planted with fast and slow growing trees wherever they entered my land. In a few years, all evidence of their existence was erased. Before making the move and having a cabin built, I returned to visit my parents. Oh, sorry, I'm going off on a tangent."

"No," Aaron answered. "Please, go on."

"Okay. So when I got home, I was shocked to find both of them in failing health. I hired a health company to arrange and manage their care in a retirement community that also provided for more advanced care as their health deteriorated. I also hired an attorney and kept her on retainer to manage whatever legal matters arose and an investment banker to manage my money, who, it turned out, was an ex-GI whose life I'd saved back in Iraq.

"I had to put my plans on hold. I moved into my parent's home to remain close by, but I continued to research living off the grid. I visited my friend, the physician, and told him about my land. He was happy for me, but he made me promise to stay in touch after I moved away.

"Within six months, both of my parents died, first my father, then my mother a month later. As their only surviving child and sole beneficiary, it wasn't difficult to have their estate settled. Almost all the money I'd given them the year before was untouched, so I donated all of their estate to the Emergency Department of the hospital where I used to work.

"Once I had no ties to the outside world, I focused all of my attention on my new home. In the spring of 1998, I hired an architectural company to design this cabin and a construction company to build it. They helped me to select a plot on my land that best suited the design.

"By early that summer, a temporary lumber mill had been set up and as the land was cleared, the best cuts of timber were set aside for the cabin. Any construction materials that couldn't be provided by the forest were flown in by a helicopter air transport company, and it was costly, but what did I care? I was rich.

"The building crews were flown to the site in a helicopter without windows to prevent them from knowing exactly where they were working. To ensure their sworn secrecy about the cabin's general location, I spared no expense in taking care of them. To keep them comfortable, I had luxury trailer homes flown in by helicopter once enough land had been cleared.

"I had an entire refrigerated long-bed trailer flown in and kept it stocked with any and every form of food and beverage the crews could have wanted. I also paid for each crew member to be flown back home on a revolving schedule for one week's leave each month. As it turned out, a few of the construction workers were gay, and I engaged in brief flings with them, but they never developed into anything beyond sex.

"I took advantage of every conceivable technology and modern convenience that would allow me to live comfortably and remain off the grid. After the cabin was built, I had the stockade constructed so that it held the cabin and a good chunk of cleared land. Then I added the other structures and the livestock.

"To minimize the encroachment of wildlife near the exterior of the stockade, every tree that stood within fifty yards of its perimeter was felled. Another twenty yards deep into the surrounding forest, all the trees were trimmed of their branches to twenty feet off the ground.

"Once I was on my own, I tried to live off the land as much as I could. As you've seen, I developed an extensive book and video library over the years to occupy my free time, but there really isn't much of that in the spring, summer, and autumn because of my chores and hunting. The forest can provide me with all the meat, fowl, and fish I could ever eat. For any of the other things I couldn't provide for myself, I hired the same air transport company to fly in supplies a minimum of twice a year, as soon as the snow melted in the spring and again in mid-autumn.

"Every now and then, I've invited some of the guys back up here for a weekend of hunting and fishing. In addition, they've provided me with all the physical comfort and sexual release that I could ever want. Their visits have allowed me to engage in three or more days of passionate, and unbridled ménage à trois sex and have taken care of any need I might have for outside physical contact. Since that time, my life has been an uncomplicated one."

Jason fell silent. Aaron took his hand. "Jason, I don't know what to say. You've been through so much, and you've had to do it all by yourself. I can't imagine how difficult it all has been for you, and I can understand why you've lived the way you have."

"I know it sounds like a lot, Aaron, but there's more, much more. I don't know if I can even speak of it. I've never told anyone about it."

"I'm not going to ask you to, Jason. It's not my place."

"No, it seems like it's about time to let it out, Aaron, but hold on to your hat, it gets pretty rough."

Over the next hour, Jason revealed the story of his trial for sexual assault to Aaron. When he began to speak, Aaron motioned for him to move from the chair to beside him on the bed. Aaron began to caress his arm with his good hand. When Jason instinctively moved closer, Aaron reached for his face and whispered words of encouragement and understanding. Several times, Jason began to cry, and Aaron allowed him the time he needed to let the tears flow. By the time he'd finished, Jason's tears had dried.

"That's why I didn't return to that base after my first tour," he said as he sat up. "I didn't want to run into Corporal Garrison again. The thing is, Aaron, twice in my life I've had the religious construct of Redemption held over my head for being nothing more than who I am. "Will I ever be free of it? Will any of us? I can't help but wonder what it is that we've done to deserve such condemnation for being ourselves. Do they think we've chose this life, knowing what the world thinks of us? Is the whole world that insane? I mean, who would to that the themselves?"

"No wonder you retreated, Jason. No wonder." Aaron held out his left arm and invited Jason in. "Jason, you're the kindest man I've ever known." He kissed Jason's brow, his cheeks, his eyes, and finally, with all the tenderness he could muster, Aaron kissed him on the lips, and Jason didn't pull away.

"You did nothing wrong, Jason. There is nothing for you to feel guilty about, and as you said, the court recognized that when they expunged your military record."

"I know in my head that you're right, Aaron, but I've just been carrying this guilt around with me for so long, even if it was unjustified. I felt I would never find redemption for what happened with that corporal. Even if I didn't intend for it to happen, it happened because my hands were touching him. Then there was that crazy lady outside of a bar that one night. Not until now have I realized just how traumatized I've been by all of it."

"Well, it's over now. You've shared it with someone else. I've got broad shoulders, Jason. Let me carry some of it for you."

Jason felt like a weight had been lifted from his soul, but he wasn't ready for what Aaron wanted. Not yet.

"Aaron, I have to go milk Heather," he said after several minutes had passed. "Weird isn't it, how life goes on. Here I am, unburdening my soul and then next thing you know I'm going out to milk a goat."

"Jason, you go do what you have to do. I understand there are things that have to be done around here, and I can't help you with them. Yes, life does go on. I'll be fine. Go."

"Aaron, there's one more thing."

"What's that?"

"Yesterday was the anniversary of September 11th, when our country was attacked by those terrorists in passenger planes, remember?"

"Yes, I remember. I'd just turned fifteen."

"Well there's something I do every year that I forgot to do yesterday, so I'll be a bit longer than normal."

"What is it that you do? Could I help or do it with you?"

"It's outside. I raise the American flag on my flag pole and say the Pledge of Allegiance. Then I say a prayer in remembrance of those who lost their lives. And I remember Mark Bingham, a gay man who was on the plane that crashed in Pennsylvania. He was part of the group who overtook the terrorists and prevented them from crashing the plane into the White House. Because he was gay, his partner didn't receive any of the benefits that all the other family members of those who died received. I remember him, because he was a hero who our government refused to acknowledge because of who he was."

"Oh, Jason, if there's any way that you'd be comfortable with me participating, I'd really like to."

"Thank you, Aaron. That means a lot to me. Do you think it would be okay if I hung the flag in here from the rafters? Then we can do it together."

"Oh, yes, Jason. Yes. I'd be honored."

****

While Jason was with the animals, Aaron realized he had just grown up. Suddenly, he had been able to put someone else before himself, and somehow, he had found the right words to say.

****

Saturday, September 12, 2009, 8:15 AM

When Jason returned to the cabin, he washed up and hung the flag. The ceremony took only a few minutes, but it meant the world to Jason that Aaron was there, and it meant the world to Aaron that Jason included him.

When they finished, Jason took out a spiral-cut ham from the freezer for the next day and put it in the refrigerator to defrost. He began to take out what he needed to cook a late breakfast, but immediately he thought better of it. He looked over at Aaron, who he could see was watching him. "Aaron, are you getting tired of eggs and bacon and pancakes?"

"No, not really, but what did you have in mind?"

"I've got loads of cereal in the pantry. Interested?"

"If that's what you want, it's fine with me."

Jason carried in two boxes, one of Frosted Flakes and the other of Fruity Hoops with milk, bowls, and spoons, on Aaron's tray. "You having any pain?"

"Not really."

"None?"

"Well, some."

"Okay," Jason said, "I'll get you some aspirin and acetaminophen."

Chapter Ten
We can take this real slow

After cleaning up from breakfast, Jason assembled the dressings and the soap and water for Aaron's bath. When he returned to the bed, Aaron stopped him.

"Sit down for a minute, Jason."

Jason sat down. "Okay, I'm sitting."

"We've just bared our souls to each other, Jason. We can take this real slow."

"Aaron, please hear me. I do understand what you're asking of me, but please understand, I'm not ready for it. Please give me some time."

"Okay, Jason, but what am I going to do about this?"

Aaron uncovered himself to reveal a tremendous hard-on. Jason sucked in his breath and turned red. Aaron watched his face. Jason's eyes were locked on it. *Is that longing I see in his eyes?* Aaron wondered to himself.

Jason answered in a moment, "I don't know, Aaron. You're making this very difficult for me. I not only feel a humanitarian obligation towards you, I also really do want to help you to get better, whatever that may entail, but I'm not ready for what you ask. Please respect that. Do you not understand that right now you're practically recreating the traumatic event I experienced before my trial? Can't you see that?"

Immediately, Aaron recognized what he had done.

"Jason, I- I ... I'm sorry. I'm so sorry. Please forgive me. I just told you all those things about how I felt about you and being realistic about our situation and everything, and then I listened to you tell your story, and what do I do? I completely disregard your feelings. I can be a selfish prick at times! Please, Jason, please forgive me."

Good God, Aaron, he thought to himself, *and you thought you'd grown up? What a joke. What a joke you are. You're nothing but a horndog and an ass, too.*

****

After their emotions had settled down, Jason began to bathe Aaron. When he got to his groin, Aaron was hard as a rock. Aaron turned his face away while Jason lathered him up. Though he made no sound, his cock quivered and throbbed beneath Jason's touch. When he felt his pre-cum begin to flow, Aaron bit his lip.

"I'm sorry, Aaron," Jason said, "It'll be over soon."

The moment Jason finished, Aaron turned and looked him straight in the eye.

"Jason, I have to ask you to leave me alone for a few minutes. I know you'd be uncomfortable being present while I take care of this, but I have to come. I can't take it another minute."

As Jason rose, Aaron asked, "Would you please leave me a towel?"

Jason nodded and walked out to the barn.

****

Saturday, September 12, 2009, 10:05 AM

When Jason returned, he found the towel folded up next to the buckets of now cool water on the tray at Aaron's side. Aaron's eyes were closed, but Jason couldn't tell whether he was asleep or not. After emptying and cleaning out the buckets in the bathroom and dumping the linens into the hamper, Jason checked on Aaron again. His breathing told Jason that Aaron really was sleeping, so he left him alone and went to sit down in front of his computer.

Jason remembered downloading some medical journals that contained articles about human sexuality earlier in the spring so he started to scan the titles. He found one he thought might be helpful. It was titled, "The Denial of Sexual Needs: One of the Greatest Atrocities Committed Against Long-term Hospitalized Patients by Healthcare Systems in the United States".

After reading the article, Jason thought long and hard about the way he reacted to Aaron's request for sex. He'd given priority to his own misgivings without considering Aaron's needs at all. Aaron was right about one thing. To justify his feelings, Jason had held himself to a professional standard that didn't exist.

Jason also knew that morality wasn't the issue. He was a gay man who'd had gay sex, infrequent as it may have been. If he had met Aaron on the street, he would have definitely been interested in him. Here was a perfect opportunity for him to have regular sex with a man, even if he had to be careful about Aaron's injuries. As Aaron said, he was throwing himself at Jason, and Jason was rejecting him.

The problem was, Jason no longer trusted people. At the time he'd moved to the cabin, he was hurting, fearful, and confused by everything and everyone around him. He took comfort in knowing that at least here in the wilderness, no one could ever hurt him again. The truth was, though he was also lonely and afraid of love, he was more afraid of being hurt.

Finally, Jason realized that it was more than just the fear of getting hurt. He could never live with himself if he hurt another person and caused them to feel the depth of pain he'd felt, especially Aaron, who, he now finally admitted to himself, he had strong, physical feelings for.

Jason couldn't even remember when he began to believe love was not in the cards for him, but he had a good idea that the incident with the corporal was at the heart of it all. He remembered reading an article about the Human Sexuality Spectrum, where at one end were heterosexuals and the other end were homosexuals. People could fall anywhere along that continuum.

For all he knew, had he not been seduced by that senior medic while on his first tour, he very well may have found a girl who would have had sex with him. He might have been comfortable or even happy in a heterosexual relationship. Heck, had he gotten married, his life could have gone in a completely different direction, but that was water over the damn now. He'd talk to Aaron when the time was right.

****

Saturday, September 12, 2009, noon

When Aaron woke, it was lunch time.

"Hey, sleepyhead," Jason said from the other side of the bed, "you hungry?" He put down the book he was reading.

"Jason?"

"Yes, Aaron, it's me, Jason."

"No, I know it's you, but what are you doing on the bed?"

"Sorry, I was reading. Did I wake you?"

"No. No, you didn't wake me, but after what happened this morning and after my bath, the last thing I expected was to find you here."

"Aaron, everything is fine, I promise," he said, laying his hand on Aaron's shoulder.

A chill shot through Aaron's spine, right through his belly into his loins, all the way down to his toes and up the back of his neck. "Really?"

"Yes, Aaron, really. There are some things that I need to say to you, but why don't we talk after you eat."

"Jason, I can wait. Talk!"

"Let me get you some food, and then we'll talk."

"But..."

Jason got up and went into the kitchen to make Aaron a sandwich with the last of the tuna salad and poured him a glass of cool well water. After setting him up to eat, Jason began.

"Aaron, I've done some real hard thinking, some soul searching, and I've also done some research to boot about what we talked about this morning. I may fumble through all this a bit, so please be patient with me."

Aaron nodded his head.

"First, I read an article about the sexual needs of long-term hospitalized patients and how the healthcare system has ignored those needs for many reasons. The main reason is the moral beliefs of caregivers and hospital managers which then become translated into policies that govern practice. This coincides with what I call puritanical morality."

Aaron raised his hand, but Jason went on.

"I know, I know, you're not in a hospital, but you have made it very clear that you need sexual release, and I know that I have balked at that. I also took a look at myself and realized that I've been afraid for a very long time. Afraid of being hurt by being in a relationship or even being in love, but that's my problem, not yours.

"Even though I was completely innocent, and I knew it from the start, the idea that I was accused of sexually assaulting a fellow soldier, let alone another human being, enabled me to imagine being in the position of becoming the victim. The absolute horror I imagined from that experience made me wonder whether

I was capable of doing such a thing, and it prevented me from allowing myself to be put into a situation where I might possibly do so. That idea became warped in my own head, to the point that I would never be able to live with myself if I did. As a result, I've prevented myself from forming any kind of emotional attachment because I simply couldn't risk it. I realize now that that's why all my encounters after the service were one night stands. I know this doesn't make much sense, but compound that with my PTSD, and I've been a tragedy just waiting to happen.

"I also believed for a very long time that love was not something that I would ever find. That probably stemmed from a combination of being shy, which made me a loner, the trial over the corporal and everything I just said, and being seduced by a senior medic during my first tour in Iraq. I was still a virgin back then and unsure of my sexual orientation. My self-imposed and nonexistent professional standard I was imposing on you was my excuse to hide behind my fears, even from myself. For that, I apologize."

"Jason, you don't have to apologize. I can't imagine the struggles you've been through. I knew I was gay from the time I was a little kid, I just didn't know what to call it … and because of what I'd been told about it as I grew up, I hid it from my family and from my friends. And now, as an adult, I've had to hide it from the world because of my profession."

"Yes, Aaron, but at least you had found someone. I'm sorry to bring up Nathan, but at least you were being true to yourself. I was hiding."

"I don't think I'll ever get over Nathan," Aaron said, "and I'm still struggling with his loss, but right now I have to separate myself from that, for your sake."

"You don't have to separate yourself from

anything on my behalf, Aaron," Jason said as he gently patted Aaron's thigh, "particularly Nathan. I know how important he was to you."

"It's strange, Jason, but it's like I've put the loss of Nathan into a box that I open at times. There are moments when I'm overwhelmed with grief when I think about him, and I can't quite make heads or tails of why it happened. I can still see the plane exploding into a fireball when I close my eyes, and I'm horrified by the memory. It's like I'm living it over and over again, but also, I somehow find comfort knowing that he died instantly and didn't suffer.

"There have also been moments when I've become overwhelmed with guilt when I think about what I've proposed to you about us. Then I remember what happened to Nathan, and the grief rushes back in. Sorry, I didn't mean to change the subject, but I wanted you to know how I'm dealing with those memories right now."

"Aaron, it's important for you to feel comfortable talking about Nathan. I understand that, and I want to do whatever I can to help you through it. I'm not a psychiatrist or psychologist, but what you're describing, putting your memory of Nathan into a box, is called compartmentalization. It's how people who are stressed or overwhelmed by too many things cope with them all."

"Yeah, that's exactly what it's like."

"Aaron, you've been through so much trauma, both physical and psychological. It's amazing to me and a testament to you that you're handling it all as well as you are."

"Oh, I'll probably freak out at some point in time," Aaron said with a weak smile, "but I'll deal with that when it comes."

"And I'll be here to help you. Can we promise each other something?"

"What's that?" Aaron answered.

"That there's no subject off-limits, and that we'll respect each other's feelings."

"Yes, Jason, I can agree to that. Speaking for myself, I need to know that I can trust you enough to be able to tell you or ask you anything, and that you won't judge me or reject me. I'm asking you to allow me to be free to talk about anything. I know that I may appear to be handling all this, but to be honest, I'm barely keeping it together. I never admitted to myself before all this happened just how fragile I am, emotionally."

"And all I ask, Aaron, is that you open yourself up to the possibility that before your trauma you had the same degree of emotional strength that everyone else does. Trauma puts a tremendous amount of stress on not only the body, but also the mind. Really, you're still in shock, and it will take some time before it eases. What you're feeling about being fragile could be because of that."

"Thanks, Jason. So back to what we were talking about before, what do you want to do, right now, I mean?"

"Wow, I can't even remember how this conversation started."

"You started talking about love and fear and sex."

"Oh, yes, now I remember. Okay, hear me out. Aaron, I'm willing to help you in whatever way you want or need. I know that I'll probably be uncomfortable about some things, but as long as I'm being honest ... I'm sorry, but this is kinda awkward to say."

"Go on, Jason. You can tell me anything. I asked to be able to do that with you. It's only fair for you to feel free to do the same."

"Okay. I have to admit that I find you very attractive, both physically and as a person."

Aaron smiled such a huge smile that his pupils dilated.

"Gee, Jason, thanks. I thought I'd lost my touch! Ha-ha! Sorry, just kidding."

"Aaron, you're a great guy. I told myself when you were asleep a little while ago that if I'd have met you on the street, and got to know you like I have now, I would've certainly been interested in developing a relationship with you."

"So then where do we go from here, or where do you want to go?"

"The next time you need or want me to help you ... with sex I mean, all you have to do is ask."

"Well, truth of the matter is, I came just a little while ago. Normally, I'd be able to go again by now, but as you can see, I'm not up to snuff. I will, though, take you up on the offer and soon."

"Okay."

"What about you, Jason? Do you have any needs right now? I could try."

Jason blushed. "I ... I ... didn't think you'd want to. I was really only thinking of you."

"Really, Jason?"

"Well, ... I thought it might happen later, way later, after you were much better and if you really wanted it. I just didn't think ..."

"Well, I can't do much, but I'm willing to try. Whatever you want."

"I don't think I'm ready for that just now. I know I said a lot, but it all still needs to settle in for a little while. Maybe we could watch a movie together?"

"Sure, that'd be great. But ... you'll lie next to me on the bed?"

"Okay. That'll be fine. What would you like to watch?"

"You pick. Hey, I just had a thought."

"What's that?" Jason asked.

"Well, it's just that right now, with the way the bed's set up, I can't touch you with my right arm being all screwed up, and I'd like you to let me do that. Nothing sexual or anything, I promise."

Jason nodded.

"And speaking of the bed. It's your bed. You shouldn't be sleeping on the floor."

"You mean sleep ... in the bed ... with you in it? I don't know, Aaron, what if I bump you or roll over on you when I'm sleeping?"

"Do you toss and turn at night? You certainly didn't last night!"

"No, I guess not, and that was a fluke, falling asleep I mean. I didn't mean to, and I'd be afraid ..."

"Well, don't be. It's settled from now on, you're sleeping in your bed."

"Okay, but I'm gonna put a body pillow between us when we go to bed ... um, sleep ... you know what I mean. I'll feel better about it if I can do that."

"Deal." Aaron chuckled. "So, here's what I was thinking. My left arm is the good one. Is there any way I can be moved to the right side of the bed so that I can reach you with the good arm? Remember, nothing sexual."

"I can't move the pulleys, not the way they're attached to the rafters, but let me think. Yes, I could hoist you up in the air on the slings and then slide the bed over and let you down on the right side."

"That'll work. Yeah, great!"

While Aaron was in the air, Jason moved the bed and changed the sheets on the two twin mattresses that covered the two halves of the bed.

"That's great, Jason," Aaron said after he was

back down, "now I'll be able to touch you."

Jason didn't recognize that Aaron had said touch.

"Okay, so do you want to pick one? A movie, I mean?" Jason asked.

"No, like I said, you pick."

"Well, I may not look it, but I like romance or romantic comedies and dramas. That okay with you?"

Aaron smiled. "Whatever you want."

"Okay, what about Philadelphia?"

Chapter Eleven
Inspired by his touch

Saturday, September 12, 2009, early afternoon

Before the movie started, Jason added two logs to the central wood stove, then he raised the heads of both sides of the bed and put a pillow down for himself. He laid down on Aaron's left but kept about a foot of space between them. About thirty minutes in, Aaron motioned for Jason to move closer and then reached his arm under Jason's neck and pulled him in tight. His hand remained on Jason's shoulder.

"That's better," Aaron sighed. "I've missed cuddling."

Jason soon snuggled in closer and turned into Aaron, resting his arm across his bare chest.

At different moments in the movie, Aaron would hear Jason sniffling, and he too shed a few tears of his own. When Aaron's arm went to sleep, he went to pull it from behind Jason's head. As he removed his arm, a poignant scene in the movie unfolded. Jason hugged himself to Aaron. Aaron reached down and patted the top of Jason's thighs as if to say, "there, there," but he left his hand resting on it. Before Jason realized it, Aaron was caressing the inside of his thigh just below his groin, and his loins responded.

"Oh," Jason whispered.

Aaron could feel a bulge beneath the fly of Jason's pants, so he gently lifted the bulge and squeezed.

"That feels nice," Jason said wantonly as he looked into Aaron's eyes.

Aaron went to unzip the fly, but Jason stopped

him. Aaron raised his eyebrows. "Should I stop?"

"I don't know," Jason whispered, yet he began to unbuckle his belt and unzip his fly himself. In a moment, his pants were down around his knees. He guided Aaron's hand beneath the waistband of his boxers to his now, fully erect cock.

"Plaid, flannel boxers? Oh, Jason, how virile!"

Aaron was very gentle. He caressed, squeezed, and gently tugged at Jason. When Jason began to moan, he reached for Aaron's cock and found he too was fully aroused.

"Can we just do this, Aaron?"

"Whatever you want, Jason. Like I said, I don't think I could come just now, but this is enough. It's beautiful. You're beautiful!"

As the movie continued, they caressed each other, stopped for a while and then began again.

****

By the time the movie was almost over, both of their cock heads were slick and oozing. Though they both were very aroused, neither acknowledged the pre-cum.

Aaron wanted Jason. He wanted to feel Jason shoot his load all over his hand so he could taste his essence, make his essence a part of himself, but at the last moment, he thought better of it. *I have to let him make the first move.*

When the protagonist died, Jason began to sob into Aaron's chest. "This part always gets me," he choked out, as his erection eased.

Aaron felt it happen, and then his erection began to fade, but only partially. They held each other, each in his own thoughts, each affected by the movie for different reasons, though Jason seemed more affected than Aaron. Aaron kissed Jason's forehead and held him tight. When he was calm, Aaron eased his hold, and Jason leaned back.

"Thank you for watching that with me, Aaron. I've always hated watching it alone."

"You're welcome. It was a great movie."

"It's a true story, you know."

"Really? I didn't know that. I've heard of the movie, but this was the first time I've ever seen it."

"And thank you for not forcing me into anything."

"Jason, I promised you we'd move at your pace, and I meant that, though I have to admit, I was more aroused than I thought I'd be." Aaron reached down and lifted his still semi-hard cock. "It's gone down some, but I was oozing quite a bit a while ago." As the seconds passed it became limper.

Jason smiled weakly, "Truth is, Aaron, and I'm embarrassed to admit it, so was I."

"I know. I could feel it happening. It's okay, Jason. You shouldn't be afraid to allow yourself to feel things."

"I gotta go pee. I'll be right back," Jason said.

"I'll be here."

****

When Jason returned, he slid off his boxers and scooted over next to Aaron's hips. He reached out and lifted Aaron's cock in both hands, examining it closely.

"Is this okay?"

"Definitely, um sorry, I mean yes," Aaron answered with more enthusiasm than he meant.*Oh, my God, he's touching it on his own*, Aaron thought.

"It's just that it's so beautiful, Aaron, I mean aesthetically. It's exquisite, like what should really be on a Greek sculpture. Those penises are so small. How big is it?" Aaron's cock slowly filled with blood under

Jason's touch.

"Jason, we agreed that we could say anything to each other, right?"

"Yes."

"Then I gotta tell you, that feels really, really good right now. I can't believe this is happening again, but I'm really getting turned on. Sorry, but you said I could tell you anything."

"Yes, Aaron. Thank you for telling me, but I know. I can see it growing." Jason licked his thumbs and began to gently massage Aaron's cock with both hands. He focused them just beneath the corona's edge. "Is it okay that I'm doing this?"

"Yes, Jason. You don't ... you don't have to ask me ... anymore. You can ... you can do whatever ... whatever you want to it."

"You didn't answer my question. How big is it?"

"Seven inches soft and ten inches, sometimes more, fully hard."

"I thought so. It's got some heft to it, too. I'd say two and a half inches in diameter from what I remember when it was completely hard before."

"Yes, Jason, yes."

"I'm not hurting you, am I?"

"No, Jason, no."

"I know I'm being rather clinical right now, Aaron, but I want to see if we can do this without you moving any part of your body."

This? This? What's this? Aaron's mind was reeling.

"I understand your sexual needs," Jason went on, "but I'm not going to be the cause of you displacing your fractures. You've got to be able to remain completely relaxed, and just let me do it."

Aaron had never considered being a passive

participant in sex before. He'd always taken the lead and rarely was a bottom. He was trying to think clearly, but Jason's touch was testing his limits.

Jason stopped abruptly, so much so that Aaron let out a grunt.

"What's wrong?"

"Nothing's wrong, Aaron. I just wanted to see what would happen."

"You mean that's it?"

"No, not necessarily, but I want you to seriously think about what I just said. I know you're really turned on right now, but I want to take it slow so we can figure out how I can help you while at the same time not jeopardizing you in any way."

"The only thing I can say, Jason, is that I'll try. I just realized that I've never been submissive during sex."

"Should I continue?"

"Yes. Please."

"Okay, but if I see you moving, I'm going to stop. Agreed?"

"Yes. Agreed."

As Jason began again, Aaron tried to relax and think about something else, but he was failing miserably.

"It might help you if you try to focus your mind on the sensations you're feeling and just let happen whatever's going to happen on its own," Jason said encouragingly.

"Thanks, Jason. I'll try that."

"Focus your mind on your, sorry for the word, uh … cock, not only the way my touch makes it feel but also how you feel inside, emotionally. Let your mind go free. Tell me what feels really good, what doesn't necessarily, and if you're getting close to orgasm. Okay?"

Aaron nodded his head and closed his eyes. His head was swimming. Jason pressed Aaron's cock down against his belly and slowly and firmly ran his palm up and down the underside of the shaft. When it grew to its full length, the glans extended two inches above his naval. Aaron moaned, but he held still. "Oh God, Jason. It feels like it's going to burst. It's so hard it's almost uncomfortable. And no, don't stop."

"Aaron, when was your last HIV test?"

"It was right after the last time I'd seen Nathan, a week before we went away. I got the results Friday morning, the day we left for our vacation. Why?"

"What were the results?"

"Negative. Why?"

"Did you have sex with anyone else between those times?"

"No, I've been faithful to Nathan since we were together, but I could never be absolutely sure he was, faithful I mean. Why do you ask?"

"Just thought I should know." Jason focused his fingertips again around the corona, drawing them up and down from the frenum to the tip of the glans. At the same time, he grasped the massive shaft firmly with his other hand, barely reaching around it. He began to slowly pump it up and down. Soon a bead of pre-cum formed at the slit. Jason leaned forward and placed his lips just over the bead and sucked it into his mouth, rolling it around his tongue.

Aaron gasped, opened his eyes, and looked to see Jason removing his mouth from his cock. He couldn't believe it, and forced himself to say the words, "Jason, that felt really, really good," but what he thought was, *Oh, my God, suck me. For God's sake, suck me!*

"Aaron, there was a bead of pre-cum there. I wanted to know what it tastes like. Was that okay? It's really sweet, really good."

"Oh," was all Aaron could manage.

"I said, was that okay?"

"Yes, oh, yes!"

"You're doing really well, Aaron. I'm watching your leg and arm, and you haven't moved them at all yet. Good for you."

Aaron croaked out, "Thanks."

"Are you feeling any pain right now?"

"God, no. This couldn't be any further from pain."

"Good. I want to try to bring you up closer to orgasm. Is that okay?"

"Definitely."

"Do you think you might be able to have an orgasm?"

"Jason, I'm pretty damn well sure there's nothing I could do to stop it at this point."

"Good. Okay, here we go, but remember, I'm keeping an eye on your limbs."

****

For the next thirty minutes, Jason projected calm from his mind, hoping that it would somehow reach Aaron and help him relax. He squeezed the shaft firmly with one hand and reached down to Aaron's sack with the other, lifting his massive balls into his palm. They were nearly the size of plums. A deep rumbling growl began to rise from Aaron's chest, and his body went completely limp. His sack relaxed and flattened out over Jason's palm, so that each globe hung over the edge like a piece of dangling, succulent fruit.

"I'm not moving, Jason. I swear, I'm not moving!"

"I know, Aaron, you're doing great!" Jason shifted his hand and began to scrape the tips of his fingers under Aaron's scrotum, drawing it away from the base of the penis while moving his other hand to work the corona again with his fingertips.

Aaron's face began to twitch. "Not moving. Still not moving!"

Jason rolled the globes around and between his fingers, gently massaging and squeezing them to encourage them to release their nectar. Aaron began to pant as his sack started to tighten up until his balls hugged the base of his now-dripping cock.

"So good. It feels so good, Jason," Aaron moaned.

Jason made a ring with his thumb and fingers to pull the ball sack down and stretch it away from the cock's base. At the same time, he put his mouth to the tip of Aaron's cock and then slid down over it, engulfing the glans to just past his teeth while gently and rhythmically sucking. His other hand moved down the shaft and began to pump it up and down, just as slowly as he sucked. He was immediately rewarded with a steady trickle of pre-cum that soon turned into a stream.

"Oh!"

"Oh!"

"Oooooohhh!"

"Jason. Jason!"

"Oooooohhh!" were the only words that escaped Aaron's throat between deep, panting breaths.

"Are you close?" Jason asked.

"So ... close."

"So ... so ... close."

"Now don't move, Aaron."

"No!

"No ... move."

"No move!"

Pre-cum now flowed freely from Aaron's swelling glans and Jason drank it down, greedily. No other man had ever tasted so good to him.

Jason slowed his pace. He wanted to be sure Aaron could endure this without moving. Aaron pleaded with him to finish him off, but Jason kept him like that for another fifteen minutes, just beneath the point of no return. The only part of Aaron's body that moved was his head, steadily rolling from side to side. He groaned. His groans turned to moans, then whimpers, then he began to squeal.

"Please, Jason. Please. I can't ... can't take it ... can't take it anymore."

Jason pulled Aaron's straining sack away from the base of his cock while ever so slowly driving his mouth further and further down his shaft. He grasped the shaft tightly to form an extended ring of pleasure while he moved up and down, up and down, with his mouth.

"This is it. This is it, Jason. Oh, my God. Oh, my God! The pressure is building. It's building. It's building! I can't hold it back anymore!"

Intentionally, Jason allowed his teeth to gently graze over Aaron's burgeoning, inflamed glans.

"I'm gonna come, Jason. I'm gonna come!"

Jason became lost in what he was doing. His own cock felt like it was going to split open as pre-cum flowed from him as well. He forgot everything he'd said about not moving to Aaron. He sucked deeply and applied all the pressure he could muster against the underside of Aaron's cock with his tongue, flicking it several times as it passed over the frenum, all the while increasing the speed of the pumping he applied to the shaft.

"I'm coming. Oh, my God, I'm coming. I'm coming. Jason ... I'm coming!"

The first wave of Aaron's viscous nectar pounded the back of Jason's throat, coating his tonsils. He nearly dislocated his jaw when he forced his mouth down the thick shaft so far that the pulsating head met his tonsils. Several loads were driven right down his throat before he was able to pull back. He felt Aaron's thick, hot man-cream rush across his tongue, so he lingered there allowing himself to savor every luscious gush. He held the final surge in his mouth and rolled it over and over his tongue, relishing the sweet and musky notes that floated over the savory, saltiness that was the essence of Aaron.

When it was over, Jason's mind began to clear. Soon he was able to think, but he was too spent to even speak or move. He rolled to his side and ended up in a fetal position against Aaron's flank where he began to shiver. Images shot through his mind as he remembered what he'd done, what Aaron had said, and how Aaron responded to his touch.

****

After a few minutes, Jason pressed his hand against the mattress and pushed himself up. Aaron's eyes were open, but he had a faraway look on his face. Then Aaron blinked and turned to face him. He opened his mouth. His lips quivered, but no words came out. He reached for Jason and pulled him down to his chest, caressing his back. Finally, he spoke.

"No words. There are no words, Jason, to tell you what happened. I was in another place, floating in another time, yet it was like I was in your mind too, feeling what you were feeling for me. It was the most beautiful thing I've ever experienced.

"Oh, Jason. Jason. My eyes were closed, but I could see you caressing me, and I could feel the deep caring that you felt for me. It was as if I was in your mind while at the same time feeling every moment of pleasure I was receiving. I've never known such calmness and a tremendous sense of love swept over me, caressing my body and mind. It was as if I'd left my body, watching from above, while at the same time still being in it."

"It's okay, Aaron. It's okay. I felt it too."

"Yes. Oh God, yes."

Jason suddenly rose and squatted at Aaron's side, furiously checking his left leg. "I'm sorry, Aaron, but I forgot myself. I forgot all about your injuries. I'll never forgive myself if something's happened."

Jason climbed off the bed and walked around to the other side to check Aaron's right arm, then he let out a sigh of relief. "Please tell me you're not feeling any pain in your bones, Aaron."

"Jason, I'm fine, wonderful in fact. I can't believe that I was able to do what you told me to. It was like I was in a trance, completely detached from my physical body, yet I was able to feel every moment of pleasure you gave me. Oh, Jason, it was incredible."

Jason returned to his side and pulled a sheet and blanket over them. "I'm so relieved you weren't hurt, Aaron."

"I'm fine, Jason. I'm better than fine."

They lay there holding each other until together, they fell into a deep, restful sleep.

Chapter Twelve
Progress report

Saturday, September 12, 2009, early evening

While they dozed, the sun continued to fall towards the horizon. When it reached the tops of the trees, a sunbeam entered the window, brightening the room, waking Jason. He gently dislodged himself from Aaron's arm, pulled the blanket up over him, dressed, and then left him sleeping while he took care of the animals. Heather gave them another two quarts, but when he checked for eggs, there weren't any. Before he left the animals, he mucked out the stalls and then headed back to the cabin.

****

When Jason returned, he put away Heather's milk. Aaron was still asleep, and with the longhorn roast and chicken salad all gone, he put together a simple dinner of canned ham salad sandwiches. Then he remembered the pickled eggs and beets he'd made two weeks earlier but had forgotten about since he'd found Aaron. By now they would be perfect so he added them to the meal.

While putting the meal together, he got to thinking about supplies, particularly food. He took a stenographer's spiral note pad and pencil to the pantry and inventoried each can, bag, and box and then the contents of the refrigerator and freezer, the kitchen cabinets, what was in the root cellar and smokehouse, and what he remembered of what remained in the garden. While he was going over the list at his table, Aaron woke up and called him over. "What are you doing?"

"I was inventorying our food supplies and calculating our needs." He walked to the bed and sat down next to Aaron.

"Is there a problem?"

"Well, I haven't finished, but I know we'll be okay until my next delivery arrives in a couple months. I've kept the pantry well stocked to cover myself, knowing that if for some reason they're late, or I don't get another one until the spring, I'd be okay. It isn't that I was worried we won't have enough food, but more whether we'd have enough of the right food."

"What do you mean?"

Jason got up from the table and walked to the bed. "You're injured, and your body is going to need a variety of foods to provide all the proteins, calories, and vitamins and minerals necessary to heal and to rebuild your bones. I can't leave you alone while I go out and hunt, as I can be gone for hours and hours."

"You're amazing, Jason. I'd never think of those things. I'm so lucky to have you."

Aaron smiled, and Jason blushed.

"We'll be all right, I'm sure. Between what's in the smokehouse and the pantry, and don't forget the eggs from the chickens, there's plenty of protein," Jason patted Aaron's shoulder.

"Aren't you running out of the stuff you've been using on me? You know, all the gauze and stuff?"

"No, not by a long shot. There's plenty to cover what you'll need. I'll just order more when the time comes."

Aaron took Jason's hand and kissed his palm. It sent a shiver through Jason's body and a buzzing sensation to his loins.

"I'm so lucky," Aaron said again, looking at Jason adoringly.

"You hungry?" Jason asked, changing the subject. "I made some ham salad sandwiches, and there's pickled beets and eggs."

"Sure, I'm starved. You really drained me earlier," Aaron said with a wink.

"Then we'll just have to be sure we replace your fluids." Jason shook his head, chuckling to himself, and went into the kitchen to get dinner.

After they'd finished and Jason had cleaned up, he returned to bed and laid down to read a book.

"Jason," Aaron said.

"Yeah."

"I want to understand something."

"What's that?"

"Well, earlier, after the movie, what was that all about?"

"I took your advice and went with the flow. It seemed right to me."

"Why?"

"Because, you held me and comforted me while we watched the movie. I've never felt so close to anyone before except my mother. I felt secure. No, not secure, protected and safe. I've never felt so safe with a man. I could sense your caring."

"But you were so into it."

"I've thought about that too. When this began, I mean when I found you, I was caring for you clinically, but as the days went by, I began to feel a deep, emotional connection with you that grew and grew until it became so strong that your needs have become my needs. All the different levels of what I've felt for you over the past week are still there, but they've combined to the point where I don't know where one ends and the next begins. Does that make sense?"

"Yeah, it does." Aaron stroked Jason's arm for a

few minutes while he read, but then soon fell asleep. By ten o'clock, Jason was yawning uncontrollably so he got up, stoked the central wood stove, and removed all his clothes. He figured he'd slept naked all his adult life, and there was no reason to be conservative any more. Before he turned in, as promised, he put not one but two body pillows on the bed between himself and Aaron. He was sound asleep within a minute of turning off the light.

****

Sunday, September 13, 2009, 7:00 AM

Jason had been up for more than an hour. The animals had started to make a good dent in grazing down the yard around the barn, but they still had quite a way to go. After carrying in Heather's milk and six eggs, he mixed up a batch of cornbread from scratch and put it in the oven. The ham was still partially frozen so he put it in the sink to finish thawing, and he doctored two large cans of baked beans and put them in a casserole dish.

"Good morning," Aaron called to him.

"Ready for breakfast?" Jason answered back.

"Sure am. I'm starved!"

"Cereal okay again?"

"Absolutely."

Jason carried everything over to the card table. Aaron had already raised the head of his side of the bed so Jason set him up for breakfast and then ate himself sitting cross-legged next to Aaron with his bowl in his lap.

"Ham, baked beans, and cornbread okay for dinner?" he asked Aaron.

"Sure, sounds great!"

"There's also about a half a dozen cabbages still in the garden. I could bring one of those in and either simmer it or fry it up on the stove if you'd like."

Aaron smiled, then chuckled. "Just how much farting do you think you can put up with?"

Jason laughed out loud. "I didn't think of that. Should I make something else?"

"Hell, no. I haven't had ham and baked beans in like forever. I can't wait! Mmmm, I think I smell the cornbread now."

"Oh … shit!" Jason jumped off the bed and ran to the oven. "Phew," he called back, "it's okay, it's okay. Still needs a few more minutes."

Jason returned and finished eating. After cleaning up, he took the cornbread out of the oven, placed the ham in his cast iron Dutch oven and poured a can of ginger ale and honey over it and then put it and the doctored beans in to bake.

While bathing Aaron and changing his dressings, Jason noticed how much better his wounds looked.

"Aaron, I've been putting antibiotic ointment over your wounds, but I'm going to leave the dressings off. They can be opened to the air now. Your sutures will be ready to come out in another few days, probably Tuesday—that'll make ten."

"Ten? Sutures?"

"Oh, no, sorry, I meant ten days. Ten days since I put in the sutures. Almost without exception, sutures come out within seven to ten days after they're put in. That's how long it takes the skin to grow back together.

"I was also able to remove the drains I put in your penetrating wounds, but they'll get dressings until there's no more drainage. How's the leg and arm? Any pain?"

"Some, but it's like it's almost normal to me now. They ache and sometimes I get sharp, shooting pains, but I've just accepted that that's how it's going to be until they heal."

"Well, the alignment looks good. Thank God

none of them were compound fractures. That would have been real tough to deal with outside of a hospital."

"What's compound mean?"

"When the broken bone ends punch through the skin creating a wound right over the fractures. It's a perfect setup for infection. Fortunately, the wounds you had weren't directly over the fracture sites."

Aaron turned a little green at the thought. "Oh God, I could puke right now just thinking about it."

"Sorry," Jason said apologetically, "I shouldn't have mentioned it."

"No, it's okay."

"Just one thing to finish up, and we're done," Jason said pointing to Aaron's groin.

Of course, Aaron got an erection when Jason was soaping up his penis and scrotum. He didn't ask for sex, but he did offer a comment. "Feels real nice, Jason. You're so gentle. It's more like you're caressing me than washing me."

"I'm just trying to be gentle, that's all. No urges?"

"I could if I really wanted to, get into it I mean, but yesterday, God, Jason, yesterday! All my sexual tension is gone."

"All done," Jason said, drying him off. "Oh, one more thing, those nasty scrapes down there at the folds where your thighs meet your abdomen, from when the parachute harness straps dug in, they're going to take a lot longer to heal. If you can manage to move your right foot to the edge of the bed or bend your right knee and let your hip roll outward, that will let some air in and help to keep the moisture down."

"Will do, and yeah, it is sore down there."

"I've been applying the antibiotic ointment there each time I've finished bathing you."

"Ah, is that the slick stuff I've been feeling under my balls?"

"Yeah, probably, and one last thing. I was thinking it's about time your hair was washed, and you had a shave. It's been over a week."

"How is that going to work?"

"Washing your hair is easy. I'll roll up a blanket and put it under your neck, and I'll move it up around the left side of your face, over the top of your head. Then I'll put a trash bag over the blanket to keep the sheet dry. With both ends of the rolled blanket hanging off the edge of the bed, it'll make a trough, and the water will drain into a bucket on the floor."

"I never thought of that."

"Yeah, it's not difficult at all. I'll be right back with shampoo and the other stuff. You good?"

"Yeah, good."

****

"Your head sutures look great!" Jason said when he finished with Aaron's hair. "I was able to work out most of the crusty scabs that had formed up against your scalp. They can make suture removal a little difficult, but for the most part, they're gone now. The drain's been out for two days, and I applied some antibiotic ointment over the suture line to protect the wound because the scabs aren't there any more to keep it sealed from the air. The sutures can definitely come out on Tuesday."

"Great, one step closer to normal."

"Now, let's get you shaved."

"I don't know … Jason, you've got a beard, and I've thought about growing one every now and then. I wasn't allowed to have one on the team, but I think I'd like to try it out for a while, that is unless you don't think it'll look good on me."

"Too soon to say. It's only a week old, and it's a

bit scruffy right now. It's actually begun to lift some of the pine sap I couldn't get off and the scabs where there were scrapes and cuts. But okay, let's give it another few weeks, and you can let me know what you think of it then."

"You got a mirror?"

"Yeah, I'll bring you the one from the shower."

A minute later Jason returned with the mirror.

"Here … have a look."

"Wow, I see what you mean. I look like crap. My face is thinner. I've lost weight!"

"Aaron, you fell thousands of feet through the air and landed in a tree, and you've been flat on your back, not working out with the team. It's to be expected."

"I guess."

Chapter Thirteen
Here's to you, Gordon Merrick

After dumping out the bucket of water and throwing the towels and a set of sheets into the washer, Jason laid down on the bed with a book, but before he started reading he said, "So do you want to do anything? Watch TV, play cards? I've got a few board games in the closet."

"Nah, how 'bout a book. What do you have?"

"Really?" Jason looked surprised. "I thought you said you didn't like to read."

"Yeah, I did, but I figure I might as well, coz that's what you do. We can read together, and that way I'll always have a book handy. I might as well take advantage of this time and expand my mind."

"Okay, sure. What subject do you think would interest you?"

"I have no idea."

"Well you know, I love romance ..."

Aaron screwed up his face mockingly. "No way, Jason! Just kidding, just kidding. Whatever you think is fine with me."

"I've got mysteries, adventure, a few sci-fi, and gay? Anything sound appealing?"

"I'd say gay. Is it porn?"

"No, though there's sex in all of them. They're more gay-themed novels."

"How 'bout you just bring me a few of each, and I'll page through them until I find something."

Jason returned from his collection with a stack of books and set them on the bed within reach. Aaron skimmed or leafed through all of them until he got to *The*

Lord Won't Mind, by Gordon Merrick.

"This must be a gay one," Aaron said, pointing to the two handsome male figures facing each other on the cover.

"Yeah, it's one of the first gay novels I ever read. It's really, really good, Aaron … but prepare yourself."

"Well, it's got a great cover," Aaron commented. He reached down and grabbed his dick and balls, lifting them up from between his legs and draping his shaft over his left thigh.

"Yeah, and both characters are hot as all get out. I think you'll like it a lot," Jason said encouragingly.

****

About an hour later, Jason got up and went to the kitchen to check the ham and beans.

"Wow, Jason," Aaron called to him, "I never knew there were books like this, This is really great!"

"Sort of like we are," he called to Aaron. "Right?"

"Yeah, right," Aaron answered, "just two people who happen to be gay."

****

By dinnertime, Aaron had read over a hundred pages and was getting close to the middle of the book. If he'd had two good hands, he would have kept reading while he ate, but he had to put the book down to hold his fork. "Jason, I'm really amazed by this book."

"How so?" Jason asked while he set Aaron up to eat.

"He's writing about people like us—Gordon Merrick, I mean. Charlie and Peter are real people, just like us."

Jason smiled. "I know, that's why I kept it, coz it was the closest thing to real life I had read up to then."

"Yeah, and it's not porn."

"No, it isn't. Shocking, right?"

"Yeah, and I'm grateful to him for portraying gay characters as normal people. I hope I can meet him one day and tell him."

"Aaron, I felt the same way when I read it, but I'm sorry, he died over twenty years ago. My heart really ached when I learned that."

"Damn. Now I'll never be able to tell him. Well, here's to you, Gordon Merrick," Aaron said, raising his glass of milk towards the ceiling.

"Wait, let's do this properly." Jason got two tumblers and the bottle of scotch and poured some for each of them.

"Here's to you, Gordon Merrick, and thanks!" Aaron toasted again, and they drank to the author's memory.

****

After Jason cleaned up after dinner, he went out to take care of the animals. Once he put Heather's milk in the fridge, he took a shower, then put on a pair of workout shorts and a tank top and joined Aaron on the bed. He'd started to read when Aaron interrupted him.

"Jason?"

"Yes?" he answered with his face in his own book.

"Do you have any gay videos that are like the book?"

"No, not really. Well, wait a minute. There's one called Latter Days."

"Can we watch it?"

"If you like."

Chapter Fourteen
An arc of ecstasy

When the movie began, Jason was lying close to Aaron with his ankles crossed and his arms behind his head. After the first minute and a half, the movie got hot and steamy. Unconsciously, Jason uncrossed his legs and spread his thighs and then slowly worked his hand beneath his waistband. Aaron immediately noticed.

"Jason, can I ask you something?"

"Yeah," he answered, his eyes locked on the screen.

"Can I do that?"

Jason turned to Aaron who was pointing towards his junk. "Well." Jason immediately blushed.

"Hey, after what you did for me yesterday, let me at least try to give you the same pleasure. Come on, we talked about this."

Jason let go, and Aaron moved right in with his muscular, quarterback hand. "Mmmm," Aaron said softly, "Nice. I love the feeling of it growing under my touch."

Jason slowly let out a breath.

"Don't be uncomfortable about this, Jason. We'll take it nice and easy."

"I know. I know," Jason answered.

"Take off your shorts."

Jason lifted his hips and began to pull them off, when his erect cock got stuck in the elastic, pulling it downward. He winced.

"Here, let me help you with that," Aaron said as he lifted the waistband, freeing Jason's manhood. As it thwacked against Jason's belly, Aaron asked, "Better?"

"Yes."

"Your shirt too."

When he was completely naked, Aaron ran his fingertips through Jason's thick chest hair, then down his belly, following the treasure trail to the base of his now fully erect and throbbing cock.

"Oh, my!" Jason said, an octave higher than normal.

"Feel good?"

"So good."

"You just watch the movie and leave it to me," Aaron said as he caressed the inside of Jason's thighs.

"Okay."

"Oh! Oh! Oh, Aaron!"

"Yeah baby, I know. I'm gonna take such good care of you."

When nearly thirty minutes of the movie had passed, there was a scene where one of the main characters put a bandage on another guy's butt cheek. The wound was just above the strap of his black jock.

"That guy's got a hot ass," Aaron commented, "and so do you."

Jason was biting his lower lip trying not to be embarrassed that he was oozing pre-cum all over Aaron's hand. Aaron's touch was amazing.

"Jason, man, don't fight it. Just enjoy whatever's going to happen, and go with it. Okay? Isn't that what you said to me?"

"Yes." Jason squirmed.

"Then let me do the same for you."

"Okay," Jason said, letting go of his lip.

"You got any lube?"

"Yeah, right here." Jason reached into the nightstand drawer and pulled out a large bottle.

"Mmmm, industrial size. Great! Squeeze some in

my hand."

The moment Aaron touched his slicked-up hand to Jason's shaft, Jason let out a groan. "Oh God!"

"Yeah, baby, I know. You feel so good, baby. So hard. So swollen. So big. Close your eyes. Picture my mouth, slowly sucking your cock!" Aaron exclaimed.

"Oh! Oh!"

Aaron kept it up, alternately stroking Jason's shaft, squeezing it, palming the glans, sometimes firmly, sometimes barely touching him, allowing just enough time to lapse in-between so that he didn't push Jason past the point of no return.

"Aaron, please. Please, Aaron. Please make me come. Please!"

"All in good time. All in good time."

After ten minutes, Jason couldn't take it anymore. "Oh, Aaron, please! Oh God! Oh God, please!"

"You want to come, baby? You wanna?"

"Yes! Yes!"

Aaron grasped the shaft a little firmer and increased the pace of his strokes. Twice over the glans, once down the shaft. Twice over the glans, once down the shaft. Three times over the glans, twice down the shaft. Then he avoided the glans all together.

"Mmmm, yes," Jason moaned.

"Say you want it, baby. Say you want it. Beg for it!"

"I want it, Aaron. Please, Aaron. Please. I want it. I want it. I want it!"

"Oh baby, you've been such a good boy. Such a good boy. Daddy's gonna give it to you." Aaron tightened his grip and with long slow strokes; he worked Jason's cock from the tip to the base. Rather than speeding up, he kept the pace steady, forcing Jason's orgasm to build slowly, so slowly, but build it did, until

...

"Oh God! Oh God! Oh God!"

Aaron saw Jason's balls pull up tight. Then the glans swelled and turned crimson. Jason began to thrust his hips upward. "I'm going to come! I'm going to ... Here it comes! Here it—!"

The first shot flew in an arc right over Jason's head and splattered against the wall.

The second as well.

The third landed on the headboard.

The fourth hit his face.

Then his chin.

Then his chest.

Then his belly, and his belly again, and again, and again.

When Jason was spent, there was a large puddle on his abdomen. Aaron scooped up the cum and brought it to his lips, sucking it in, savoring the muskiness of it, and then he swallowed it.

"Like honey," Aaron whispered, "just like honey, baby."

Jason went limp. Aaron smiled to himself, pleased that he could give this to Jason, though he was sure what Jason experienced was nothing compared to what Jason had given him the day before.

Chapter Fifteen
You deserve better

Tuesday, September 15, 2009, 10:00 AM

Jason brought a suture removal kit to the bed along with Aaron's bathing supplies. While he bathed him and moved from one sutured wound to another, he inspected the scars and then removed the sutures. By the time he'd finished, all of Aaron's sutures were gone.

"They may itch for a few days, Aaron. I put antibiotic ointment on the scars. It has anti-itch medication in it to minimize your urge to scratch, but I caution you, keep your fingers off them. The scars are still fresh and still healing. You could open them right up and drive bacteria down into them. Then you'd be in real deep shit."

"Oh, I'll keep my hands off them. Believe me, I will."

"Good." Jason had been debating whether and how to broach a touchy subject. As much as he felt for Aaron, he knew Aaron would face tremendous hurdles once he returned to civilization. He had to put Aaron's needs first. "I've had a thought that I wanted to discuss with you, Aaron."

"What's that?"

"This probably isn't going to make a lot of sense to you, and I'm having trouble reconciling it myself, especially in view of what we've done the past few days, but ..."

"Go on, Jason. Tell me."

"You really should be in a hospital. I'm doing everything I can for you, but I have to think of what's best for you."

"You're what's best for me, Jason."

"No, Aaron, really I'm not. Look, if my satellite antenna hadn't been destroyed, you'd have been flown out of here the day I found you. I'd have called the forest service or the state troopers or somebody, and they'd have flown you to a trauma center."

"Don't you want me here anymore, Jason?"

"Oh God, Aaron, it's not that. It's not that at all. It's what's best for your care and recovery, and that's not me. I'm in way over my head here. Hell, I was a medic almost two decades ago. What I did was stabilization and not much more. You have no idea how lucky we've been. I haven't said this before, but because of your immobilized, broken leg, you could develop a blood clot in it.

"What if that blood clot breaks off, Aaron? It could kill you instantly, and there's not a damn thing I could do about it. I've been giving you aspirin twice a day, telling you it's for your pain, but it's really the only thing I have that can thin your blood. And it's dangerous. Very dangerous.

"I'm not running blood work on you every day to check your coagulation profile, but I check your stool every time you go for blood, a sign of internal bleeding. That's the only thing I can do."

"Jason, you saved my life and besides that, you can't possibly know how deeply I feel about you."

"Yes, Aaron, I think I do, but you have to look at this long-term. You've just started a promising career. Each day you spend with me puts you further and further down the road from returning to it."

Aaron became silent and turned his head away. He was done discussing it. Jason became frustrated, so got up to leave Aaron alone.

"I've got work to do outside, Aaron. I'll be back in a while."

****

Jason went to the barn and harnessed Nellie and Sarah to the wagon, then led them to the wood shed where he began to load firewood into the bed. Once the wagon was as full as the girls could handle, he led them out into the middle of the yard where he began to lay out timber into twenty foot letters that read 'S O S'. The animals had made a huge dent in the tall grass and since it was nearing autumn, the grass wouldn't grow any more until next spring.

After several trips back and forth to the shed, he'd finished. Though he hadn't seen or heard a search and rescue plane or helicopter yet, he figured they couldn't miss his distress signal if they flew overhead. It wasn't much, but he had to try.

****

When he came back in, Aaron called to him, and he went to the bedside. "Jason, you were right about me being in a hospital. I'm sorry about acting so childish about it. Thing is, Jason, you're so important to me, way more important than I realized until we began to argue. I don't want to lose that, lose you, I mean."

"Aaron, we can't know what the future holds, but please know that I've come to cherish these days that we've been together. You've helped me as well, more than you could ever know. So ... this is what I've done. I just wrote out S O S in twenty foot letters made from firewood. It's the only thing I could think to do other than hike it out of here, but as I've already told you, that would leave you alone for too many days, and at this point in time, I'm still not willing to do that.

"Not only do I think you wouldn't make it on your own, I failed to consider that autumn is approaching, and the predators are becoming more active. We've got grizzly bears, black bears, wolves, cougars, badgers, coyotes, foxes, and bobcats and lynx, not that I think the last three would be a threat. Even though the stockade is electrified and topped with razor wire, if they got in here, you'd be defenseless."

"Thanks, Jason. I do know you want what's best for me. I just can't think of my life without you anymore. This is where I want to be. Here with you."

****

Tuesday, September 15, 2009, 3:00 PM

After lunch, while Aaron was napping, Jason cleared off his work table. As the hours passed, and with pencil in hand, he began to draw on a large pad of sketching paper while referring to several books. By the time Aaron woke up, there were papers spread out all over the place and open books were scattered here and there.

"What are you working on over there?" Aaron called from the bed.

"It's a surprise."

"What kind of surprise?"

"I'm almost done, just give me a few more minutes."

When he was finished, Jason picked up the pad and carried it over to Aaron. "Take a look at this and tell me what you think."

"What am I looking at?"

"Haven't you ever seen plans before?"

"What kind of plans?"

"Construction plans, silly. Floor plans!"

"For what? Tell me?"

"For the Aaron addition, that's what."

"Addition?"

"Yeah."

"For me?"

"Yes, for you. For both of us, but it's because of you. I figured, if you're serious about making a life with me here, then I've got to build you facilities that will help you recover. Then, once I got started, I thought about our future beyond that, so ... this is your gym and therapy room. This will be the sauna, and here's the hot tub."

"Jason, this is too much! Really, too much! And I can pay too! I just signed a huge three-year contract with the Bighorns. It's for fifteen million, and I got a four-million-dollar signing bonus. You don't have to pay! Hell, I'll pay if you're willing to have me."

"Willing? Shit, Aaron, I want you. Willing? Ha ..."

"Thank you, Jason. I needed to hear you say that."

"Wanna see more?"

"Yeah!"

"Here's going to be the library. I've got books and videos stacked in too many places around here now. This way there'll be a room dedicated to my collection, and there'll be plenty of space for it to grow. Now here, off the library, will be the theater."

"Theater?"

"Might as well plan big! We shouldn't have to lie in bed every time we want to watch a movie."

"Looks great, Jason, but what about porn?" Aaron winked.

"Well," Jason said with a twinkle in his eyes, "this is the play room. Just let your imagination run wild for a moment."

"Ha! Ha! Oh, baby, a play room!"

"Right next door, over here, will be our master

bedroom, complete with a master bath. It'll have an oversized, multi-head, glass shower, a double-sized, sunken tub with jets, a towel warmer, two toilets with bidets, a double-sink vanity and anything else you can think of or want."

"What's wrong with what we have right here?" Aaron indicated their bed.

"This area will be turned into a dining room and the kitchen will be expanded. I've also added three guest bedrooms, with their own bathrooms in case we have guests who stay over for a visit, and another bathroom here. Do you have family?"

"Yeah, but they don't know about me ... being gay, I mean."

"Well, we'll cross that bridge when we get to it. Now there's more. Off the back entrance where the wood shed comes in will be a large, twenty by fifteen-foot mudroom with floor drains and a built-in shower. It'll have two large stainless steel sinks and work tables so that when I hunt, I can process the meat inside."

"Wow, you've thought of everything. What's this that runs along the whole side of the addition?"

"It may not actually be there, but one half is going to be a sunroom and the other half will be a greenhouse so I can start vegetables while there's still snow on the ground in early spring and grow more vegetables over the winter with a hydroponic setup. That way I won't have to deal with pots and soil. Since you've been here, I realized how important salad and greens are to a healthy diet. I'll have to have an architect design it and situate it best along the southern exposure. The whole thing is going to be paved with flagstone and it'll have floor drains installed just like the mudroom. This is all just a rough draft. The architect will do it right."

"So, what's on the second page?"

"That's the upstairs."

"Upstairs? How much more room could we possibly need?"

"Have you ever thought about children?"

Chapter Sixteen
Please look down

Wednesday, September 16, 2009, 8:00 AM

After waking from dreaming about their future together, and everything that might entail, Aaron was excited to see what the day would bring. He was also horny as hell and needed to come. It had been four days since his last orgasm, but he knew Jason would insist on bathing him first. That gave him an idea. Jason had always tried to conduct his baths with clinical efficiency, but Aaron was hoping to broaden their horizons. The thought of coming while Jason was soaping him up became almost too much to bear.

Aaron finished his eggs, bacon, and buckwheat pancakes in record time to try to speed things along, and he hoped Jason didn't have anything else planned for the morning since he'd already taken care of the animals. He was relieved when Jason went straight to the bathroom to collect the bathing supplies as soon as he had finished cleaning up after breakfast.

"Okay, Aaron, ready for your bath?"

"Yes, sir!" Aaron said with a wink and a smile.

"What's that supposed to mean?"

"What?"

"That wink!" Jason said with a chuckle.

"Oh, nothin'…"

No sooner had Jason begun to bathe him, Aaron asked, "Hey, Jason, what would you say to spicing things up a little?"

"What do you mean?"

"Oh, I don't know, maybe combining my bath

with a little titillation? Draw it out, talk dirty to me. You know."

Jason smiled a shy smile. His cock jumped beneath his jeans. Aaron noticed a twinkle forming in his eyes.

"Oh, my big, manly stud is hurt. He has a big ..." Jason rubbed Aaron's cock through the sheet. "Oh my! A big, big manly problem, doesn't he?" Then Jason began to squeeze it.

"Yes, he does, and there's only one man who knows how to give him what he needs," Aaron sighed, curling his toes.

"Does it hurt, baby? Does it hurt down there?" Jason squeezed again, then traced the outline of Aaron's growing hard-on with his fingertips.

"Oh, it hurts. It hurts real bad!" Aaron moaned.

"Well, has my big, manly stud been a good boy today?"

"No. No, he's been bad. He needs to be punished. Punish me, Daddy. Punish me."

Jason gathered a handful of Aaron's hair from the top of his head in his fist and mockingly pulled his head back. "Aaron's been bad. He needs to be scrubbed, and there's nothing he can do about it!"

"Oh, please don't hurt me. Please don't hurt me," Aaron answered in a fake whimper.

Jason took the soapy, dripping washcloth out of the bucket and began to scrub Aaron's chest and abdomen. The soapy water ran down his sides, soaking the towels beneath him. He lingered over his nipples, applying deep pressure and pinching them through the washcloth's material. Aaron drove the back of his head into the pillow and arched his back, pushing his chest up and out from the bed.

"Oh, too much?" Jason asked.

"No, it felt great."

"Thing is, Aaron, you lifted your right arm up with your chest. I'll need to check it." Jason scooted off the bed and walked around to the other side. "Phew, the splint is good, but I think we need to reconsider this. That could have been disastrous."

"Really? I didn't feel anything, any pain, I mean."

"Still, Aaron."

"Okay. Okay. Why don't you just do it when you're soaping up my cock... Linger there. You know."

"I think that's all you really want anyway. Right?"

"Yeah, right," Aaron answered with a devilish smile.

When he was nearly finished with the bath, Jason uncovered Aaron's thick, growing cock. It was already semi-hard. "Hmmm. Baby has some swelling here."

"Oh, it's swollen. It's so swollen. Help me, Daddy. Help me."

"Oh, poor stud's got too much fluid in there," Jason said as he lifted Aaron's cock and measured its weight in his hand. "Needs to be drained of some fluid. And it's dirty. So, so dirty."

"Oh, so dirty. Drain me. Drain me of all that dirty fluid."

"Let's massage that fluid right out of there," Jason whispered. He soaped up the washcloth until it was so slippery he could barely hold on to it. He hoisted Aaron's turgid cock with both hands. Gently, he began to lather the soap deep into the shaft, and it grew.

****

Aaron closed his eyes and tried to clear his mind. Soon he imagined he was floating in an aquamarine sea of Jason's deep, deep love.

Jason moved on to his tightening ball sack,

working it, easing its tension, until it hung loose like a deflated balloon holding two perfect, nectar-filled globes. Aaron's cock started to jump in the air as Jason worked the lather into the sack's folds. With each spasm, the glans swelled and darkened. Its blue-green veins, snaking the length of the shaft, could barely be contained, like a cobra, ready to strike.

Deep animalistic sounds began to escape from Aaron's chest, and Jason was rewarded by a thin stream of manly nectar that trickled from Aaron's slit. So into what he was doing, Jason didn't notice the sound when it began. As it grew louder and louder, he suddenly realized he could hear what sounded like a plane. He dropped Aaron's cock so quickly, Aaron had no idea what had happened.

As he ran for the door, Jason yelled back over his shoulder, "Aaron, they've seen the sign! They've seen the S O S! They're coming, Aaron! They're coming!"

"What the fuck!" Aaron shouted as he was pulled out of the tranquil sea and back to reality.

****

Once he'd made it off the porch, Jason could see a silver glint about a thousand feet up as the plane's wing shimmered in the sunlight. The words, Search and Rescue, were painted on its side. He ran out into the yard and watched to see if the plane wobbled its wings to indicate it had indeed seen his S O S.

****

"Hey, Mason!" Joshua the spotter shouted into his helmet's microphone. "What's that over there?"

He pointed at the ground, off the plane's left wing.

"Where?" Mason asked, looking down.

"Over there," Joshua pointed, "That movement beneath the trees, by that ridge.

"Let's check it out," Mason answered as he banked left.

Both men focused beyond the wing, just as Jason's S O S came into view.

"It's just a stampede of longhorn. The whole herd is charging down the hill," Joshua shouted.

The S O S was now just below their right side, but neither of them saw it.

"Well, we've got an hour's worth of fuel left. Let's move on to the next grid," Mason shouted.

"Right. Do you think we'll ever find him?"

"Nah," Mason shouted back. "If anything, they might find pieces of him, but I'll betcha animals have already dragged off anything that was left."

"Yeah, from what they found of that Taggart guy and the pilot, he's gotta be in a million pieces. Betcha, I'll betcha."

"You're right there, Josh. Maybe some hunter will find a big gnawed up bone in a few years and wonder what the hell it came from."

"It's a shame," Joshua shouted, "From what I've heard, he had a promising career. Wonder what the team's gonna do now?"

"Oh, they always have somebody waiting in the wings."

Mason had the last word as the plane flew away.

****

Jason waved his arms furiously at the plane flying right overhead.

"Over here! He's here! He's here! Please, over here! He's over here!" he screamed and screamed.

He watched as the plane disappeared over the ridge.

****

There were tears in Jason's eyes when he

returned.

"Jason what happened? Where'd you go?"

"It was a plane! A fucking plane! A god-damned, fucking plane, Aaron, and it just flew away!"

"Jason, it's not your fault. You did everything you could."

"I know. I know. I can justify it in my head, but all they had to do was look out the right window. God damn it!"

"Jason, calm down. Come over here."

Jason climbed onto the bed and kneeled down next to Aaron. Aaron pulled him down to his chest and hugged him.

When he sat back, Jason said, "Sorry, Aaron, but I'm just not in the mood to finish you off. I just can't do it right now."

"That's okay. I'm fine. Hey, don't you ever forget, you're my hero, Jason. You're my hero."

****

After they landed, Joshua repeated what Mason had said about the quarterback's remains to another search and rescue crew, just within earshot of a reporter who was staking out the hangar.

Chapter Seventeen
I always thought I'd die alone

Friday, September 18, 2009, 6:30 PM

Two weeks after Aaron fell from the sky, life in the cabin had become a routine of cooking, eating, bathing, goat milking and egg gathering, stall mucking, reading, movies, porn, and there was sex, lots and lots of sex. Jason had been restless all day, but Aaron figured he'd talk when he was ready.

Since the plane had appeared, both of them had been vacillating between imagining a life together and what life would be like when they were apart.

After dinner, they were reading in bed. The animals had been taken care of, and the barn was closed up for the night. Suddenly, Jason sat up on the bed, crossed his legs under him, and began to caress Aaron's arm.

"Aaron, can I ask you something without you getting upset?"

"You can ask me anything, Jason. How could I get upset with you for anything?"

"Well, it's like all we do around here is eat, bathe, read, watch movies, and have sex. Aren't you getting tired of it all?"

"Tired of sex? Ha, ha. Never," Aaron winked. "And what else is there to do anyway?"

"I know, I know, but ..."

"Are you getting bored with me, Jason? Is the sex not good for you?"

"No, the sex is fine. No, that's not true, it's great. Fantastic! Better than any I've ever had, but what's gonna happen after you're rescued? We're not going to be able to keep it up, this all up, I mean. You'll be in a hospital and then rehab far, far away and probably for a long time, and I won't be able to stay with you, coz I've got the animals to look after, and besides that, my life is here. Not that I wouldn't want to be with you, but I don't know how long I would last in the city. Too much noise, too many people, too much of everything."

"What about those construction plans you drew up three days ago? Was that a joke?"

"Oh, God no! Sorry. It's just that I had a nightmare last night. We were living together, and then you were taken away, and I couldn't stop it."

"Jason, I've been dreading this conversation. To be honest, I've been thinking about it more and more. I've never been so happy, really. I know I have a life too, had a life, but all this, right here, right now seems more real to me than anything I've ever known. I'd give it all up in a heartbeat if I knew you truly wanted me, and I could live with you here, or somewhere else even, as long as we were together."

Jason got a faraway look on his face.

"Jason, I'm sorry. I didn't mean to put pressure on you. Maybe you've imagined something else after I'm gone, but I have to tell you how I feel about you. Really, I've kept myself in denial over the whole idea of not being here with you."

"No, Aaron, I've thought about the same things, but are we being realistic? Were those floor plans just a pipe dream? Fate threw us together. Are we just reacting to our circumstances, that we've been thrown together, two people who desperately need someone right now? We'd have never met if it hadn't been for your plane accident. Hell, I always believed I'd grow old up here and die alone, and my body wouldn't be found until someone flew up to make a supply run. I could be a withered, dried-out corpse when they find me if the timing's right."

"Don't talk like that! I can't bear to think of you dying alone. And I promise you one thing right now, you won't. Ever! Not if I have anything to do with it."

"I'm sorry, Aaron, but that's how I've always seen my life ending."

"Well whatever the reason, Jason, we're together now. Everything's different. We care about each other. Shouldn't we make the most of it while we can, as well as plan for the possibility of a future? Here? Together?"

"Aaron, the fact that you're here, right now. The fact that the past two weeks were real. I could have never imagined it. But are we being honest with ourselves, Aaron? Can it last? Will it last? It's just as difficult for me to wrap my mind around the idea that you could be here as it is that you won't be."

"What made you start to question this, Jason? You've been amazing. You're an amazing man. If I'd have fallen a hundred feet deeper into the forest, you'd have never found me. I've thought a lot about that. One day you'd have gone outside and wondered what that stench was, coz I'd have been rotting in a tree somewhere. You should never, and I mean never question why you found me. God damn it, Jason!" Aaron started to cry.

"I'm sorry, Aaron, I didn't mean to upset you. It's just that we said we could talk to each other about anything. Didn't we?"

Aaron nodded his head, still crying.

"Then shouldn't we think about it, talk about what to do after? After you're rescued."

"Jason, I don't want to be rescued. I don't want to be without you. I want to stay here with you forever!"

"Oh, Aaron. Aaron."

Jason leaned in and hugged him. "I'd want you to stay with me too, really I do, but we're kidding ourselves if we believe that could happen right now. You don't want to be crippled, do you? You want to get normal function back, right, to be able to walk without a limp, to use your right arm normally, get back to the game?"

"I guess," Aaron sniffled.

Jason gave him a tissue. "Then we should make plans to ensure that happens. Right?"

"Right!" Aaron answered. There was a sparkle in his eye now. "So I could live here with you? After?"

"If that's what you truly want. I'd be the happiest man in the world if that happened. Those floor plans were my wildest dream, my 'if I could have anything in the world, what would it be' dream."

"And I've been afraid that I'll never see you again too, after I make it to a hospital."

"Then let's be realistic about what will or probably will happen. Only if we're honest and true to our situation, can we work with it."

"Okay."

"So, you'll be flown out of here by chopper. Right?"

"I guess. Yeah. A plane couldn't land here, could it?"

"No. It would need a runway. There's only a helipad. Soonest that could happen is the middle to the end of October. That's when my next supply delivery will be. Which makes me realize just now that I don't have any way to contact Rod to give him my order. Shit! Sorry, Rod's the owner of the transport company that choppers in my supplies. I'll have to think about that later. So where was I?"

"The middle or end of October."

"Oh, right. So that's the earliest you could possibly be rescued. That is, unless someone sees the S O S for some reason, but the search plane that flew overhead missed it. Search and rescue doesn't go on forever. They may not look in this area again."

"Really? They'd stop?" Aaron was shocked that they wouldn't keep searching for him until he was found.

"It's more likely they will stop than they won't. So then what?" Jason said cautiously.

"I don't know."

"You'd be taken to a hospital where they'd examine you. Do tests on you. Maybe do surgery to fix whatever needs fixing. Then there's recovery. Then physical therapy and/or rehab. How long do you think that'll take?"

"A couple weeks, maybe?"

"No, Aaron, it'll be more like months. Months!"

"Okay, months. Then I'll come back."

"Months from now I could be snowed in. Then nothing could fly in or out of here until spring."

"Next spring?" Like a rag doll, discarded in a corner, Aaron's shoulders sunk, his face sagged, and he fell back into his pillow.

"Aaron, if I have to come back here to take care of the animals, and you're in the city, and your recovery takes months, when you get out, you might not be able to get to me."

"Hell, I'll find somebody to fly me up here."

"Well, if that could happen, it'd be sometime after the new year."

"Then it'll be after the new year. So?"

"So? So, what about your career? What about the team?"

"Shit! I forgot about that."

"Okay, now let's consider the best-case

scenario."

"Yeah, let's."

"Say you're out of the hospital much earlier, say November, because you didn't need surgery, and you won't need rehab, maybe just physical therapy. You might not be able to play, and if that's the case, wouldn't they want you to be suited up and present at each and every game, representing the team?"

"Fuck! Probably. Damn it…"

"So you're gonna fly up here and back how often? What about PT? They're gonna want you to go to their own therapists, right? Physical therapists who specialize in sports medicine? Every day. Right?"

"Jason, I hate you. Why do you have to know all this stuff? Why do you have to be so damn truthful?"

"Because, Aaron, you're very, very important to me. I'd never lie to you or mislead you, and I only want what's best for you."

"So even with the best-case scenario, I couldn't come back until after the season's over. Right?"

"Probably," Jason answered as he lowered his head.

"Fuck! Fuck! Fuck! Fuck! Fuck!" Aaron shouted.

"Yeah, I know."

****

Friday, September 18, 2009, 7:00 PM
National evening news broadcast

"Good evening, ladies and gentlemen. We end our broadcast tonight with an update on the search and rescue efforts to locate Aaron Jaeger, the Nevada Bighorns' new quarterback. We now turn you over to Chuck Jackson, who is coming to us live from Idaho Search and Rescue headquarters. Come, in Chuck."

"Good evening. In view of the fact that fourteen

days have passed since the private plane that was chartered by Aaron Jaeger disappeared from radar, and no trace of Jaeger has been found to date, we have just learned from Idaho Search and Rescue that their mission has changed from one of search and rescue to search and recovery.

"What that means is, they believe it's nearly impossible to consider that Jaeger could still be alive due to the weather conditions that have been present in the mountain ranges surrounding the plane's last known location. Temperatures in the region have fallen into the upper thirties overnight during the past week.

"Also, no new information has been forthcoming from the coroner's office in Hinnen Valley with regard to the ongoing DNA testing of the human remains found in the area surrounding the crash site.

"A gruesome prediction was made by a member of one of the search and rescue crews two days ago. And I quote, 'Maybe a hunter will find a big gnawed up bone in a few years and wonder what it came from.'

"That's it for now from Hinnen Valley. Back to you in the studio."

"That ends our evening broadcast. We wish you all a safe and happy weekend."

Chapter Eighteen
Wild Asters

Tuesday, September 22, 2009, 2:00 PM

Jason was up at the crack of dawn. Heather had given more than two quarts of milk, and he'd collected eight eggs, almost a record for the hens. He was also feeling a little randy so he made an extra effort at breakfast with pancakes made with frozen blueberries and eggs fried in rings he'd made from cans with the tops and bottoms cut off. He topped them with ham and cheese that he'd shaped to fit English muffins he'd cooked from scratch on the griddle. Finally, he went out into the yard and cut a few of the last remaining wild Asters and put them in a tall narrow jar.

"You're naked again!" Jason announced as he carried in breakfast.

"I know. I know." Aaron said as he laid back and rested his left hand behind his head. "Aren't you used to it by now?" Aaron spread his right leg out to the side to teasingly show off his package.

"Yes, but still, how can you stand it?"

"I'm used to it. What's all this?" Aaron asked waving his arm towards the flowers and overflowing tray Jason was holding.

Jason set the tray down on his dresser and then shook out the sheet and blanket and covered Aaron up. "Oh, I thought I'd bring a little color inside. I've made blueberry pancakes, ham, egg, and cheese-stuffed English muffins, coffee, orange juice, and, of course, Heather's milk. You hungry?"

"Starving!"

"Then let's eat."

****

As Jason was gathering the things he'd need to bathe Aaron, the image of him lying back and spreading himself wide open made his dick jump. He removed his jeans and shirt in the bathroom. Aaron raised his eyebrows when he saw Jason walk back in wearing only his boxers, but he didn't say a word.

When Jason finished bathing Aaron, he used a comb and a small pair of scissors to trim and shape his two-week-old beard. It was beginning to fill out nicely, and he thought it gave Aaron a debonair look with just a hint of nobility. He filled his hand with shaving cream and began to suggestively apply it to Aaron's neck. He lingered with the razor as he moved it from side to side and up and down his whiskers. By the time he finished, it was the longest shave he'd ever given.

Aaron reached up and pulled Jason down by the neck. When their lips met, Aaron teased his tongue into Jason's mouth, and then kissed him deeply. When they broke apart, Aaron said suggestively, "Why don't we take some time later today to...?" Jason's eyes glistened, and he nodded yes.

Aaron lifted the mirror and turned his head from one side to the other as he looked at his reflection, admiring what Jason had done. He smiled. "Wow, Jason, it looks great. Thanks!"

"You're welcome. You'll have to decide just how long you want it to be, and I'll trim it accordingly."

"So what should we do now?" Aaron asked slowly, as he reached out and ran a finger up the inside of Jason's thigh.

"Oh, my!" Jason jumped. "Well, as much as I hate to say it, I've still got to muck out the stalls ..."

Aaron cut him off, "Anything else?" Aaron

reached up beneath the leg of Jason's boxers and tickled his balls.

Jason's body jerked. "And I want to check the last cabbages in the garden. It's starting to get cold ... Oh my, Aaron. You're distracting me!"

"Am I?" Aaron snickered.

"God, yes. I can't think now," Jason said as his knees began to buckle. "It's getting cold so we're going to have to eat them before they freeze."

"There's nothing cold about this," Aaron whispered as he lifted the leg of Jason's boxers to reveal his erection.

"Oh God! Um, whatever we don't eat, I'll turn into sauerkraut."

"Mmmm, this looks good enough to eat," Aaron said as he ran his fingers along the underside of Jason's cock, causing it to twitch.

"Aaron, please, these things need to get done. Now, where was I? I'll keep what I think we'll eat over the next month in the fridge, and I'll can the rest."

Realizing that Jason had already planned his morning, Aaron ceased his teasing. "Have you ever made coleslaw?"

"Yeah, I love coleslaw! Do you eat it? Would you like some of that too?"

"If you'll make it, I'll eat it."

"Great. I'll make a big batch. I like to add a shredded carrot too for color."

"You're amazing, Jason. You can do and know so many things."

"Living alone for eleven years forces you to learn."

"Great! Then, after you're done ..."

"Yeah, baby. I'm looking forward to it."

****

After several hours, Jason came in from the yard. He was sweating and dirty and carrying a basket overflowing with vegetables.

"What have you been up to?" Aaron called.

Jason answered from the kitchen, "Well, one thing led to another and before I knew it, I'd cleaned and straightened up the barn, cut a lot of the remaining tall grass, and stacked it up in the loft so it'll dry out for winter feed for the livestock. Nellie, Sarah, Heather, and Jasper really look forward to the small amounts I give them each day. Then I dug up the last of the potatoes and some of the carrots. The rest of the carrots can stay where they are until the ground begins to freeze. I'll put the potatoes in the root cellar, and we'll have potatoes and carrots with one of the six cabbages I cut, for tonight's dinner. Venison roast okay with you?"

"Yeah, sure!"

"I'll make up the slaw with one cabbage, and the other four I'll turn into the kraut. Do you like your sauerkraut with or without caraway?"

"I have no idea. Make it however you like."

"Ok, caraway it is. You all right for a few minutes? I stink, and I need to take a shower."

"Yeah, you do stink," Aaron mockingly held his nose. "I can smell you from here."

****

After Jason had showered, he walked out of the bathroom completely naked and climbed onto the bed on his knees next to Aaron. Aaron noticed his dick appeared thicker than it normally did when it was flaccid, and it stood out ever so slightly, as if he was just beginning to get an erection. Aaron admired Jason's exquisite masculine form, and that made his own dick jump. He couldn't help but pull down the sheet and start stroking himself.

Aaron was very in tune with Jason's body language by now, and he could tell he was feeling randy, but he thought he'd hold off a while. He knew that would only serve to feed Jason's flames of passion. A bit of foreplay was called for.

Aaron let go of his own cock and reached over and ran his fingertips up and down Jason's chest and abdomen, lingering in his belly button, which he knew, drove Jason wild. Immediately, Jason's dick lurched and began to grow.

"Mmmm, baby, that feels wonderful." Jason's body shivered as goosebumps were raised under the touch of Aaron's muscular fingers. Soon his manhood was at attention, and it began to pulsate. Jason reached for Aaron's erect cock, but Aaron pushed his hand away.

"Later, baby," Aaron said seductively. Let me just linger over the look and feel of you for a little while. We have all the time in the world."

Aaron ran a finger up the underside of Jason's pulsating cock. "Mmmm, baby, you're leaking. Let me take care of that for you." Jason's body quivered as Aaron began to coax the ooze from his cock, lifting his fingers to his mouth to suck them dry.

When Jason began to thrust his pelvis forward, Aaron pushed against his hips and wagged his finger at him. "Just wait, baby. Later."

After Aaron had wiped off all traces of pre-cum, Jason put on a pair of boxers and a t-shirt and began to prepare their lunch.

****

Aaron was all smiles after Jason finished washing the dishes. "Hey, baby, I'm in the mood for porn. Got anything real hardcore in your collection?"

Jason blushed. "Hardcore?" He climbed into bed, "I've got porn, but I don't know what you consider hardcore."

Aaron winked. "Well then, let's put some on and see what happens…"

Jason brought Aaron about thirty videos from his collection to choose from. "Hey, most of these haven't even been opened yet."

"I know. I subscribe to a service that sends them up to me in lots when I have my supplies delivered. Find something you like?"

"A few."

"We could also watch a regular movie. You know how I love romance."

Aaron winced, "No way!"

"Okay, you pick."

"How about this one. It's two hours long," Aaron said, handing the disc to Jason.

Jason loaded the DVD and laid down next to Aaron.

"You get naked too," Aaron said, tugging on the waistband of Jason's boxers.

"Yes, sir!" Jason stripped down and hopped onto the bed on top of the sheets. "Better?"

"Much!" Aaron said, lapping his tongue like a dog at his water bowl. "Now hold on a minute. Let me look at you. Hop off the bed and stand in the sunlight from the window."

Jason blushed but hopped to the floor and walked in front of the window.

"Really, Jason, look at you. Turn around, slowly," Aaron said as he made a pirouette with his index finger. "That's it. God, you're beautiful, but in this light, the way the sun is coming in through the window and highlighting your body," Aaron kissed his fingers like he was complimenting a meal, "the muscular, hairy globes of your buttocks, your rippling six-pack, and your package—? God, you're stunning! Absolutely stunning. God, look at your muscles, the way the light filters through your hairy chest!"

"Oh please, Aaron, aren't you going just a little overboard?"

"Overboard? Me?"

"Yes, you."

"Ha! I'm shocked," Aaron said with a barking laugh. "Hasn't anyone ever said this to you before?"

"No," Jason said shyly.

"Well shame on them. Jason, you deserve to hear these things. The way your treasure trail leads down to your package. Oh, Jason, I could just eat you up."

Jason blushed, but he was less uncomfortable than he put on. It was actually turning him on—he could feel the blood flowing into his dick. "Sorry, Aaron, it's just that I'm not used to this kind of talk ... I mean compliments, compliments about my body that is. I'm more comfortable about a lot of things since you came into my life, but what you're saying now is too much."

"Then shame on me too for not clearly expressing my appreciation for the masterpiece that is you. I mean what I said. Now, climb over here and snuggle up to me."

When Jason climbed back on the bed, he laid on his side facing Aaron and began to gently run his fingertips through the short hair on his pecs. Aaron sighed. Jason's dick jumped as it swelled.

"I love my nipples caressed," Aaron whispered.

Very slowly, Jason made circles around Aaron's areolas then gently drew his fingernail across his nipples. Aaron shivered and turned his head to Jason.

"My turn now," Aaron said with a devilish smile. "Up on your knees, and face me."

Aaron reached for Jason's package. He lifted it in

his muscular palm and gently squeezed, then drew his fingers up the underside of the shaft to linger over Jason's glans. Jason shivered and bit his lip. "Oh!" escaped his mouth as his body jumped.

Aaron moved from Jason's shaft to his thighs gliding his fingertips down one and up the other, drawing them across his ever-growing cock whenever they passed it. Jason reached his hand down and found Aaron's cock. It was rock hard.

"I want you, Jason. I want to feel your body against mine."

"I do understand, Aaron, really I do, but please tell me. How far do you want this to go?"

"As far as we can. As far as you'll let me."

"Then give me a few minutes. I'll be right back." Without waiting, Jason hopped off the bed.

Aaron heard the shower running, then it stopped. The toilet flushed and then the shower was back on. Aaron smiled to himself.

Jason was back in five minutes, completely dry and naked. Aaron had raised the head of his side of the bed and was slowly stroking his hard-on. "My God, Jason, you're gorgeous! And your cock, thick and hanging down and free like that. God, I just want to suck it."

"Before we start, Aaron, I must insist one thing."

"What's that?"

"Please, please be mindful of your fractures. You must not move your right arm or your left leg. It's only been three weeks."

"Haven't I been a good boy so far? Of course, I promise. We're going to take this real, real slow. Now scoot over right next to me."

As soon as he was close enough, Aaron cupped Jason's balls. Jason froze in place and sucked in his breath. "Feel good, baby?"

"Oh God, yes," Jason moaned.

"Good. Get the lube?"

"Already done. It's right here."

Jason pulled the bottle from behind his pillow then leaned his hips toward Aaron. He began to put some lube into Aaron's hand, but Aaron pulled it away. "No, Jason, straddle my face."

"Really?"

"Oh yes, really."

Jason lifted his left leg across Aaron's chest and rested it on the bed beyond his right arm. Then he leaned his hips forward.

Aaron drew the fingertips of his left hand beneath Jason's sack, causing his cock to begin to jump and grow. When he was completely hard, Aaron grabbed his sack and guided his cock toward his face. He began to run the tip of his tongue across the slit. Jason's cock jumped and his body jerked. "Mmmm, your pre-cum is starting," Aaron said, licking his lips.

Jason knees began to buckle as he started to shake uncontrollably. "Never!" Jason panted as he spoke, "Never have I felt ... never have I felt anything ... anything like this before. Oh my. Oh, my God, Aaron. Oh, my God!"

"Mmmm, so good," Aaron whispered. "Mmmm, Jason cock. Mmmm, yummy, luscious Jason cock." Aaron leaned his head forward and drew Jason's quivering shaft between his lips, gently sucking on the tip. Then he took in some more, then more, drawing in the entire length of Jason's shaft until the head stopped at the back of his throat.

"How are you not choking?" Jason asked as he watched his cock slide in and out of Aaron's mouth.

"Practice," Aaron mumbled as he pulled back for

a moment. "How big are you, Jason?"

"I'm eight inches, I think."

"That feels about right. The perfect length, and the perfect thickness. You're about two, two and a quarter inches wide?" The veins along Jason's cock became engorged as they strained against the blood surging into the shaft. Aaron sucked Jason in again, then pulled his head back, darting his tongue along as the head reached his lips. As Jason pushed his cock in, Aaron felt the swollen head hit his tonsils.

Jason struggled to speak. "Oh God. Never before. Never, never before."

Aaron reached back and teased the backside of Jason's balls, tickling them with his fingertips. Jason let out a yelp as pre-cum began to ooze from his slit.

"That wasn't pain, Aaron. I just wanted you to know that."

"I know, baby, I know." Gently, Aaron began to press against Jason's perineum until Jason thrust his hips forward when Aaron hit his P-spot. Aaron pressed his thumb up into the sensitive nerve endings while he created tremendous suction with his mouth on Jason's glans. Jason couldn't help himself and began to thrust his hips, driving his cock deep into Aaron's throat, past his tonsils. Aaron gently withdrew his mouth and whispered, "Slow down there, big boy. We've got a long way to go."

"Sorry, Aaron, I can't control it."

"I know," Aaron said wickedly. "Have you ever had your anus probed?"

"Not really. I don't think so. I've only been opened up before, for anal."

"So you've never had your prostate massaged, your anus caressed?"

"No. Massaged? Like with fingers? Caressed? Like with a hand? No. God, no!"

"Oh, baby, then you're in for a treat. Did I hear right? Did you clean yourself out?"

Jason nodded. "Yes. I have a rectal douche in the bathroom."

Aaron smiled up at him. "Good boy. Then pick up the lube, and slide your cock back down my throat." Jason squirted more lube on Aaron's fingers than he intended. His hands were shaking so much, he could barely control them as he leaned his hips towards Aaron's face.

Aaron inhaled his cock and began to work his slick, dripping middle finger around the opening of Jason's anus. Jason's body began to quake with spasms and his head fell back. "Oh, my. Oh, my. Oh, my God. Oh, my God!" Jason yelled to the rafters.

Aaron pulled his head back so he could focus his lips tightly on Jason's glans, darting his tongue back and forth along the underside of his throbbing cock-head again and again, while continuing to explore Jason's anus. He pressed his muscular thumb up into the P-spot until the external sphincter succumbed to his advancing finger. He worked it in ever so slowly so he could gauge the internal sphincter's resistance.

"Oh, Aaron, what are you doing? I can't take it. The pleasure. Oh, the waves of pleasure. How? How is this possible? I'm losing ... Aaron, I'm losing my mind!"

"There, there, baby," Aaron whispered as he withdrew his mouth from Jason's quivering shaft. This is just the beginning."

Aaron sucked him in so hard and fast that he gagged when the swollen helmet hit the back of his throat. He continued to probe Jason's anus so gently that soon the internal sphincter not only relaxed, but drew him in. He searched for the swelling, golden orb until he found it.

When Aaron caressed it for the first time, Jason thrust his hips forward so hard that Aaron choked for a moment. He continued to stroke the orb back and forth, back and forth, then round and round, round and round. Jason clenched his buttocks tightly together, causing pre-cum to trickle freely from his slit. His prostate swelled and hardened as turgid as his cock-head. Aaron felt a puddle forming on his belly. He too was pouring out pre-cum uncontrollably.

"Ahhhh," Jason screamed. "Help me! Help me! Oh God! Help me!"

"Do you want me to stop?" Aaron asked wickedly.

"Are you kidding? No! Oh, my God. Oh, my God. No!"

"Sit down on my belly for a minute," Aaron instructed while he kept his finger in place. When he did, Jason felt moisture.

"That's my pre-cum, baby. You did that to me. Now I'm gonna use it to finger-fuck your ass for all it's worth." He scooped up some of the slick puddle and guided Jason to rise again while adding a second finger to Jason's convulsing hole. Slowly he slid them in and out together, in and out, in and out. Jason's anus was begging to be finger pounded, but Aaron held back. He wanted Jason to beg for it.

Just when Jason thought he couldn't take any more, Aaron increased the pace, as he tightened his lips and sucked Jason's shaft, rubbing his cock head against his soft palate, probing his ass deeper and deeper, twisting his fingers round and round like the agitator on a washing machine.

"I'm going to cum. Oh, my God, I'm going to cum! Aaron, please!"

Aaron drove his fingers in to their hilt and

pressed down firmly against Jason's hard, swollen, aching prostate. He furiously worked Jason's cock with his tongue, sucking the glans, as if he was pulling a strawberry from its stem.

"It's happening. It's happening, Aaron. I'm coming. I'm coming!"

Aaron braced himself as Jason thrust his hips forward. The first jet of cum was so enormous, it made Aaron choke. He pressed his fingers against Jason's spasming orb, causing wave after wave of thick, milky cum to shoot from Jason's engorged, pulsating head, coating the back of his throat. It had been a long, long time since Aaron had taken that much cum, but he hungrily gulped down stream after stream. He lost count at thirteen, but it was worth it. Jason was worth it.

Jason collapsed and fell to Aaron's side. Aaron laid there in the afterglow of Jason's orgasm, immersed in his own thoughts. *How'd I get so lucky to find such a guy? He's amazing. I think I might be in love. I really might be in love with him. But is it really him, or is it because he saved me? Am I being unfaithful to Nathan?* As he fell asleep, his last thought was, *Wow, we never even started the DVD. I must still have it.*

Chapter Nineteen
Search no more

Friday, September 25, 2009, 6:55 PM, evening news

"Finally, we end our evening broadcast with some sad news. Three weeks ago tonight, the private plane that was chartered by Aaron Jaeger, the newly-signed CFL quarterback for the Nevada Bighorns, disappeared from radar as it exploded and crashed in pieces to the ground.

"Idaho Search and Rescue reported today that it has suspended its search and recovery mission in view of the fact that they have found no traces of Jaeger since they began to search for him the morning after the crash.

"You may remember that things turned grim last Friday when their mission changed from search and rescue to search and recovery. We send out our deepest condolences to Jaeger's family, friends, and the entire Nevada Bighorns organization, and to the family and friends of Nathan Taggart, Jaeger's trainer, and the pilot, Samuel Johnson, on their losses.

"Good night, and have a safe and pleasant weekend."

****

Monday, September 28, 2009 10:15 AM

From: Rod Livingston
<pacificnorthair@pacifictel.com>
Subject: Visit & Next Supply Delivery
Date: September 28, 2009 10:15:46 AM PDT
To: Jason Ackerman
<JAckerman@pacifictel.com>

Hey Jason,

Wondering whether Jack and I could come up for a three day visit this coming weekend. We could arrive Friday morning around ten. What do you say?

We'll go over your next supply delivery at that time. We've found a few new gadgets you might be interested in.

Hope to hear from you soon,
Rod Livingston
Owner, North West Air Transport

****

Wednesday, September 30, 2009 7:15 AM

After Jason had finished his morning chores, he took the two, ten-pound chickens from the fridge that he'd started to defrost two days earlier. They could eat off them for at least two days. He rinsed and dried them, then slid rosemary sprigs from the small herb garden on the kitchen windowsill under the breast skins, and then stuffed them with two packages of dehydrated stuffing mix from the pantry and several cups of bread cubes from a loaf of whole wheat he'd baked on Monday.

To make up for the extra bread, he added extra chopped onion, sage, a little garlic, parsley, dried celery leaves, and two cups of chicken bouillon broth. He'd made so much stuffing that he had to bake half of it in a lidded casserole dish. After the chickens were in the oven, he washed five pounds of potatoes for mashing, put the giblets and necks in a pot to simmer on the stove, and then made breakfast.

****

Aaron woke to the smell of banana pancakes, bacon, and fried eggs.

"Wow, these are great!" Aaron said as he dug in after Jason brought him his tray.

"Jason, how'd you make banana pancakes? Where are there bananas?"

"There aren't any, but I have dried banana chips that I rehydrated and mashed up. Make sure you clean your plate and finish up all your juice, and Heather's milk. You're gonna need to be well-hydrated today."

Aaron was shoveling his breakfast into his mouth. He lifted his head but was unable to speak with his mouth so full of pancakes. "Huh?" he mumbled.

Jason smiled wickedly. "Sorry, pal, but I'm real randy for you right now, and I'm going to need all your strength and all the fluids you can muster to quench my thirst."

Pancake spewed from Aaron's mouth as he belly-laughed. "You got a deal, mister," he said after he regained his composure.

"Your choice. Before or after lunch?" Jason asked.

"After. I can smell chicken roasting in the oven, so I'll fuel up on that. Then we can have the whole afternoon and maybe even into evening if you think you're up for it, wink, wink."

"I like! I like!" Jason said with a big smile.

****

After breakfast and Aaron's bath, they spent the next few hours reading in bed. Jason left the dishes until he had to get up and finish with the chickens. He was reading several articles on erotic male massage to learn some of the finer points, hoping that he could apply the techniques to Aaron and lessen the chance that he'd move his fractures and re-injure himself.

Aaron had just started the second Gordon Merrick novel, *One For The Gods*, in the three-book series, and he was getting upset by the way the wife of one of the main characters was treating him. "What happens,

Jason?" Aaron asked, as he tilted the book towards him.

"I can't tell you. I'd ruin it for you if I did."

"Not even a hint?"

"Nope. You'll thank me for it later."

"Well, what's with the wife? I thought you said it was a gay trilogy."

"It is, and no, no hints!"

"Does Charlie figure it out?" Aaron asked. "Does Peter come back into the picture?"

"Not telling," Jason answered with an upward lilt in his voice.

****

Wednesday, September 30, 2009 11:35 AM

Jason cut up the giblets and neck to add to the gravy and stuffing. He washed the pot with the breakfast dishes and checked the chickens with a thermometer. They were done so he moved them to the proof box. After he'd prepared all the side dishes, he began to carve the birds. "So, do you like white meat or dark meat?" Jason called to Aaron.

"Both!"

"Are you going to pig out on it? Remember, I need you at your best this afternoon…"

"Oh, you're evil. You go and make a terrific meal, and then try to keep me from enjoying it."

"I'm not trying to keep you from enjoying anything. I'm just reminding you of what's to *come*," Jason emphasized the word, come. "The fuller your belly is, the less blood there'll be for something else," he said with a devilish laugh.

"Just you wait! Just you wait! 'I'll get you my pretty, and your little dog too!'" Aaron said with a cackle in his voice.

Jason bent over, he was laughing so hard. Finally,

he recovered. "Is that a promise?"

****

"Wow, baby," Aaron exclaimed, "a drum stick, breast meat, mashed potatoes and tons of stuffing with gravy, homemade biscuits, peas and carrots, cranberry sauce, and Heather's milk…? A man and his stomach could fall in love with you! This is too, too much."

"You're welcome … now, eat up."

"Oh God. I just thought of something. Is this one of *the chickens*?" Aaron asked in shock, emphasizing the words.

"Oh God, no. Sorry. I should have told you. No, I don't eat my chickens. They're family. And besides, they're a lot smaller than a roasting chicken. Only a couple of pounds. No, the chickens came from frozen ones I ordered. I get about twenty of them with each supply delivery."

"That's a relief. You know, Jason, I was wondering. I've been here for nearly a month now, and I have no idea who Nellie, Sarah, Heather, or Jasper are, or the chickens for that matter. I've drank Heather's milk, eaten her butter and the chicken eggs, and I can hear Nellie and Sarah making their donkey noises."

"It's called braying," Jason interjected.

"Yeah, braying, and Heather and Jasper call to you when you go out to them, yet I've never seen them."

"Goats bleat," Jason said with a wink.

"Right, and the rooster wakes me in the morning, and yes, I know, it's called crowing," Aaron said before Jason could chime in, "and the chickens have lulled me to sleep with their clucking and cooing. All of them, in their own way, have either nursed me back to health, sustained me, or entertained me, and I've never seen them let alone thanked them or shown my appreciation to them. I wish there was a way I could do that."

"Aaron, that's really sweet of you, but it's impossible. You can't get out of bed, and I can't bring them in here... Wait! I have an idea."

"What's that?"

"I could record them with my digital video camera, and then copy the file to my computer and play it for you on the TV. Heck, I can videotape the entire yard for you. You could see their stalls, the barn, Heather's milking table, the chicken coup, everything!"

"Oh, Jason, that would be fantastic. That way I can see what it looks like outside. Oh, thank you! Thank you!"

"Everyone's most active in the morning. How about I do it tomorrow?"

"I can't wait!"

"Oh, and save room," Jason added. "There's pumpkin pie for dessert."

****

After lunch was cleaned up, and all the food was put away, Jason and Aaron napped together until midafternoon. Jason woke first, then Aaron was coaxed from sleep by the most wonderful sensations coursing through his body. "Mmmm," Aaron moaned as he opened his eyes, "Oh, wow, what are you doing to me?"

"Just caressing your body, that's all," Jason whispered.

Jason got up from the bed and walked to the microwave to turn it on. After it beeped, he removed the large mug he'd filled two-thirds full and stirred in enough cold water from a pitcher to top it off and cool it down just enough to drink. He raised the head of Aaron's side of the bed and handed him the mug. "Here, drink this. You're going to need it."

"What is it?"

"Vegetable bouillon. Now drink up, but don't sit

up. I want your body completely relaxed for what's coming next," Jason answered with a devilish smile.

Aaron did as he was told. When he finished with the broth, Jason took the mug and sat it next to the microwave. He lifted Aaron's right leg and pulled his foot out to the edge of the bed. "Your face looked so serene," Jason continued as he walked back around and climbed back onto the bed. "Then your cock began to swell." He raised Aaron's left leg in the sling and moved it far to the left while he lowered it back down.

Aaron's legs were now spread-eagle, providing unrestricted access to his most sensitive areas. "I couldn't resist adding some pleasure to your dream so I began to trace my fingertips over every part of your body that wasn't covered by the sheet. Did you like it?"

"And then some! Just look at what you did." Aaron nodded towards his cock.

"You did most of that yourself. I just added a little melody to the notes your body was humming."

"Are you going to keep this up?" Aaron asked, "I should probably pee if this is leading to what you asked for this morning."

"No, baby. The fuller your bladder is the better it will be for you."

"Well then, start singing, Jason. Start singing."

Jason pulled the sheet towards him so slowly that Aaron wanted to scream for him to get on with it, but the delay just increased his anticipation for when Jason would finally touch his cock, and it drove him mad with desire. Soon Aaron's eyes glazed over as he fell deeper and deeper under the spell of Jason's masterful hands until his growing cock became a dripping, raging hard-on. "Oh. Oh. Oh, Jason. Jason."

Aaron closed his eyes when Jason began to add moments of deep muscle manipulation, using massage cream combined with the puddle of pre-cum from Aaron's belly. He alternated his hands between barely touching Aaron's skin and intensely rubbing and squeezing his largest muscle groups.

"Jason. Jason. Jason," Aaron sighed.

When he lingered over a muscle, kneading it deeply, Aaron would draw in a breath and hold it until Jason released it. Seconds passed before he was able to take in another. Soon, a deep, barely audible growl began to rise from Aaron's chest until it became a constant, low-intensity grumble. "Ah. Oh. Oh. Oooooohhh," he moaned.

Jason spread his touch across Aaron's entire body with no discernible pattern so that Aaron would have no way to predict where he'd be touched next. This increased his anticipation and surprise each time Jason paused and then began anew.

The moments Jason spent on Aaron's erection were few, but he lingered there, gently caressing it with the tips of his fingers. He lifted several drops of Aaron's dripping pre-cum from the slit and traced up, over, and around the glans with one finger alone, then traveled down the entire length of the underside of the shaft, making Aaron's toes curl while he panted as intensely as a dog on a hot summer's day.

Aaron began to drift between dreams and the here-and-now as he was lulled into one and then drawn back to the other, until he could no longer discern between the two. When Jason noticed that Aaron began to make sucking noises with his tongue and lips, he knew that Aaron was reliving his most deep-seated memories of comfort, suckling at his mother's breast. Aaron was now ready to move into the next phase of pleasure.

Jason shifted all of his attention to the insides of Aaron's thighs. As his caresses moved from one thigh to the other, he teasingly lifted Aaron's swollen testicles from where they rested against the mattress and raked the tips of his fingernails across the thin skin of his scrotum. With his first pass, Aaron's cock spasmed. A thick stream of warm pre-cum was expelled with enough force to reach his chest. Jason moved from thigh to testicles to thigh, to testicles again and again, beckoning more pre-cum to ooze from his loins. With each successive pass, Aaron was pulled further and further from the tranquility of his dream state.

Aaron's breathing deepened and slowed, and his nostrils flared. He opened his eyes and watched as his bulbous, swollen, crimson glans disappeared beyond Jason's lips. He tried to speak, but his voice failed him.

With each passing moment, Jason applied more and more suction to pull Aaron's sweet nectar into his mouth as his shaft advanced further and further until it was enveloped by Jason's throat. "Mmmm. Oh. Oh." Aaron murmured.

Aaron's breathing quickened when Jason cupped and lifted his balls in his palm, jiggling them gently. A squeal escaped his throat the moment Jason squeezed them and pulled them away from the base of his cock, stretching his sack to its limit. "Oh no. No. No. No. Yes. Yes. Please, Jason. Please."

Slowly, Jason slid Aaron's shaft out of his mouth. He lingered on his glans, sucking it like a lollipop on a stick then just as slowly slid the shaft back down until he could smell Aaron's musk rising from the beads of sweat that formed beneath his manicured pubes. Over and over again Jason repeated the sequence, never increasing the pace. It was minutes before Aaron approached the edge.

As Jason sensed Aaron's orgasm near, he slowed his pace to ensure he experienced just enough pleasure to suspend him at the precipice of release. Aaron began to glisten as sweat oozed from every pore on his body until it covered him like a steaming blanket. "Oh my. Oh my. Oh, Jason," Aaron whimpered.

As the surge in Aaron's loins grew, so did his revelation that Jason was devoting all of himself to his pleasure. No lover had ever shown him so much passion. Tears began to fall from his eyes as he opened himself to the single greatest moment of adoration he had ever experienced, and that was enough to push him over the edge.

Soft moans began to slowly leave Aaron's mouth.
"Oh yes."
"Oh yes."
"Yes."
"Jason."
"Jason."
"Jason!"

As slow as the build was, so was Aaron's release. Thick, musky cum began to flow from his cock in a steady stream that never diminished and never increased. It continued, and it continued. Jason sucked greedily on Aaron's glans, swallowing mouthful after mouthful of his seed until it abruptly stopped, but he continued to suckle none the less until Aaron's cock became as limp as his body.

When Jason released him, Aaron was completely still. His head was turned slightly to the left, and a thin trickle of drool dripped from his chin. His eyes remained closed, and his breathing was shallow. Jason covered him with the sheet and then curled up next to him and immediately fell asleep.

****

When Jason woke, it was dusk. He dressed and left Aaron to sleep while he went out to the barn to put the animals down for the night. He returned with a pail of milk and two eggs, and put them away for the morning.

Aaron was still asleep, so Jason took out a book and crawled into bed to read until he felt Aaron stir. Aaron's face glowed, his movements were slow, and his speech soft. "Jason, I have never known such devotion, such love as you have shown to me today. I will never forget it. Never. Thank you."

"Oh, Aaron, I couldn't help it. It didn't start out that way, but it began to grow from a place I didn't know was inside me. You gave yourself to me completely, and I will never forget that."

Aaron reached out for Jason, and Jason leaned into his embrace. They lay like that until the sun had long set, and moon began to rise. In the distance a wolf called to the moon and was soon joined by others. "I know just how you feel," Aaron said to the wolf. "Just how you feel."

Jason went to the kitchen and spooned leftovers into two serving bowls, smothering everything with giblet gravy, and then covered the bowls with plates. After putting the leftovers away, he carried the bowls to the microwave and heated them together, one on top of the other. While their dinner was heating up, Jason put on an old movie, and they ate together in silence. When it ended, they fell asleep with Jason curled in Aaron's embrace at his side.

Chapter Twenty
Nellie, dare I tell him

Thursday, October 1, 2009 7:30 AM

After Jason returned from the barn with the milk pail, eggs, and his camera, he made breakfast. Once they'd eaten and the dishes had been put away, he loaded the video segments he recorded into his laptop and then connected it to the TV. As the videos ran, he described the scenes to Aaron.

"So, this is me walking through the front door to the porch. You'll see me pan right and left and then walk down the steps. That's the barn over there," Jason said, pointing to the screen, "There's the chopping stump where I split the firewood, and there's the well."

"Jason, this is so cool!"

"Now I'm turning around so you can see the cabin."

"Wow, Jason! That's no cabin! It's a friggin' mansion!"

"Well ..."

"It's huge!"

"I wanted to be sure I'd be comfortable, that's all."

"Comfortable, my eye!"

"Okay. Okay. Now I'm walking into the middle of the yard. Here's where I stop and start panning all the way around."

"How big is this place?"

"The stockade encloses three acres."

"Good God! That must have cost a fortune!"

"Like I said, I'm comfortable. Now I'm walking

towards the gate. I'm turning off the electric fence. That's the big slide latch. Okay, the gate's open. Now you can see how I had the timber cleared around the stockade. That's the hill where the helipad sits on top. There's fifty yards cleared all around it."

"Jason, this just boggles the mind! Really!"

"Now I'm walking back in. I'm locking the gate and turning the electric fence back on. Now I'm heading towards the barn. Okay, back near the cabin now. You'll see me turn to show the ... Yes. There it is. That's the wood shed."

"Wow, how much firewood is in there?"

"About two years' worth, but it has to age a good year or two before it's ready to burn. It's a constant process of use some, cut some, stack some then use some, cut some, stack some, over and over again."

"So, here's me turning around and heading to the barn. That's Big John, the rooster, on the fence post. I used to have a split-rail fence all the way around the one side of the barn to keep the animals in, but then I realized, what the hell, I could just let them have the run of the stockade. I left a short section up so that Big John could perch on it to do his crowing."

"He's beautiful. What kind of chicken, I mean rooster, is he?"

"They're all Japanese Bantams. Oh, here are the girls coming up to greet me. They really just want feed and scratch. Their coop is right over there. Its back end opens into the barn so they can get heat from the heating system and stove in there when it gets too cold. You'll see them walking all around me until I get them their feed."

"How many are there?" Aaron asked as he tried to count them.

"Right now there's ten, but the number goes up

and down, depending on whether they've just hatched some chicks or one or two have died."

"Died? How long do they live?"

"Over ten years, but I have to be sure there's always a few new chicks every year. They can get taken by hawks and the like."

"What if there's too many chicks?"

"I can control that by leaving only so many eggs for the hens to sit on and hatch. Most are fertilized by Big John, but the embryo dies after the egg's been refrigerated. Usually it's just a red dot in the middle of the yolk. Their eggs are smaller than the eggs you buy in a store. When the girls get older, they slow down and often produce double yolks."

"Oh, I see."

"Okay, now I'm opening the barn door all the way to let in light for the camera. It'll get brighter in a minute."

"Is that Nellie and Sarah?" Aaron asked, pointing to donkeys.

"Yes, that's them, the pair of them are mother and daughter. They're standard Jennets or the common, Jennies."

"What's that?"

"Regular-sized female donkeys, but they're at the upper end of the category."

"Category?"

"There's standard, miniatures, and the mammoth donkeys."

"Oh, okay. Ooh, and there's Heather and Jasper! Hello, Heather. I love your milk. And look at those horns on Jasper. They're impressive!"

"Now I'm headed over to the windows to open them too. Okay, I've just turned on the overhead lights. That's as bright as I can make it for the camera now."

"Here I am scooping up some feed and scratch from the barrels for the chickens. Watch this!" Jason exclaimed as they watched him scattered the food outside the barn.

"Oh, wow. Look at them go! Wow! Wow! They're really going at it, aren't they!"

"They're hungry is all, but they really could get enough by foraging in the yard after it's warmed up in the spring. Right now, there's not much left for them to eat. All the bugs are done."

"Now the camera's gonna jostle here in a minute ... oops, there it goes. Heather just butted me. She wants to be milked. I don't get it, though ... I milked her last evening. For all I know, she was showing off for the camera."

"That's so funny."

"Try it some time. It can hurt!"

"The stables are getting a little small right now coz I'm walking over to a table to set the camera down. I need two hands to pick up their feed and grass and do the milking."

"Okay, Heather's ready. She's turning towards the milking table."

"Why's that?"

"I trained her to go up there coz it's easier to milk her. That way I don't have to bend down to the ground."

"Oh, I see."

"Ha! Ha! See, she's stopped, coz she's waiting for her bucket of oats. It started out as my way to bribe her when I was training her to get up there, but now she won't hop up without it, unless I've missed a milking, and she's overflowing."

"You might have a little trouble seeing here, coz the camera isn't so close, but I've just started washing her teats before I milk her."

"She's ready now. Okay, now I'm milking her."

"Cool!" Aaron exclaimed.

"Now I'm walking back to turn the camera off to save the battery. Milking takes a few minutes."

"I've just turned the camera back on. That's how much milk Heather gives twice a day," Jason said as the camera tilted to show the inside of the pail. "It comes to around a gallon each day total."

"Now here's me walking out and over to the coops. See, the girls have left us seven eggs. See their size? They're smaller, like I said, but they taste so much better."

"Wow, Jason. Look at the colors of the shells. That's so cool!"

"Okay, I'm done and headed back to the cabin."

"But you didn't close the barn door!" Aaron said, alarmed.

"I'm letting Nellie, Sarah, Heather, and Jasper roam right now so they can work down all the tall yard grass. It's also good for them to get out in the sun and walk and run around … Okay, I'm walking up the porch steps. I'm opening the door, and there you are lying right here."

The TV screen went dark. "Well, that's everything," Jason said as he turned off the TV.

"Thanks, Jason. Thanks for doing this for me. It really means a lot."

"You're welcome, Aaron," Jason answered as he leaned over and kissed him on the forehead.

When Jason leaned back, Aaron pulled him in and kissed him on the mouth. "You're the best, Jason. The best!"

****

Friday, October 2, 2009 9:30 AM

"Hey, Jack. I haven't heard back from Jason. What do you think?"

"Oh, I don't know, Rod. You know how he disappears into the woods sometimes. He's probably havin' the time of his life out hunting. Give him a couple days, why don't ya."

"Yeah, you're probably right. I'll send him another e-mail. You wanna go up next Friday instead?"

"Hell yeah," Jack said, rubbing his hands together. "I can never get enough of his sweet, tight ass and cock, but then you know that yourself. Right?"

"Damn right!" Rod laughed and laughed.

****

Friday, October 2, 2009 10:02 AM

From: Rod Livingston
<pacificnorthair@pacifictel.com>
Subject: Visit & Next Supply Delivery - 2nd email
Date: October 2, 2009 10:02:27 AM PDT
To: Jason Ackerman
<JAckerman@pacifictel.com>
Hey Jason,

Haven't heard back from you about my email from this past Monday. Jack and I were thinking of flying up for three days to visit. You know, hunting, drinking, and all the other fun stuff. Maybe next weekend? How about it? Let me know, okay?

Also, we've found a few cool gadgets you might be interested in. We'll go over your next supply delivery too.

Looking forward to hearing back from you soon,
Rod Livingston
Owner, North West Air Transport

****

Friday, October 2, 2009, 1:30 PM, after lunch

At the four-week mark since his injuries, Aaron felt like he could climb a mountain. Jason was getting worried that his overconfidence would lead him to try something he wasn't ready for and really injure himself. His fractures appeared to be healing nicely, but Jason had no real way of knowing how they looked anatomically. Even so, there was no denying Aaron's stamina was growing. His escapades under the sheets were truly impressive. Regardless, they were headed for an argument. Of that, Jason was sure.

****

"Hey, Jason," Aaron called.

"Yeah?" Jason answered from the bathroom while brushing his teeth after lunch.

"I've been feeling better and better for the past couple of days."

"Yeah," Jason said as he rounded the corner with the toothbrush clenched between his teeth. "You are definitely getting better," he said around a mouth full of toothpaste. "You're doing really well. What about it?"

"I've been thinking, I'd like to try to get up, walk around a little."

Jason spit the toothpaste into the wastepaper basket. "Are you out of your mind? Really? You've got to be kidding!"

"No, really. I'm feeling great."

"You may be feeling great," Jason said, shaking the toothbrush at him, "but your fractures are only four weeks old. Bones don't heal for at least eight. And in your case, you haven't had proper orthopedic care from a board-certified orthopedist. Yours will probably take twelve. You're crazy if you think I'm gonna let you get out of that bed, let alone let you try to walk on that leg!"

"Don't be such a mother hen."

"Aaron, I'm not kidding!"

Aaron raised his voice. "Yeah, well you don't know what I'm capable of!"

"I know you're capable of crippling yourself permanently, if not killing yourself, that's what I know!"

"Jason, I can't stand to be in this bed one more day. There's no way I'm gonna put up with this for another two months! Now, help me up!"

"No fucking way! And don't you even think about trying something when I'm not here. You hear me Aaron? I'm not kidding about this!"

"We'll see!" Aaron laid there fuming, defiantly staring straight ahead.

"Jesus, Aaron. If you can't promise me right now that you'll do as I say, I won't be able to take care of the animals! I'll be scared shitless any time you're not in my sight. Now promise me! Promise me you won't try anything stupid."

Still Aaron wouldn't answer. Tears began to stream down Jason's face.

"You promise me, Aaron!" Jason's voice broke. "Right this minute!"

Aaron immediately felt terrible when he saw Jason's tears. They were having a fight. Their first fight, and it was his fault. He couldn't stand to see Jason crying especially because of him. "Jason, baby, I'm sorry. I won't. I won't do it."

"You promise?"

"Yes, Jason, I promise."

"Don't ever do that to me again, Aaron! Ever."

"I'm sorry, Jason. I'm so sorry."

"You better be… Jesus H. Christ!" Jason threw the toothbrush on the bed, stormed out the front door, and jumped right off the porch. He pulled his axe from the splitting stump and started pummeling logs from the wood pile, splitting them into pieces. They certainly didn't need any more firewood at the moment, but he felt like he had to smash something.

****

"Fuck! Fuck! Fuck!" Aaron yelled as he fell back onto the bed.

****

Jason heard Aaron yell. He bolted from the log pile and rushed back inside, unable to believe what he found. "Jesus Christ, Aaron! What have you done? You promised me! You promised me! Aaron, wake up! Wake up, Aaron!" Jason shouted as he smacked Aaron across the face several times.

Aaron's buttocks, back, and head were lying on the bed sideways. His legs were down with his heels on the floor as if he had been sitting and then fell back.

"What? Huh? What happened?" Aaron said as he came to.

"You tell me, you asshole!" Jason shouted. "What the fuck did you do?"

"Oh Fuck! Fuck! Sorry. Sorry, Jason. I was trying to get the TV remote. It wasn't on the bed. I saw it on the tray table, but it was just out of my reach, so I sat up and reached for it. That's the last thing I remember."

"Liar! You're a liar, Aaron! You tried to get up! You tried to get up, didn't you?" Jason was so angry and scared that he was shaking. "What if I lost you? What if you threw a blood clot? I couldn't live with myself if I let that happen! You bastard, Aaron! You bastard!"

"Jason, I swear. I wasn't trying to get up. Please believe me. I love you, Jason. I'd never do that to you."

"You lied to me!" Jason shouted as his tears began again. "You lied to me! You bastard! You bastard!"

Aaron started to cry too. "Jason, I did not lie to

you! I love you! I love you! I would never break a promise to you! I swear it! Please believe me! Please!" He reached for Jason.

"Don't touch me! Don't you dare touch me!" Jason screamed as he backed away and began to sob. His whole body shook. "I could have lost you! I could have lost you, Aaron!"

Jason turned away, crying with his face in his hands. He couldn't bear for anyone to see him like that, especially Aaron. Even as angry as he was, he knew Aaron was telling the truth. It was fear racing through his mind that made him say those things, but he was too overwhelmed to say that to Aaron.

After a few minutes, Jason turned around and went to Aaron. He placed one arm under his shoulders and the other beneath his thighs and with one smooth motion, lifted and pivoted him back onto the bed.

Immediately he began to assess Aaron's leg and arm and the splints supporting them. He could find nothing wrong, but he was still worried. If bruising began to show within the next several days, he would know that Aaron had displaced the bone ends, disrupting the calluses that had formed, causing him to bleed internally. He had no idea what he'd do then.

Jason laid down and held him. Aaron's sobs turned to whimpers and sniffles, again and again he confessed his feelings. "Jason, I love you. I love you. I love you."

****

When Aaron fell asleep, it was well after dark. Jason went out to the barn and took care of Heather's milking. Then, as he'd done many times in the past when something was bothering him, he pulled a stool into Nellie's stall. He needed someone to talk to, and Nellie was a good listener.

Jason sat down and rested his forearms on his thighs and slowly rubbed his face. Sensing something was wrong, Heather and Jasper stuck their heads through the slats that separated their stalls from Nellie's and Sarah leaned her neck over the top rail. They wanted to offer their support too.

Jason lowered his head. "Oh, Nellie, dare I say it? Can I say it? Can I say it back to him?" Nellie moved forward and rested her neck over his shoulder. She laid her chin against his back and gently caressed him with her big donkey lips.

"I do love this man, Nellie, really I do, but am I in love with him?" Nellie stopped her caresses. "Oh God, yes," he said. Nellie began to caress him again. "Yes, I am, but what if he realizes he really wants to go back to his prior life and play football after he recovers? Oh, to be young and free again." Nellie stopped and lifted her head. She backed away, turned, and then leaned her cheek against Jason's forehead.

"What if I say it to him, and he gives it all up because of me, because of some sense of duty or obligation or even debt he believes he owes me? I'd ruin him. No! No, I can't tell him." Jason felt a shiver ran through Nellie's body.

"No, I'll not be the cause of him giving up his chance at a remarkable career, Nellie, at fame and fortune, at his chance to be loved and respected and honored for his abilities. No. No, I have to let him go." Nellie pressed against Jason with her chest, making him sit up. Then she leaned back and looked directly into his eyes as if she was peering into his soul. A single tear formed, slid down her cheek, and fell into Jason's lap.

****

Saturday, October 3, 2009, 8:15 AM, before bath

time

"You better let me have a look," Jason said.

Aaron was afraid that he'd really screwed up his bones, and he didn't want to let Jason see.

"Aaron, please. I'm not mad at you anymore. Really, I was only mad for a few minutes last night. Most of it was fear. The fear that you'd done something and the fear that I could have lost you."

"Jason, I'm sorry, but I don't know what happened. I started to sit up, and then I don't remember anything else. Not until you hit me in the face."

"I was smacking you so you'd come to."

"What happened to me?"

"It's called postural hypotension. You've been flat on your back for an entire month with only your head being elevated a bit at a time. Your cardiovascular system is out of shape, and your heart and arteries have forgotten how to adjust your blood pressure. When your head went up and your legs went down, all the blood slid into your legs. There wasn't enough blood for your brain, and your brain turned off. That's about as simple an explanation as I can give you."

"So, my heart is out of shape?"

"Yes, and your arteries and even your veins, but they come back real quick. Usually within a day or two of starting therapy, even if you've been flat on your back for months. They'll put you on a tilt table to raise your head and lower your legs in increments until your cardiovascular system equilibrates, and you regain your vasomotor tone."

"Wow. I had no idea."

"I know you didn't. What we can learn from this is when I tell you to do or not do something, it's because I know the physiology behind it, and I can't necessarily explain it to you every time. If you had a medical background, it would be a lot easier. Understand?"

"Yeah, sorry. And Jason, I didn't lie to you. I really was just trying to reach the remote."

"I believe you, Aaron. I do."

"Good. That's a relief. I don't know what I'd do if you thought I was a liar."

"I don't. Now put it out of your mind."

"Okay, it's gone."

"Good, now let me look at that leg and arm and that meaty beast that lies in between."

Jason smiled and winked, and Aaron laughed out loud.

"Oh baby!" Aaron said as he whipped off the sheet. "I'm all yours…"

"Be that as it may, Aaron, we're not going to do anything for the next twenty-four hours. Not until I'm sure there's been no damage done. Agreed?"

"Yes, Jason, agreed, but I'm going to hold you to that. Come twenty-four hours, brother, you better hold onto your hat."

Chapter Twenty-One
A deep, penetrating massage

Sunday, October 4, 2009, 1:45 PM

When Jason returned from putting away Aaron's bathing supplies, he sat down on the edge of the bed. "I'm feeling a lot better about your fractures, Aaron. I can't find any evidence that you caused any new damage, but that should serve as a warning to us both."

"Yeah, no more fancy foot work on my part."

"Good," Jason said relieved.

"So, in view of my clean bill of health, you wanna fool around a little?"

"You've got a one-track mind, Aaron. A one-track mind."

"That's not an answer."

"Yeah, I'm all in for fooling around. Just give me a few minutes to get ready. All right?"

"I'm not going anywhere."

****

Jason picked up the lube as he passed the night table getting into bed. He also brought a few toys he thought Aaron might want to play with and a bucket of hot water.

"What's with the bucket?"

"We might need it. You'll see."

"What's in the box?"

"Toys."

"Toys? What kind of toys?"

"Man toys, that's what kind."

"Hmmm. Let me see!" Aaron looked through the box and picked out several, still sealed in their packages.

"Oh, this could be interesting. And this. And this one too. You're feeling a little ambitious, aren't you?" he said with a sly wink.

"Well, you never know," Jason answered. "You want porn on?"

"Baby, I don't think we'll need it," Aaron said waving his hand over the small pile on the bed. "Not with all this. There's so much to play with."

"Good. Then let's not waste any more time. Do you trust me?"

"How can you ask such a thing. Of course, I do. Go for it!"

"Ever use one of these?" Jason held up a thin silver cylinder about three inches long and inserted it into the flat base of an oddly-angled, bulbous, rubberized shaft. "It's a prostate massager."

"No, I usually top, so I haven't had much butt play."

"Well, let me introduce you to this little miracle."

"Hey, I thought you said you never had your prostate massaged," Aaron said accusingly.

"I haven't, that is until you, last week. I've never opened one of these before, but I've read about them."

"So why do you have it, then?"

"Aaron, I've gotten lots and lots of stuff I've never used or even opened. I know what they are and what they're used for, it's just that I haven't used them. Like with the porn DVDs, I have lots of toys shipped to me by the service I contracted with. That way I've got plenty to keep me busy on those long, cold, lonely winter nights I've lived through over the years. So … do you want to try it or not?"

"You think it's safe?"

"Aaron, I'd never offer you anything I even remotely thought was unsafe."

"Okay, I'll give it a try. What do I do?"

"I'll do it for you, and from this point on, no more talking about toys. Let's just get to it."

"Yes, sir, Daddy, sir!" Aaron saluted.

Jason pulled the cylinder out of the prostate massager and then dropped the massager into the bucket. He hopped off the bed and walked around to Aaron's right side. He began to caress his thigh and then raised his knee gently bending and guiding it to fall out to the side.

Once Aaron was in position, Jason opened a small box and took out a bottle with a long tube on the cap and warmed it up in the microwave for fifteen seconds.

"What's that?" Aaron asked.

"It's an enema, and before you object, it isn't bad and it's really a good idea to clean yourself out for what's to follow. You should try to hold it in for a few minutes."

"I trust you, Jason."

****

After Aaron was finished and cleaned up Jason said, "Okay, you gotta stay soft for this one," as he picked up the largest T-shaped, ball-splitter/cock ring he could find. He put it on Aaron's ample package, leaving his heavy balls to hang between the soft, lined, leather strap. Jason began to caress them with his fingers. With each pass, they pulled up tighter and tighter. Unaccustomed to being separated, they fought against the strap like lovers who couldn't bear to be kept apart.

"Oh, baby, my sack is so sensitive. It's like your fingers are supercharged!"

"Haven't you ever used one of these before?" Jason asked with a devilish smile as he continued to tickle Aaron's ballsack.

"No, I never thought to try one, but it's fantastic! And my cock is becoming hard in half the time."

"The splitter separates your sack and stretches it tight. That makes its nerve endings more sensitive, and the cock ring restrains the blood from leaving your shaft. We'll need to be careful because you could get too engorged, and that can be painful. You've got a huge cock, Aaron. The bigger the cock, the more blood it holds, and the longer it usually takes to fill.

"There've been men whose cocks are so big—and I mean like a friggin' hard salami in a deli case—they come close to passing out when they get hard, if they can even get fully hard. Because so much blood is needed to fill their cocks, there isn't enough left over in their general circulation, and their brain pays the price, just like what happened to you two days ago. Just be mindful of what you're feeling."

Jason applied a new, thicker lube to his fingers and began to work them around Aaron's anus, gently massaging the external sphincter until it relaxed. Aaron closed his eyes and began licking his lips as Jason teased it open. His straining cock was already dripping pre-cum, and Jason hadn't laid a finger on it. "God, Jason, that's incredible. Ooh. Ooh. Oh, baby. Baby. So, so good."

Jason worked his finger in past the internal sphincter and massaged the circular muscles between his thumb on the outside and finger on the inside. Slowly it relaxed more and more until he was able to add another finger inviting the muscles to relax further. Before long he was able to add a third.

Aaron's belly was soaked with so much pre-cum it was draining down his sides and onto the towels beneath him. Aaron was so turned on he was nodding his head and smacking and sucking his lips. "Jason. God, Jason, what are you doing to me? I feel like I'm having

... like I'm having ... having some kind of orgasm, but I'm not."

"No, you're not having one yet, not like you're used to, but just you wait. There are many kinds of orgasms, Aaron. This is just one of the ones you've never experienced. There's more to come. You'll see."

When he felt Aaron was good and ready, Jason took the warm prostate massager from the bucket and reinserted the cylinder. After lubing it up, he slowly eased it into Aaron a little, then pulled it back, then in a little more and back out some more, until it was sucked right in. The base stopped it at just the right depth so that the angled shaft rested its thick bulbous end against Aaron's prostate.

"Now, gently try to squeeze your sphincters and see what happens," Jason encouraged.

Each time Aaron contracted, the massager slid in further and rocked forward, gently pressing against his prostate while at the same time pressing against his P-spot with one of the external arms. When he relaxed, it slid out a little. "Oh, wow. That's amazing! Oh, Jason, it's wonderful, and it makes the head of my cock swell even more."

Jason pressed the button on the cylinder and it began to vibrate. "Jesus Christ! What is that? My asshole is spasming," Aaron yelled.

"Oh, baby. That's the vibrator. It's on the lowest setting right now. I don't want to push you into overdrive even before we get started. It's supposed to be just enough, but just you wait, baby. Just you wait. How are you feeling otherwise?"

"Wonderful. It's nice and warm, and warm waves are starting to flow through my body. This is something else."

"I'm so glad, Aaron. Now I'm going to lower the

top of the bed all the way down and take the pillow out from under your head. You ready?"

"Whatever you want, Jason. Whatever you want. I just can't believe how good I feel right now. This is incredible." Aaron closed his eyes.

Jason straddled his hips over Aaron's head with one knee at each shoulder. Slowly he lowered his chest down to Aaron's abdomen until he could feel the heat that was radiating off his body. "Remember, Aaron, don't move your right arm or your left leg."

"I won't, I promise," Aaron moaned softly.

Jason lowered his hips to just above Aaron's face and then took Aaron's cock into his mouth. He knew Aaron figured it out when he felt Aaron's nose nuzzle his balls and engulf his cock with his lips allowing them to inhale each other's scent while eagerly sucking down the nectar that flowed from their loins.

Jason gently ran his fingertips over the globes of Aaron's stretched ballsack making him shiver with each caress, and causing his cock to strain inside his mouth. He could feel the vibrations from the cylinder travel through Aaron's shaft and tickle his tongue, so he knew it was in the right place and doing its job.

For the next forty-five minutes, Jason would turn the cylinder off when he sensed Aaron getting close to climax to allow him to ease back from the edge. After things would settle down, he'd turn it back on to bring him back up, renewing Aaron's moans and whimpers. As the cycles repeated, Aaron's ejaculatory ducts swelled with nutrient rich fluids, preparing his seed for its impending release.

****

Aaron was in another world. His need for relief from his swollen, aching ecstasy reduced him to grunts and groans, hardly aware that he had Jason's cock shoved down his throat or that he was sucking it furiously. He was so ensnared by the pleasure waves originating in his loins and traveling throughout his entire body that he wasn't prepared for what happened next. His loins had filled beyond their capacity and could no longer be contained.

Aaron found himself floating above the straining moans and sweat-slicked rhythm of their passion. He became aware of a gentle, humming warmth deep inside him, deeper than he had ever experienced pleasure before. The warmth grew as the humming turned into waves of pulsations. It intensified, but it didn't burn, rather it supported him.

Jason felt the changes that were taking place in Aaron's body. His cock was so rigid that Jason could barely move it with his tongue and mouth. At the same time, he felt his own orgasm building uncontrollably as if Aaron's mouth was drawing it from him. Jason reached down to the silver cylinder and pressed the button to high.

****

Aaron was lifted higher and higher as wave after wave of pleasure washed over him, until finally an overwhelming feeling of release engulfed his entire being and began to flow out every part of his body. He was helpless to hold back the quakes of ecstasy as his body opened up to a pleasure he had never known before—all he knew was, it was wonderful. Aaron opened himself to Jason, and Jason felt Aaron's warmth pour through him. In that moment, their bodies became one. In a synchronized storm of passion, their flood gates opened at the same moment.

With each orgasmic wave, Jason drove his hips downward, pressing Aaron's head deep into the mattress. Aaron drank greedily as if he'd been in a desert for days, and the only thing that would save him was Jason's cum.

Though Aaron sucked with forceful abandon, the rest of his body lay motionless. Jason was amazed by the power that propelled Aaron's seed deep into his throat. He swallowed as quickly as he could but was overwhelmed by the sheer volume that surged from Aaron's core. Cum poured from Jason's mouth then poured some more.

When it was over, Jason could barely hold himself from collapsing onto Aaron's body. His legs were so weak, he couldn't even lift his cock from Aaron's mouth. Finally, he found the strength to roll to his left. It was the only way he could free his still rigid cock from Aaron's sucking lips.

Aaron protested. He was sure there was still more to suckle from Jason's cup, and he wanted it, no, he needed it.

⚡⚡⚡⚡

Monday, October 5, 2009 9:30 AM

"Yo, Jack."

"Yeah?"

"Still no word from Jason. You think I should do something?"

"Oh, Papa Bear, you're nothin' but a worrier," Jack said playfully. "Leave the poor guy alone. He'll write back to you in his own good time."

"I guess."

"Remember that time a few years back when he was trekking out every day, setting up blinds along his trails, and didn't check his e-mail for nearly a month? He's just fine. I'm sure of it."

"Yeah, I guess so," Rod answered, shrugging his shoulders, "but if I don't hear from him by next week, we're headin' up there. Unannounced."

"He won't like that. I'm tellin' you right now. He won't like it one bit!"

"Well then he'll just have to lump it, Jack. Him being pissed off at me will be way easier to take than me not doing something if he's in trouble."

****

Monday, October 5, 2009 9:47 AM

From: Rod Livingston <pacificnorthair@pacifictel.com>
Subject: Visit & Next Supply Delivery - 3rd email
Date: October 5, 2009 9:47:36 AM PDT
To: Jason Ackerman <JAckerman@pacifictel.com>
Okay, Jason, now I'm starting to get worried. I've sent you a couple emails, and I haven't heard anything back. Where the hell are you? Jack says you're out on your trails, but I'm not so sure.

Get back to me, will ya?
Rod Livingston
Owner, North West Air Transport

Chapter Twenty-Two
Driven by DNA

Tuesday, October 6, 2009 6:45 AM

Jason stretched, yawned, and turned his head. As he rubbed away the crusts of sleep from his eyes, he found Aaron watching him. "You're up early."

"I want you, Jason," Aaron said with a longing expression on his smiling face. "I want to feel myself inside you. I want to fill you with my seed."

"Whoa, Aaron, where's this coming from?"

"I don't know, but this feeling has been building since yesterday, that I must mate with you. It's like I need for us to become part of each other at the deepest level to ensure we'll never forget."

"Hold on, Aaron, slow down. We've got more time. Not that I'm saying no, but what started all this?"

"This isn't just passion talking, Jason, it's become an overwhelming need. It's like I'm being driven at some deep, animalistic level, like it's coded in my DNA or something. I can't explain it. As the minutes tick by, I sense that we're running out of time, and I need it to happen before it's too late. We've only got a few more weeks before your supplies arrive."

"I'm sorry, Aaron, but can you hold that thought a couple minutes? I really need to use the bathroom. I'll be right back." Though Jason could have waited, he realized he'd also been uneasy for the past twenty-four hours, but he couldn't identify what it was. He needed a few minutes to collect his thoughts. Now both of them were being hounded by something they couldn't quite define or deny.

****

When he returned, Jason sat on the bed and took Aaron's hand. "Aaron, we're going to have to plan for this. It's not something I can just do. I've never taken anyone as big as you inside me, and baby, you're huge."

"So, you'll do it?"

"Of course. I thought we were working ourselves up to it, but there's your leg to consider. How's that going to work?"

"I don't know, and I don't care. All I know is I want you."

"Okay, Aaron, we'll make it happen … but I have to ask, and I know this is still very sensitive for you."

"Go on, ask me anything."

"How did you and Nathan do it?"

Aaron was silent for a moment, swallowed, and then continued. "After things got really heated during our foreplay, he'd do poppers just before I was ready to enter him. He said it helped to relax him and open him up."

"What about yourself? Did you ever bottom?"

"Sometimes, but he wasn't as big as me. I think it was my girth that made him need the stuff. And anyway, he really liked to bottom, and I liked to top, so it always worked out."

"You're probably right—about your girth, I mean—but I don't have that stuff here, and I'd probably never use it. It can be dangerous. It causes your blood vessels to relax, and you can pass out if your blood pressure drops too low, sort of like when you tried to reach for the remote, remember?"

"Yeah, I remember."

"There's a huge difference between a cock that's two inches and a cock that's two and a half inches thick, and I need to be sure I can take you inside me."

"So how can we make this work, Jason? We can't

wait. We just can't!"

"Let me go through the toy closet, well, really three shelves and two chests in my closet. I'll see if I have anything that will help. I've got so much stuff in there, and I can never remember it all."

****

"Look what I found," Jason said a few minutes later, showing Aaron a strange-looking metal object and the largest porn-star-replica dildo Aaron had ever seen. "I had no idea I even had them."

"Hmmm, they look ominous, Jason, even dangerous. Good God, look how big that dildo is! It's a monster! And what in the world is this thing?" Aaron asked picking up the metal object by its handle. "Maybe we should forget it. Maybe this is all just nonsense."

Jason took the object from Aaron. "Now, let's just wait a minute and talk this out. Look, this is an anal speculum. It's inserted into the anus," Jason noted as he slowly squeezed the mechanism to demonstrate. "You slowly spread it open to widen the opening, and I also measured the dildo. It's just over two and a quarter inches wide and just under eight inches around."

"Please, they look like they could rip you apart," Aaron begged. "We better just forget the whole thing."

"No, we're going to try, and anyway, you said Nathan could take you. The speculum opens to about three inches so if I can open it all the way, I'll have no problem with your size." Jason held up the dildo. "And by the way, did you know that you're bigger than this is?"

"No way!"

"Yes, way!"

"Yeah, but I also said Nathan used poppers."

"And he wasn't ripped apart, right?"

"No, but ..."

"Poppers are a nitrate compound. Nitrates dilate or relax smooth muscle. Your anal sphincters are made of smooth muscle. They're what hold your ass tightly shut. Where do you think that little blue pill came from?"

"You mean the 'V' drug? I don't know."

"A pharmaceutical company was looking for a new drug that would be more effective than nitroglycerine for angina, you know, chest pain. When they tested one compound, they found that many male test subjects began to report that they were suddenly getting erections when they hadn't had one in years. Voilà, the company markets it as the new wonder drug for impotence and charges beaucoup bucks for it. And what's the warning on the package?"

Jason imitated a company spokesperson, "'If you are already taking nitrates for chest pain, check with your doctor first to see if you're healthy enough for sex.' Cause they don't want men dropping dead during sex when they've taken one of their little blue pills."

"What does that have to do with this stuff?" Aaron asked pointing at the toys.

"They're a speculum and a dildo, and it doesn't, but I wanted you to understand how and why those poppers made it easier for Nathan to take you. And besides, we pass stools as big as two inches sometimes, sometimes even bigger, and they don't rip us apart, so if two inches can come out, two inches can go in. I think if we take it slow, I'll be able to handle you, once I've prepared myself properly."

"Really? I don't want you to be hurt."

"Aaron, think about it. I'm going to be on top, and you can't use your leg. You're not even going to be allowed to thrust your hips—you'd have to use your legs to do that. I'm going to be doing it all, so I can control the depth and speed of penetration. Human tissue has more give to it than this silicone does," he said squeezing he dildo, "so there'll be more give in your penis when it's inside me. I promise, if I don't think I can do it, I'll stop."

"All right, but you'll be careful, right?"

"Yes, of course. If it makes you feel better, I'll measure the girth of your shaft after I get you good and hard. I know how much you like the way I tease you up."

"You're right about that, but you'll measure me first, right? It's not worth it to me if you could get hurt."

"I just said I promise. And don't worry, if it doesn't happen," Jason winked, "I'll still give you an orgasm to remember. Now I have to go milk Heather."

At the mention of Heather, Aaron laughed out loud, and Jason joined him.

"And when I'm done milking Heather, I'm gonna milk you to within an inch of your life."

"I believe you! I believe you! You big braggart," Aaron answered.

****

After the animals were cared for, Jason served breakfast, washed the breakfast dishes, and gave Aaron a bed bath, giving his nether regions some extra attention. Then he showered and cleaned himself out in the bathroom. Aaron never questioned why Jason had given him an enema again. He figured it had to do with whatever Jason had planned, and he was certainly looking forward to it, but he was still nervous for Jason.

When Jason returned, he was carrying a seamstress' tape measure and a bucket of hot water. He dropped the speculum into it. "It's going to take some time, Aaron, so why don't I load up a couple porn videos and start the DVD player. I'll just let them run one after the other."

"Whatever you think is best, Jason."

After a few minutes, Jason remove the warm speculum from the water and lubed up its three prongs and himself.

"Here goes, any suggestions before I start?"

"What do you mean, suggestions? You've never done this before?" Aaron's eyes widened. "Good God. Look how long that thing is, Jason! You're going to insert the whole thing inside yourself?"

"Aaron, you're longer, remember? And no, I've never done this, but I've used other things to open myself up, and I know how to use a speculum. I learned about them in one of my classes when I was in the army. It's no big deal. So, again, any suggestions before I start?"

"No, Jason, but please be careful."

Jason smiled but didn't answer. As the sounds and voices played from the television, he laid down on his side on the bed close to Aaron. Aaron reached out and ran his hand along Jason's back in a show of support.

"Thanks, Aaron, that helps." Slowly, Jason worked the closed prongs up to the first sphincter. He advanced it a little further until he felt the second sphincter and started to take deep breaths as he advanced it further. It slipped right in. "Well, that was a whole lot easier than I thought!"

"Really? You're okay? You're not just saying that?"

"No, Aaron, really, I'm fine. I think warming it up helped a lot. It just went right in."

"What are you feeling, baby?" Aaron asked.

"It's a weird sensation because it's so hard. There's no give to it at all, but it's not painful in the least, though it's certainly not a butt plug or dildo. That's for sure."

"Well, just be careful. Do you think it would help if I masturbate you?"

"I'd love that, but staying curled up right now helps me to relax, and I can reach the handle easier. Maybe in a few minutes. Okay, I'm going to start to open it up. Here goes."

Aaron held his breath. *I can't believe he's going through this for me. I should have never started any of this.*

The locking mechanism on the speculum clicked as Jason began to squeeze the handle. After three clicks, he stopped and took some slow, deep breaths. "Well, it's going better than I thought. Can you tell how far it opened?"

Aaron tilted his head down. "Sorry, I can't see it from this angle. How long do you keep it in?"

"That's okay, don't worry about it. It'll stay in until I've either opened myself up to its limit or I can't take it anymore." Jason felt for the opening. "It feels like about an inch. I can put two fingers inside. There really weren't any directions other than to use lube, but I think I'll take it out when my sphincters are so relaxed that I don't feel any more pressure."

"Shit, Jason, this just seems like too much work!"

"What, you have some pressing engagement to get to?" Jason asked with a smirk. He started to giggle, and Aaron couldn't help himself. He started to laugh too.

Chapter Twenty-Three
Making love

After forty minutes, Jason had taken the speculum to just below its maximum opening. "Okay, I'm gonna take this out and put in the dildo, but I want to try something first."

"Please be careful," Aaron cautioned.

"I will. I will," Jason said as he lubed up the dildo. "Here goes." Jason released the lock allowing the speculum to close. As soon as he'd removed it, he began to slide in the dildo. It began to go right in without any problem until it got close to the base. "Oops, that's it for the moment, but I can really feel a big difference between the metal and the silicone."

Aaron had a stunned expression on his face. "I can't believe you did it, Jason!"

"There's much less give in the dildo than you. The way I feel right now, I don't think you're going to be any problem at all. I'm going to turn onto my back now."

"Please be careful. Do you think it would help if I masturbate you now?"

"I'm in new territory here, Aaron. I have no idea, but yeah, go ahead and try it. I'd be grateful."

"How's that, baby?" Aaron asked as he gently caressed Jason's limp cock.

"It feels wonderful! Mmmm."

"I'm not hurting you, am I?"

"God, no. It's wonderful!"

After a few seconds, Jason's cock began to twitch. Soon it began to engorge and lengthen.

"There you go, baby. It's working now," Aaron said, encouragingly.

"Yeah, that's so nice." Jason closed his eyes. "You wouldn't believe the sensations shooting through my ass and cock right now."

"Jason, I can't believe you're going through all this for me."

Jason smiled, "I'm doing it for both of us, Aaron."

After a minute, Jason got up and then sat down on Aaron's belly with his back to Aaron's face and the dildo slid all the way in. "Aaron, I'll be ready for you in just a minute. Are you ready?"

"Yes, but I need to say this first. Jason, I'm sorry this created so much work for you. It's not like this has been spontaneous, has it?"

"No, but it should get easier each time. Sex isn't always spontaneous. Sometimes it has to be planned, and anyway, I'm planning to keep this up from now on. The time spent on a little preparation and experimentation now will have a big payoff for us later. Can you reach to my butt and keep the dildo from sliding out? I'm going to suck you to get you partially hard, and I want to feel the blood surging into your cock while it's in my mouth. When you're where I want you, I'll slide the dildo out and then slide myself right onto you. That way you'll be inside me before you reach your full size."

"Baby, it won't take much."

"I know. That's why we're going to go slow. Oh, and there's one more thing."

"What's that?"

"This!" Jason pulled the prostate massager out from under his pillow. He'd already inserted the thin silver cylinder.

"Oh, baby, you think of everything!" Automatically, Aaron bent his right knee upward.

"Yeah, I do, and it wouldn't be fair for my

prostate to be hammered and not yours. I even put a fresh battery in it for you, so ..."

"Put it in me! Put it in!" Aaron begged as he rolled his leg outward.

Jason didn't even have to take time to open Aaron up. He began to work his outer sphincter with the tip of the lubed-up massager. The sphincters just relaxed and sucked it in, but Jason didn't turn it on.

"Oh, Jason. This is going to be so good!"

Jason latched onto Aaron's growing shaft. It was the first time he'd ever gone down on him when he wasn't fully erect. "Oh, baby, that feels amazing," Aaron said encouragingly. "I only hope that I can make you feel just as wonderful when I'm inside you."

Jason began to manipulate Aaron's spongy cock with his mouth. As soon as Aaron was erect but not completely hard, Jason pulled Aaron's cock out of his mouth. "Mmmm," he said as he came up off the leaking glans, "pre-cum. Yummy. Now, let me quickly measure you."

Jason picked up the tape measure and wrapped it around the base of Aaron's growing shaft. "It's eight inches exactly, just like the dildo. You're not going to get much thicker. Ready?"

"Yes, but wait a minute. I want to put the bed up some so I can catch as much of your load in my mouth as I can when you shoot."

"See," Jason said, "now you're thinking along the same lines. All we need is a little preparation."

Jason turned around and straddled Aaron's waist and squatted down over him. He poured a liberal amount of lube into Aaron's glans and worked it along the entire length of his cock. The pre-cum that continued to drip from his slit mixed right in with it. Once Aaron was lubed up, Jason pulled the dildo out and lowered himself until Aaron's bulbous head pressed against his gaping hole. Immediately, he lowered himself.

"Oh, Jason, it feels so good! Oh, your hole sliding over the head, it's amazing! Oh, my God, Jason. My asshole, every time it clamps down I can feel the massager tapping against my prostate."

"Yeah, baby. That's all you. You're manipulating the massager all on your own. Each time you squeeze tight it's gonna hammer your prostate. Now, let me amaze you some more."

Jason lowered his hips a little further, and Aaron's cock head disappeared into his depths. "Aaron, I can feel your warmth filling me up. My ass is so hungry for you. Feed me your shaft Aaron, feed me."

As Jason continued to lower himself, inch after inch of Aaron's shaft disappeared inside him. Aaron began panting. "My prostate is quaking, Jason. It's quaking. Oh, my God, Jason. Something's building inside me. Oh, God. What is it? I can't stop it. Here it comes, Jason. Here is comes." A tremendous gush surged from Aaron's loins. When Jason lifted himself up, his hole was oozing.

"Oh, my God! What was that?" Aaron yelled.

Jason raised himself further and reached down. He felt a viscous liquid. "It's pre-cum, baby."

"Jason, I just shot a huge load of it when I was inside you, and I wasn't even completely hard! It wasn't like coming, it just poured out of me. It was a completely different sensation, and it was amazing."

"How did it feel?"

"It felt wonderful. Wonderful. Like midway between coming and when you start to pee with a bladder that's just about filled to bursting. Just whoosh!"

"Yeah, me too. I'm dripping like a leaking faucet right now. Wanna rest?"

Aaron furiously shook his head no.

"Didn't think so. Okay, baby, let me blow your mind!" Jason leaned back and turned the massager on low. "Now, I'm gonna take in all of you."

"Oh yeah. Do it. Do it to me." Aaron moaned.

Ever so slowly, Jason rocked back sliding Aaron's shaft deeper inside. He could feel the pressure spreading his hole the further down he went, taking in more and more of the ever-thickening shaft until he was actually sitting on Aaron's lap. "Aaron, it's incredible. You're all the way inside me."

Jason rocked forward, sliding the shaft out until he felt the head ready to pop out, then back down massaging the shaft and Aaron's very, very sensitive glans. It drove Aaron wild.

"Oh, Jason. Oh, God. I'm inside you. I'm inside you. Oh, my prostate. My prostate. It's quivering. It's quivering! It's so beautiful, baby. Oh, fuck me, Jason. Fuck me!"

As he lowered himself down, Jason easily made it to Aaron's lap again. Aaron's shaft felt hot and hard against his straining hole and tremendous waves of pleasure began to course through his body. The pleasure continued to mount as Aaron's cock swelled, exerting more and more pressure against him. He knew he was being stretched wider than the speculum, wider than the monster dildo, and it was wonderful. He eased himself up a little and grabbed Aaron's shaft.

"Aaron, baby, your shaft has no give to it at all and something's happening. I feel this warmth building inside me. God, it feels like it does just before I'm going to come. Your cock, it's rock hard, and it's huge, bigger than I thought it would get, but it feels so damn good, Aaron. God, it feels wonderful! I must be completely filled because I'm stretched to my limit. It's more than

I've ever taken before, and I know I couldn't possibly take any more. Are you doing okay?"

"Yes. Yes. Great. Can't talk. Can't..."

Jason eased himself up and down Aaron's shaft. It quivered as the massager thrummed deep inside him. "Oh! Oh! Oh, Jason. My shaft is so sensitive," he murmured. "I've never been fucked so slowly before, and the head of my cock is so sensitive. There's so much more I can feel. More than I've ever felt with anyone, even Nathan."

"Oh, baby, me too. I can count every bulging vein on your shaft as they squeeze one by one past my straining hole. They're amazing. You're amazing, Aaron. Amazing."

"Jason, I can feel more pre-cum flowing out of me. It's not as strong as the first time, but it just keeps flowing." Jason became so full of pre-cum, it began to ooze out whenever he rocked forward and his own bobbing cock began to spew threads of pre-cum across Aaron's nipples and chest.

"Is this okay, Aaron? Am I going too slow?"

"Jason, please don't stop what you're doing. Please don't."

Jason lowered himself to sit on Aaron's belly and in short bursts rocked his pelvis forward and backward.

"Oh, my God! What are you doing now? My cock. It's banging against you ... inside. Oh, Jason, it's more than I could have hoped for. The sensations are incredible. Are you okay?"

"Yes, baby," Jason answered, "I'm wonderful. Your shaft is striking my prostate, and it's incredible for me too. No more talking now. Let's focus our attention on each other."

"Yes, baby. Yes," Aaron said as he wrapped his left arm around Jason's back.

Jason was overcome by the strength of Aaron's loving embrace. It cradled and caressed him while he was filled from the inside all at the same time. As Aaron's cock swelled, it became a beacon of vibrations and sounds through which Jason could hear Aaron's voice calling to him to pledge his love, his devotion, and his dedication. He began to feel Aaron's heartbeat and his own merge into a passionate rhythm. He leaned his head back as he rocked Aaron's cock back and forth, squeezing his sphincter to embrace its heat.

A new and different sensation began to echo between their bodies, a passion of total openness, an unbridled desire for each other, and a love released from their two bodies made one. As the sensations quickened and surged, Aaron's loins began to fill with his essence.

All Jason could think of was Aaron, and Aaron was lost in his love for Jason. Jason felt the vibrations of Aaron's cock intensify. He thought his mind was going to explode when Aaron's meaty hand enclosed around his shaft and stroked it.

Each moment brought new ways to give pleasure to each other bringing their cocks closer and closer to release. The helmet of Aaron's thick shaft hammered Jason's swollen orb. Each time it passed, Jason's gland grew firmer and firmer. The more it swelled the more each thrust became like pounding, like a pounding on a door, demanding that it be answered. Unconsciously, Jason slowed, then quickened, then slowed the pace, again and again, driving himself as wild as he was driving Aaron.

Aaron's anticipation grew as he felt himself coming closer and closer to exploding, but more than that, he imagined himself filling Jason with his essence, his seed, and the idea that Jason wanted him became almost more than he could bear. Aaron wanted Jason to feel as much pleasure as he was feeling, so he held himself back from the edge and forced himself to focus all his attention on him.

"Oh, Aaron, your cock against my prostate, and your hand milking my cock, it's ... it's ... I have no words. No words."

Jason reached back and pressed the button on Aaron's prostate massager again, bringing it up to high. Aaron responded. "Jason, I'm getting close. I'm close. I can't hold it back. I can't hold it back anymore!"

"It's building, Aaron. It's building. Oh, God! Oh, my God!'

Jason's loins finally answered the pounding at his door. It burst wide open.

"Aaron. Oh, Aaron. Now. I'm coming. I'm coming! Now!"

Thick, white ribbons shot out of Jason's shaft. Aaron felt them strike his face, his hair, his beard. He pointed Jason's cock into his mouth.

Aaron's shaft grew harder than it had ever been. Jason felt as if he was being ripped apart to the point that he could no longer take all of Aaron in, but the waves of ecstasy became so intense all he could think of was how he needed all of Aaron inside him, so he thrust down ever harder.

As the taste and smell of Jason's cum filled Aaron's mouth and throat, he could no longer be contained. "Here it comes, Jason! Here it comes!" Aaron screamed. He exploded so forcefully, he was sure that his cock had burst open.

Jason's geysers continued shooting across Aaron's tongue, and he swallowed greedily, mindlessly as his own seed pumped into Jason in an uncontrollable flood of gush upon gush of thick, nectar while his balls squeezed tight against his shaft, emptying themselves with complete abandon.

Each time Jason lifted his hips up, he squeezed tightly against Aaron's spasming shaft, milking the cum right out of him. Wave after wave of Aaron's hot cream continued to shoot deep into Jason's colon with an almost burning heat until Aaron grunted with his final release, emptying himself completely.

Jason's body began to twitch and spasm with uncontrollable ecstasy, causing him to slide violently up and down Aaron's massive, engorged shaft, so that with each lunge Aaron's cock was driven deeper and deeper inside him, until finally his ass was once again pounding Aaron's hips.

"Please, Jason! Please, stop! I have no more to give. Please!" Aaron pleaded.

"I can't! I can't stop!" Jason couldn't stop. He had no control over what was happening.

When it was over, Jason couldn't move. Aaron couldn't move. Their balls had emptied, their cocks were drained, and their sacks hung like two sets of over-ripened pears, ready to fall to the ground. Jason fell forward onto Aaron's chest.

They remained motionless for minutes. When Jason finally pulled himself from Aaron, his anus failed to close. So massive was the assault from Aaron's shaft, it would need hours to recover. Cum and pre-cum poured from him as if a bucket had been dumped, covering Aaron's groin, his hips, his thighs, and the bed.

Jason collapsed and fell back onto Aaron's chest, curling into a fetal position as Aaron held him close, caressed his back, and ran his fingers through Jason's hair. Jason could feel Aaron's love as he dozed off into bliss. Aaron lay there in awe, grateful but spent as if everything he had ever wanted in life he had won in that moment.

Chapter Twenty-Four
Imbedding memories

Thursday, October 8, 2009 2:00 PM

Aaron and Jason thought often of the love they had made just two days earlier, but they couldn't shake the thought that they would soon be apart for months at best, possibly even for life. They couldn't bring themselves to talk openly about the possibility that their life together might come to an end. They had slowly come to accept the fact that they might have only two, possibly three, weeks remaining before they would be separated, and they resolved to make the most of it.

They spent many moments talking about different things, but they always talked around their pending separation. Eventually one of them would say something that brought it right smack in front of their faces and when that happened, they did their best to deal with the truth, but sometimes that realization would drive them to silence as they turned inward, overcome by their fears.

Finally, it was Jason who pulled them from their melancholy, at least for a little while.

"Hey, Aaron, I'd like to try something."

"What's that?"

"Do you trust me?"

"Of course."

"Then follow my lead."

Jason leaned his ear to Aaron's chest and then his abdomen to listen to his heartbeat and the growl of his belly. He traced his fingers along Aaron's shoulders, lingering over his collarbones then down his breast bone and across his lower ribs. He leaned his nose into

Aaron's armpits and inhaled deeply and then moved to Aaron's groin and inhaled again. While he was there, he lifted Aaron's balls and took them each into his mouth one at a time, savoring their salty musk.

Jason turned his body around so he could move down Aaron's body. He lifted his leg and straddled Aaron's face. Aaron sniffed the inside of Jason's thighs, and when Jason lowered his pelvis, he drew Jason's sack into his mouth and buried his nose behind it, taking in breath after breath of Jason's scent. Aaron traced the fingers of his left hand over the globes of Jason's muscular buttocks and up his spine then back down again to linger in the indentations behind his knees, making Jason shudder at his touch.

For several hours, they explored each other's bodies, sensing with their tongues when they might otherwise have used their fingers and using their fingers when they might have used their eyes. Whatever part of Jason that Aaron wanted to explore, Jason would move to within Aaron's reach until together, they had created mental images of every inch of each other's bodies. They spent long moments focusing their attention on the curves and prominences of bones and joints, often pausing to return their gazes to each other's eyes where they found the reflection of the love they felt for one another. When Jason told Aaron he was beautiful, tears formed in the corners of Aaron's eyes. Jason placed his lips over them and drew the tears across his tongue, imbedding the saltiness of Aaron's essence into his mind.

When dusk arrived, they had discovered and imprinted more in their minds than some couples who had been together for decades might have known. They'd become aroused, sad, giggled with childish laughter, and then aroused and sad all over again until they found themselves in each other's arms reflecting on what they'd learned.

"Jason," Aaron whispered.

"Yes?"

"What did we just do? I'm not complaining at all, it was incredible, but I would have never thought to do something like that."

"I read an article that said making those kinds of memories can be really powerful and last a lifetime. I want to be able to carry you with me for the rest of my life, Aaron."

"Thank you for saying that, Jason. I feel the same way, yet I can't begin to find the words to describe what's going through my head right now. It's all so powerful, overwhelming really. I think I really know you now, like I've never known anyone before. Thank you, Jason. Thank you."

"Oh, Aaron, I'm feeling the same thing. I'm so glad we were able to have this time."

****

After Aaron had fallen asleep for the night, Jason got up and took out his stenographer's pad and began to write up a list of all the supplies he'd need for his next delivery, including replacing all the supplies he'd used to care for Aaron. He also considered what they'd need if Aaron actually could return to him before next spring, even if there was only the slightest chance.

Then Jason's deepest fears returned. Aaron may not come back at all. He dropped the pencil and wept.

Section Three
With this parting

Chapter Twenty-Five
Not another minute

Friday, October 9, 2009 8:32 AM

"Where the hell you been, Jack?" Rod yelled.

"Yo, Rod, what the fuck!"

"You're late!"

"Hell I am!"

"It's 8:32! You were due in by 8:30!"

"Jesus H. Christ, Rod! What's got your tit in a ringer?"

"You asshole, there's no word back from Jason."

"Rod, calm down."

"This is not like him, Jack. For all I know he's hurt and alone somewhere in the forest. I can't wait another minute. I gotta get up there right now and find out for sure."

"I thought you said you were gonna wait 'til next week."

"Fuck that! And if it turns out he's okay, I'm gonna kick his tight little ass from one end of the stockade to the other for making me worry. Now, get Little Bubba fueled up and do the preflight. We're takin' off and headin' up there, as soon as he's topped off."

"Okay, okay, cool your jets. But..."

"But what?"

"Shouldn't we take Big Daddy? If you're right, and he's really hurt, how are we gonna get him back in Bubba? He's only a two-seater!"

"Fuck! Fuck! You're right! You're right. Sorry."
Jack ran for the hanger and yelled over his
shoulder. "I'll have him ready as fast as I can."
****

At 9:47 AM, Big Daddy lifted off the ground. It
would be another thirty minutes before Rod and Jack
learned the truth. Minutes later, news crews would
scramble and the Internet would explode.
****

Friday, October 9, 2009 9:20 AM

Jason had finished in the barn, made and cleaned
up breakfast, and completed Aaron's bath. They were
lying in bed when Aaron ran his fingers through Jason's
chest hair. He was only fifty pages from finishing
Gordon Merrick's *One For The Gods*, while Jason read
an article on greenhouses from an online magazine he'd
downloaded the year before.

"Hey, Jason?"

"Yes," Jason mumbled, not looking up.

"I have something to tell you and something to
ask you."

"Huh?" Jason said, blinking and turning his head.

"I need you to hear me, Jason."

"Okay, I'm listening." Jason put down his laptop.

"Jason, I love you."

"I love you too, Aaron."

"No, I love you. I'm in love with you. Do you
understand?"

"Yes, Aaron."

Jason had wanted to say those words to Aaron so
many times, but he hadn't. He couldn't. He wouldn't do
that to him.

"Jason, I want to marry you."

Jason blinked, "Aaron, baby, that just isn't

possible yet."

"Yes, it is. We could go to Massachusetts and get married there, or any other state where it's legal."

"But Aaron, it wouldn't be legal here. We'd have no legal rights as a married couple."

"Then hell, why couldn't we move there, live there?"

"You're right. We could move there." That's all Jason could say. Time would tell whether they'd really make a life together. He could see that this was really important to Aaron right now, and he didn't want to take that away from him.

"Oh, Jason! Really?"

"Yes, Aaron. Really."

Aaron reached for Jason and pulled him in close, then kissed him deeply. "Why don't we explore each other's bodies some more," Aaron said, showing his white teeth through a big smile.

Soon they were doing just that as if it was their first time. Jason was latched onto Aaron's eager erection, sucking all the sweetness he could draw from it while Aaron had Jason's sack in his mouth, massaging his balls with his tongue. Jason's pre-cum was dripping down onto Aaron's chest, and Aaron was scooping it up with his hand to bring it to his lips to add to his saliva, making the sensations of his tongue all the more slick against Jason's balls.

Neither of them noticed the subtle sounds as they rose from over the ridge until they became unmistakable. Not letting go of Aaron's leaking cock, Jason tilted his head to listen. Then he recognized the sound. He pulled his mouth off Aaron so quickly that his cock banged against his belly. "Aaron, let go! Let me go! They're here!"

"Huh?" Aaron mouthed around Jason's balls.

"Aaron, let me go! A chopper's here!"

Aaron expelled Jason's sack like he was spitting out peach pits and turned his face toward the window.

"No!" Aaron wailed.

Jason leapt from the bed and ran to the door just as the lumbering helicopter set down. He threw the door open and ran onto the porch, naked, with his erection still full and dripping pre-cum. It was Big Daddy. It was Rod and Jack.

"Not now! Not yet!" he yelled. His life was over. Their life was over. It had all finally come to an end.

Jason went back inside and started to talk quickly to Aaron. "Baby, it's those friends of mine who deliver my supplies. They're real good guys. We knew this day was coming, but it arrived a lot sooner than we thought. A lot's going to happen and real fast. I'm gonna get dressed and meet them outside to give them a quick rundown of what's been going on. Do you need anything?"

"No," Aaron answered, dumbfounded. "Oh, my God, Jason! It's over, isn't it? It's really over!"

"Yes, baby, but we'll get through this. I promise."

****

Friday, October 9, 2009 10:15 AM

Rod spoke calmly into the microphone. "ATC Salt Lake, this is Henry Three Kilo Whiskey Six. We've sort of got an emergency."

"ATC Salt Lake. We've got, you Henry Three Kilo Whiskey Six. State the nature of your emergency."

"Henry Three Kilo Whiskey Six. We've found Aaron Jaeger. I say again, we have Aaron Jaeger on board. He's been injured, but he's well. Can you patch me through to Hinnen Valley Medical Center? We're heading there straight away."

"ATC Salt Lake. Henry Three Kilo Whiskey Six. We read you as recovering Aaron Jaeger alive, injured, but well. Confirm, Jaeger is the football player who went down in a plane five weeks ago."

"Henry Three Kilo Whiskey Six. That's affirmative. Request direct patch to Hinnen Valley Medical Center."

"ATC Salt Lake. Henry Three Kilo Whiskey Six. Stand by."

The air-traffic controller turned to his supervisor. "Hey, Phil, you're not going to believe this!"

****

Friday, October 9, 2009 10:25 AM, breaking news

"Good morning, ladies and gentlemen. We're interrupting our regularly scheduled programming to bring you the following news…

Aaron Jaeger has been found. Again, Aaron Jaeger, the recently signed CFL quarterback for the Nevada Bighorns, who was presumed to have perished in a horrendous plane crash five weeks ago today has been found alive and well. We do know that he has been injured. however, we do not know the nature or extent of his injuries. It's reported that Jaeger is being flown in a private transport helicopter to Hinnen Valley Medical Center at this time.

"That's all the information we have, but a news crew has been dispatched to Hinnen Valley Medical Center to bring us an update as soon as it becomes available. You may recall that the twin-engine charter plane carrying Jaeger, the pilot, and as we later learned, his trainer, Nathan Taggart, lost an engine from a lightning strike during a thunderstorm and disappeared from radar at approximately 5:50 PM on September fourth. Taggart and the pilot's partial remains were recovered among the debris at the widely dispersed crash site in the Bear River Mountains on September eighth and later identified from dental records. At this time, we do not know where Jaeger was found.

"Jaeger recently signed a three-year, fifteen-million-dollar contract with the Bighorns that included an initial signing bonus of four million. Jaeger was to start as quarterback in the Bighorns' first game of the season this past September 13. We will continue to keep you updated on this breaking news story as new information comes in to us. We now return you to our regular programming."

****

Friday, October 9, 2009 10:50 AM
Hinnen Valley Medical Center

"Ladies and gentlemen, this is Chuck Jackson, live at the helipad just outside the trauma unit at Hinnen Valley Medical Center. The helicopter that's reported to be carrying Aaron Jaeger has just landed.

They're moving a stretcher up to the door.

"They're lifting someone onto the stretcher.

There, yes, that's Jaeger. Yes, that's definitely him.

It appears there are two crew members from the helicopter and there's another man who's talking into Jaeger's ear. He appears to be gripping Jaeger's hand. We don't know who any of them are yet, but we'll get that information for you as soon as we can."

Chapter Twenty-Six
Proper care

Friday, October 9, 2009 3:15 PM
Hinnen Valley Medical Center

When the hospitalist, Dr. Spencer, turned to leave, Aaron motioned for her to come closer. He whispered into her ear. She nodded, patted Aaron on the shoulder, and then led her team of interns out of the room. Aaron swore to himself that he'd keep it together when he saw Jason.

Dr. Spencer looked down the hall but didn't see anyone, so she checked the waiting room where she found Jason, sitting by himself, putting a stenographer's spiral note pad into his coat pocket.

After she gave him Aaron's message, she led her interns to a small conference room to discuss the patient they'd just seen and reviewed what his treatment and recovery would entail.

****

Jason found Aaron in his room, sleeping. He closed the door and pulled the curtain around the bed before sitting in the chair next to him. He rested his hand on Aaron's arm and in another minute, fell asleep as well. A little while later, Aaron woke. When he saw Jason, he smiled and then took his hand. At Aaron's touch, Jason slowly opened his eyes.

"There you are. Thank you for coming back, Jason. Sorry I was asleep. They gave me something to relax me. I know you have to get home to take care of the animals, but I hoped I'd have a chance to talk to you before you left."

Jason steeled himself against the feelings that were rising in his chest. "Sure Aaron," he said with an easy smile, "I wanted to be sure you were all settled in before I headed back."

Aaron took a deep breath. "Jason, I don't know how to thank you for all you did for me these last five weeks. You saved my life, you saved my life, Jason. I don't know how I'll ever be able to repay you."

"Aaron, there's nothing to repay."

"Yes, there is, now hush, I have to say this before I lose my nerve."

Jason nodded his head.

"Jason, you didn't have to put up with all I put you through. You have no idea how much you've come to mean to me, and I wanted to be sure you knew that before ... before you leave. I don't know how I could ever not see you again. I just can't get my head around that, but that's selfish of me. You have your own life to lead, and I've interfered with it enough."

"Aaron, I..."

"Please, Jason, hush, and let me finish saying this. I was a selfish, selfish person, Jason, and arrogant and a self-indulgent prick before I met you. I can never go back to being that way, not ever again. Please know you've changed me and for the better. I'll never forget you, Jason. I can't. Never." Aaron held out his left arm. "Come here."

As Jason leaned forward, Aaron made an awkward grasp for his arm. Aaron tugged and pulled Jason tight against him, then hugged him to his chest with all his strength. After a moment, Jason went to move away, but Aaron squeezed even tighter and started to cry. Deep sops began to escape from his chest. He held on to Jason as if his life depended on it.

Over and over, Aaron repeated his name, "Jason

... Jason ... Jason," more than a dozen times.

Jason had done his best to hold his emotions at bay all during the flight back to civilization and Aaron's transfer into the care of others, but he couldn't hold them back any more. He gave in to Aaron's embrace, and together they wept. It could have been minutes. It could have been hours.

Aaron finally eased his grip, and Jason began to rise, but Aaron pulled him back so close, they could feel each other's breath against their faces. Aaron looked deeply into Jason's blue eyes with their hazel lines and flecks of green. Jason smiled bravely as he memorized the flecks of gold in the bluest eyes he'd ever seen. Then Aaron pulled him down and kissed him passionately on the lips with more love than he had ever felt before. Jason did not resist, rather, he melted into Aaron and returned the loving kiss he received.

A few moments later, they broke apart. "Jason, I remember what we talked about yesterday. It was my dream, but it was wrong of me to push it on you. I can't hold you to that, Jason. I won't."

"Aaron, let's let things settle down for a bit. We have all the time in the world."

****

When Braden, Aaron's nurse, entered the room, he found the two men lying on the bed asleep. Aaron had Jason cradled in his left arm. Quietly, Braden eased himself back out of the room and closed the door behind him. He reached into his pocket and took a piece of scrap paper and wrote "Do Not Disturb" on it. He taped it to the door with a piece of bandage tape and walked down the hall, leaving the lovers in peace.

****

When Jason woke, the sun was low in the sky, revealing it was late afternoon. He eased himself from

Aaron's embrace without waking him and rose from the bed. Before he left the room, he leaned down and kissed Aaron on his forehead. Then he walked around the curtain and closed the door behind him and headed down the hall to look for a nurse.

Seeing Jason, a young man rose from behind the nurse's desk. "Can I help you, sir? I'm Braden, Mr. Jaeger's nurse. I saw you come in with him."

"Do you have an envelope?" Jason asked.

"Sure do," Braden answered with a friendly smile.

Jason took the large envelope and reached into his coat pocket to pull out his notepad. He tore several sheets from the pad, put them in the envelope, then licked the flap, sealed it closed, and wrote Aaron's name on the front. He handed the envelope back to Braden.

"Can you please give this to him when he wakes up?"

"Sure thing. He's been through a lot, but I guess you'd know that."

"Yeah, I guess I do."

"I'll give it to him as soon as he wakes, I promise."

"Thank you, Braden. You'll take good care of him, won't you?"

"Yes, of course. We'll take real good care of him. That's a promise that'll be easy to keep."

"Thank you, Braden, thank you. He's a real special guy. He deserves the best."

"You're welcome, sir."

"My name is Jason, Jason Ackerman."

"Very good, Mr. Ackerman."

"Just Jason, and thank you again. Good-bye."

"Good-bye, Mister, um, I mean, Jason. Good-bye. For now?"

Jason smiled, but there was pain behind his eyes.

Braden sighed to himself as he watched Jason walk down the hall towards the elevators, remembering how he had found the two of them together. "They're so lucky."

****

When Jason walked through the lobby on the ground floor, he was approached by a tall, tanned, and muscled middle-aged man.

"Are you the guy who came in with Aaron Jaeger?"

"Yes, sir, I am. I'm Jason Ackerman. Why do you ask?"

"I thought so. Son, I'm Hank Thompson, Aaron's coach. I just learned what you did for him from the doctors. I saw you in the footage they showed on TV. I want you to know that we're real grateful to you, son. Real grateful. If there's anything I or the Nevada Bighorns organization can ever do for you, please, don't hesitate to ask."

"That's very kind of you, sir. Take good care of him. He's a great guy."

"He is that, and we will. Good-bye."

Jason headed towards the information desk and asked the volunteer to use the phone. He placed a call to Rod Livingston at North West Air Transport to ask if he could fly him back to the cabin. Then he hailed a cab from near the hospital's main entrance. As he rode the fifteen minutes to the airport, Jason silently said good-bye to Aaron, believing in his heart that he'd probably never see him again.

Chapter Twenty-Seven
Good-bye, my love

Friday, October 9, 2009 5:15 PM

"Mr. Jaeger, I'm Braden, your nurse. Your visitor left this envelope for you."

"It's Aaron. Please call me Aaron," he said as he took the envelope from Braden's hand.

"Thanks for this," Aaron said as he nodded toward the envelope.

"Do you need anything, Aaron? Anything for pain perhaps? Or something to drink?"

"No. Thank you. I'm fine. I'm just going to read this now."

"I'll give you some privacy." Braden nodded as he backed away towards the door. "Should I close it?"

"Yes. Please."

Aaron opened the large envelope and shook it out. Several pieces of spiral-bound, green stenographer's paper fell out. He put them in order and began to read.

****

October 9, 2009 1:37 PM

My Dearest Aaron,

I've been sitting in the ER waiting room, waiting for news about you after they took you from the helicopter into a room. There's been no word, and I don't know whether I'll get to see you again.

I've done my best to honor the request you made of me in the helicopter to keep what we had a secret in order to protect your career. I haven't told anyone, but I think a nurse might suspect. I think she could tell how I felt about you from the look that must have been on my face when I relayed the treatment I provided for you in the cabin. She was very kind and patted my arm several times when I began to lose it when I described your initial injuries.

I tried to talk to an administrator for any word about you, but she's been pacing around the ER, intimidating the staff about your care. At one point I heard her yell at them, saying, "Get it done!" I guess it's because you're famous and in the news right now. I finally cornered her and asked for information, but she abruptly shouted at me, "You're not family!" and walked away. I hope I can get this note to you because there were things I left unsaid that I want you to know. So here goes.

How do I begin to accept that the past five weeks actually happened to us? They've been a whirlwind for me, and I have to believe they've been for you as well. Who could have ever predicted that we'd meet or that you would suffer as you have?

I want you to know that you've changed me, Aaron. I can never go back to being the same reclusive man I was before I found you hanging from that tree. Caring for you and nursing you back to health has been a privilege, and knowing you has been an honor.

You've made me realize how much I've missed in life and how much there is still left for me to experience in the years I have remaining. I promise you that I will make the most of those years, and I will give back to the world because I have so, so much to give of myself and of the resources I have available to me.

Right now, I cannot imagine what it will be like to return to the cabin tonight and walk through the front door to find that you're not there, waiting for me with your beautiful smile and your tangled-up bedsheets. Nor can I imagine waking tomorrow morning and all the mornings that follow without finding you lying beside me, or your sparkling eyes, or your embrace, or your kiss.

How can I go back to cooking for just myself when cooking for two is what I now do?

I'll miss the feeling of your skin beneath my hands while I washed your body clean, and the way you looked at me with so much passion and acceptance in your eyes, and the way you anticipated the next time we would make love, and the times we made love, My Love.

1:50 PM

Aaron, I'm sorry this is quick, but I've just now learned from that nurse I told you about that they moved you to a room upstairs, forty-five minutes ago. There's so much more I want to say to you, but right now I'm going to try to find you.

2:05 PM

Aaron, I made it to the floor. A nice young doctor told me I should wait in the waiting room. She was very nice to me, Aaron. I think you'd like her.

Aaron, I'm so glad we took the time on Thursday to imprint those memories of each other in our minds. Right now, I can smell your musk, and I can see the tiny flecks of gold in your deep blue eyes. I can feel the curve of your collarbones beneath my fingers, and I can taste the saltiness of the tears you shed when I told you, you were beautiful. Those are memories I'll be able to carry with me forever, and I thank you for them.

We must face that this is what the future has brought to us, My Love, for I must leave you now in the care of those who have the ability to care for you the way you need to be cared for. I want you to know that I will carry you in my thoughts every minute of every day, and that I will follow each and every game you lead down the field. I will cheer for your successes and share the frustrations of your losses, but always remember they're just frustrations. You've survived much worse, and I hope you can always keep that in perspective. Please know that I will be by your side as you pick yourself up and brush yourself off and begin again. I will be by your side every step of the way, in my heart.

I wish you all the happiness you can find as you look towards your future and all the success you can grab hold of as you return to the life you were forced to leave that fateful day. You deserve it, Aaron. You deserve to be joyful and free, and to dream, and to find someone who can share in your dreams. Please know I will rejoice in your happiness wherever and with whomever you find it.

How do I begin to say goodbye to you? I hope in those moments when you remember me and our brief time together that you will be able to do so with a smile on your face and a lightness in your heart, because that is how I will remember you.

I have never known so much kindness, such a depth of compassion, and such a degree of passion as I have come to know from you. Nor do I believe I will ever be able to find those things again, for those days and weeks, those seconds and those moments, those feelings and those experiences, could never be recreated with anyone else because they happened with you. They'll be enough, Aaron, they'll have to be, and I will carry them with me until my last breath.

My love, you have delivered me from the life of loneliness I thought was intended for me and for that I can never thank you enough. Perhaps you can find comfort and some degree of conciliation with the knowledge that through you, I have found redemption.

Oh, my Aaron, if a day ever comes when you need an ear to listen, or a hand to hold, or someone to stand beside you when life tests you or the world turns against you, I'll be there for you. I always will.

> I remain forever,
> Your Jason

                        ****

When Rod learned from Jason that the reason he'd been out of communication was because of the damage to his satellite antenna while they were preparing Aaron for his flight to the hospital, he chided Jason for having never gotten a satellite phone. The moment he returned to his hanger, he contacted a company and had one delivered that same day, paying for it out of his own pocket. He made Jason promise to keep it charged and on hand in case anything like that ever happened again. He also called a satellite dish repairman to the hanger and had him wait until Jason returned from the hospital. He flew up to the cabin with all the parts he'd need to make repairs when he and Jack flew Jason home.

While the repairman worked, Jason confided in Rod and Jack his feelings for Aaron after giving them a condensed accounting of what had happened between them. They could see that Jason was really troubled and maybe he even thought he was in love. In the end, Rod cautioned Jason that Aaron came from a different world and a different lifestyle.

Having missed their long weekend together, they offered to return the day after they'd flown the repairman back and stay for a while, but Jason said he was too tired for that and that he needed to rest, He did give Rod the list of supplies he'd been working on and asked if they could just come back to deliver them.

Rod was really fond of Jason, and both he and Jack looked forward to their intimate weekends. Yes, they were friends, and they cared for Jason, but that was all it would ever be for them, friendship and sex. They were both deeply closeted, and they would never do anything to jeopardize that.

Due to the lateness of the hour and not wanting to fly in the dark, Rod, Jack, and the repairman spent the night. When they left late the next morning, Jason didn't even walk them back to the helipad. He was lost and in a different world.

They left Jason alone in his cabin, sitting in his chair at his table with a bottle of scotch and a glass. When they returned two days later with his supplies, Jason was sitting where they'd left him among two empty bottles with a third, nearly gone. There were more than a dozen eggs and several buckets of milk, one of which had already soured, on the kitchen counter. With some pushing and prodding they were able to get Jason to take as shower. Jack scrambled him some eggs, and they sat with him until he ate them.

Chapter Twenty-Eight
Whatever it takes

Friday, October 16, 2009 11:10 AM
Hinnen Valley Medical Center

One week had passed since Aaron had last seen Jason. He'd read Jason's letter so many times, he knew it by heart, but he read it over and over again just the same, because by touching it he was touching Jason's hand through the papers that held his words. So lost in his thoughts, he wasn't even aware that people were walking into his room.

Aaron's orthopedic surgeon, Dr. Grant, stood by his bed accompanied by Dr. Douglas Carmichael, the Nevada Bighorns team doctor, their head trainer, Matt Anderson, and Coach Thompson. Dr. Grant had brought Aaron's X-rays, CT scans, and MRI results with him, several of which were now displayed on the X-ray reader next to Aaron's bed.

Dr. Grant cleared his throat. "Good morning, Aaron, I've brought these gentlemen with me because they're all invested in your recovery and your career. Is that all right?"

Aaron nodded his head. He could feel the tension in the room, but he was amazed that he felt so at peace.

While he spoke, Dr. Grant changed the films from one to another as he pointed out different structures while reviewing Aaron's injuries with him. "As you know, we chose to wait a few days after you got here to be sure your body was up to handling surgery. We went in and had to re-break your bones while they were still healing in order to get them into proper alignment, and we put in plates and screws to stabilize them. We also went into your ankle with a scope to clean out some bone and cartilage fragments that were floating around in there, and we repaired the damage to the tendons and ligaments. Those would have given you some real mobility problems right from the get go.

"I understand," Aaron answered.

"The plates and screws will keep the bone ends in the proper position while they re-heal, and you should have little or no evidence anything was ever wrong after you've gone through physical therapy in about two months. However, and I'm sorry to have to tell you this, son, too much time passed before we could get to you. That guy did a real good job doing what he did, but he couldn't prevent the scar tissue that formed in your ankle or set your bones and ankle perfectly. I guess no one could have, really, under those deplorable conditions, and your ankle was badly damaged. I'm afraid there's a good chance we won't be able to get it back to a point where it'll have the flexibility and mobility you once had on the field. At least that's what we believe at the moment."

The other men wore solemn expressions, shaking their heads while Dr. Grant broke the news.

"Jason," Aaron said quietly.

"Pardon?" the surgeon replied.

"Jason. His name is Jason," Aaron said firmly.

"Ah, yes. If you say so," Dr. Grant answered dismissively.

"What's that supposed to mean?" Aaron began to get angry.

"It doesn't mean anything, son."

"No offense, doctor, but please stop calling me, son. I'm not your son, and I'm really trying to hold it all together right now, but when you speak about him like he's nobody, it pisses me off!"

"That's a queer thing to say, Aaron," Coach Thompson chimed in.

"I beg your pardon? Queer? What the ffff ... What did you mean by that?" Aaron was shouting.

All of the men standing around Aaron's bed shot glances to each other.

"Sorry, I misspoke. What I meant was, strange. It seemed like a strange thing to say. That's all. I wasn't implying ..."

"For Christ's sake! He saved my fucking life, Coach! He saved my fucking life. You should show some respect. All of you should."

"I'm sorry, Aaron. If you say so."

"I do say so!" Aaron was fuming.

"Okay. Okay. I'm sorry, really I am," Coach Thompson offered placatingly, as he held up his hands. He didn't want to do anything that could jeopardize his relationship with Jaeger. He could still turn out to be the prime stallion he was before the accident, and a full recovery had not been completely ruled out. At least for right now. If the future played out to their advantage, Jaeger might just be able to take them to the playoffs.

"Okay then." Aaron said, still fuming.

"As I said," Dr. Grant went on, it's the ankle that's the biggest problem. Your left leg should heal just fine, and you should have normal mobility in your right forearm, again, after extensive therapy. With dedication and hard work, you should have very little deficit and should be able to live a normal life.

"Down the line, you'll likely develop some arthritis and maybe a touch of pain when it's getting ready to rain. Fractures sometimes do, but they shouldn't give you any real trouble for many, many years to come. Any questions?"

"Yeah, what does all this mean for my career?"

"Well, Aaron, it means you may never be able to play like you did before you were injured."

"Yeah, I guessed that, but can I play?"

"Yes," he paused, "you *could* play," he emphasized the word could, "but that's not really up to me."

"Matt, what can you do for me?" Aaron asked. "You know that doctors don't know everything. No offense doctor. Do you think we can get my ankle back into playing shape?"

"I don't know Aaron, but I'm sure willing to do anything and everything within my power. Right, coach?"

"That's right, Matt!" Coach Thompson chimed in. "Aaron, we'll do everything we can for you, but you'll be off the lineup until your operating at one-hundred percent." Coach Thompson shot Dr. Carmichael a concerned glance. "That's just how it has to be."

Dr. Carmichael nodded his head, smiled, and added, "Aaron we should take it slow. Your ankle and fractures went without proper medical care for nearly six weeks. We won't know the real limitations of those injuries for many, many more months down the road, but that doesn't mean we can't try. Keep positive about it. You never know. Attitude can make all the difference."

"Dr. Grant, is there anything else you can offer me?" Aaron asked, already knowing his answer.

"No, I'm sorry, Aaron. We've done all that we can. You'll stay here for another couple of weeks, and then we'll discharge you to a rehab facility where you'll continue to work at getting back as much function and mobility as you can.

"Then I want you all to know this right now." Aaron said with determination. "I'll do whatever it takes."

****

The four men left Aaron alone in his room. Leading the group down the hall, Coach Thompson dialed his cell phone. "John, looks like we're stuck with Sanderson for a good part of the season after all. Do what you can to get him at his best for next week's game."

"Damn shame about Jaeger," Coach Thompson said over his shoulder, "such a promising career in front of him. Matt, once he's out of here, keep him working to give him the best shot, but keep in mind, we can't be investing all our best resources on a losing stallion. Am I fooling myself holding out hope? I hope not, but we'll see. We'll do all we can for him, but for all intents and purposes we have to prepare ourselves for the possibility that he's through. If his recovery is anything but miraculous, we'll ease back at a reasonable pace and let him down as gently as we can, but it'll be over."

Trailing behind, Matt, Dr. Carmichael, and Dr. Grant shook their heads solemnly.

Chapter Twenty-Nine
There is no life in isolation

Autumn, 2009

As the cold autumn settled in, Jason tried to return to the well-worn routine he'd established in the past, but his memories of his time with Aaron consumed him. After caring for the animals each morning, he'd cook himself a large breakfast and then do chores, work on minor repairs to the buildings within the stockade's walls, or head out to walk the trails he'd made through the surrounding forest over the course of his eleven years there. Often, he felt tears on his cheeks before he realized he'd been crying, but then he'd wipe them away and press on.

While in the forest, with his rifle at his side, Jason was able to procure fresh meat for his table. Whatever he couldn't eat within a week would be hung in the smokehouse until it had cured.

There was a time when Jason enjoyed his solitude, but more and more he found that he had to force himself to try to recreate the life he used to lead. Aaron's absence had affected him much more than he could have ever anticipated. So accustomed had he been to his solitude, he was surprised by how much he enjoyed having another person around every day to talk to, and now he missed it and Aaron terribly.

Providing for Aaron had been no hardship at all, and he'd found a new purpose in becoming his caregiver. But more so, and even though it was brief, he couldn't shake the deep love he'd developed for him. Never believing that such a love was possible for someone like himself, Jason had been poorly prepared when it happened and less so by its loss.

The truth was as long as he remembered Aaron, he would never be free of him. The sensation of Aaron's body as he lay beside him in his hospital bed, the touch of his hands, the memory of his lips pressed firmly to his own, and the absence of his animal musk haunted Jason's days and nights. Nothing was the same, not since the day he'd left Aaron in the hospital, asleep.

The next thing he knew, Jason found himself seeking comfort in the gay porn videos he'd watched with Aaron. He'd remember specific scenes that Aaron enjoyed, and he'd lie on his bed for hours at a time slowly masturbating, trying to prolong the memories they'd shared. When he found himself talking to Aaron, only to realize that he wasn't there, Jason would quickly bring himself to orgasm, but the release was always brief and so, so unfulfilling.

At one point, Jason began to think he was losing his mind, but by remembering the techniques he'd learned to overcome his PTSD, and using them, he soon found his way out. As the days turned to weeks, Jason slowly became accustomed to Aaron's absence, but when he recognized this the memories came flooding back.

Though he regularly checked the internet for information about Aaron's recovery, after two months there was no further mention of him. He even tried to contact the Nevada Bighorns front office by internet phone to inquire about Aaron, but they refused to release any information, citing privacy policies.

Jason began to regularly send e-mails to Rod using the premise that he wanted to share something he'd learned on the internet, but Rod knew, for Jason, that was completely out of character. Jason always added a brief, roundabout query for information about Aaron, but Rod would write back to say he hadn't heard or seen anything about him on TV.

Rod would also include an inquiry with his replies asking whether he and Jack could fly up for a visit, but Jason always declined. Rod finally got the message that for now at least, Jason was off the market, and he found sexual release elsewhere.

Chapter Thirty
On the down-low

Friday, December 4, 2009 2:00 PM

Six weeks after the team had Aaron transferred to a private rehab center, Coach Thompson came to visit him with good news. Aaron's recovery was just short of miraculous, and they planned to ease him back onto the field as soon as he was discharged.

When he entered the room, Aaron was sound asleep on his bed. Several pages of green, torn-off note paper were falling out of his hand. As he reached to gather them so they wouldn't fall on the floor, Thompson could see they had handwriting on them, and he couldn't help but read a few of the words.

At the top of the first page were the words, "My Dearest Aaron," on another page the words, "and the times we made love," jumped out at him, on another he read: "Right now, I can smell your musk," and at the bottom of the last page were the words, "I remain forever, your Jason." They were all in the same handwriting.

Coach Thompson dropped them immediately. *Jason? Who's Jason?* he thought. *Shit, he's that guy from the hospital.*

At that moment, Aaron woke up.

"Hey, coach," Aaron said.

Thompson's head was reeling, *He's a fag!*

"Coach?"

Jesus Christ, Jaeger's a fucking fag!

Coach Thompson recovered almost immediately. "Hey, Aaron. I just have a minute, but I wanted to stop by to see how you're doing."

"That's darn nice of you, Coach. Everything okay? You look like you're stressed out about something," Aaron said as he gathered the papers up from his waist and put them in the table next to his bed.

"Oh yeah, I'm fine, Aaron. Sorry. Just going through the game tomorrow in my head, but I wanted to check in to see that you've got all you need."

"They're treating me real good, Coach. Real good. No complaints here. I'm up for discharge next week."

"That's great news, Jaeger! Great news! Well, I gotta be goin'. Let me know if there's anything you need. Right?"

"Sure, Coach, sure. And thanks for stopping by. I'll be up to snuff in no time. Matt thinks I'll be back on the field before you know it. You just wait and see."

"Glad to hear it, Jaeger. Glad to hear it. Well, bye for now."

"Bye, Coach."

Jesus Fucking Christ, Thompson thought, *Jaeger's a fag! Well that's it for him. He's done! There'll be no fucking faggots on my team. No, sir! No way! No how!*

****

The moment Coach Thompson closed the door to his decked out, top-of-the-line SUV, he made a call on his cell phone. He was shouting so loud his voice went right through the SUV's closed windows.

"John? John, listen to me. Jaeger's done! He's through!"

"Not any more he's not."

"No, he'll never return to my team. Not now!"

"Why? I'll tell you why! He's a fag! A fucking fag, John!"

"No, I'm not kidding!"

"Who? Him and that guy who found him, that's who! They're a couple of faggots!"

"How do I know? He had a love letter from the fucking guy, that's how I know!"

"They fucked, John! They fucking fucked! Yeah, do whatever you have to, but get rid of him as fast as you can! We can't let this get out either!"

"How? How the fuck should I know how? That's your job! We gotta do this on the down low! Hear me? The down low!"

"I don't know! Find a fucking reason, but make this happen, John! Make this happen and soon! It's gotta be handled quick! You understand me? Quick!"

"No! I don't even want him suited up on the sideline! You hear me, John? You hear me?"

December 16, 2009, 11.00 AM

There was a soft knock at the door. "Come in, come in, Jack, but I'm real busy right now!" Rod hollered, as he kept his eyes on the papers he held in his hands. Rod Livingston, the owner of North West Air Transport, was looking at one of the many orders that were spread out across his desk. When the door opened, he didn't look up right away.

"Well what is it, Jack?" he said, turning toward the door. When he realized who was standing there, Rod dropped the cigar he had clenched between his teeth right into his lap. "Holy shit!" he shouted as he shot out from behind his desk, brushing off the smoldering embers. "I mean... Well, well, what can I do for you today?"

"Mr. Livingston, sir, I need your help, and I don't care how much it costs."

"Anything! Anything at all," Rod said, extending

his hand. "You need it, I'll get it, or I'll get it done!"

"Thank you, sir. Thank you so much."

"Please, have a seat," Rod waved his arm to the chair in front of his desk. "Now, how can I be of service?"

Chapter Thirty-One
When days grow longer

December 20, 2009, 8:00 PM

Jason mixed up a batch of sourdough for bread he was going to bake the next morning. He set the dough in a large, towel-covered, oiled bowl to rise over night in the proof box above the stove. When he finished, he found an e-mail from Rod answering has latest query about Aaron. There was still no word.

****

December 21, 2009, 5:30 AM

Jason woke bright and early. He went to the kitchen and washed his hands and then punched down the sourdough sponge and formed it into a loaf before putting it into a pan in the proof box to rise. Then he took out four frozen chicken breasts he'd defrosted in the fridge and put them in a pot to simmer on the stove.

After his shower, he cooked and ate a full breakfast and then diced up the chicken and made a salad with chopped, dried cranberries, sweet onion, tarragon, and pecans in a honey-mustard-mayonnaise dressing. After putting the salad in the refrigerator, he put the pan of risen dough into the oven to bake. That completed, he figured by the time he finished his chores and took care of the livestock, the bread would be done in plenty of time to cool and have for lunch.

Rod's e-mail from the day before had started Jason to thinking. As painful as the thought was, he decided it was about time he moved on and did something with his life. He sat down at his computer and sent off an e-mail to his lawyer and accountant, asking them to investigate what would be involved in him becoming a philanthropist. He wanted to start a foundation, but he didn't know how to get started or even what the foundation would be.

As he walked toward the barn, Jason smiled to himself when he realized he was whistling. Nellie, Sarah, Heather, and Jasper greeted him enthusiastically with their brays and bleats. He could barely get their feed into the trough before they planted their faces and began eating.

He added some oats to the wooden bucket and coaxed Heather to the milking table where she greedily munched while she gave up her milk to the stainless-steel pail. When she was finished, she hopped down and joined Jasper at the feed trough where she pushed him aside as if to say, "Hey, save me some! I just gave milk!"

Jason spent the next half-hour straightening up the barn, mucking out the stalls, and shoveling dung into the pile outside the barn door.

December 21, 2009, 8:30 AM

"What in the world?" Jason heard the familiar whop-whop-whop of helicopter rotors. "Who could that be? That sounds like Rod. He didn't say anything about coming up in his e-mail. Good thing I made chicken salad and bread. I can serve sandwiches for lunch."

He turned to watch the lumbering chopper set down on the helipad and then heard the engine cut off just as he closed up the barn door. "It's Big Daddy. Why didn't they bring Little Bubba? I'm not due for a delivery. What on earth could they be hauling?"

As he carried the milk pail and eggs he'd gathered into the sunshine, the chopper's rotors were still going at a pretty good clip, so he hightailed it back to the cabin to put them away. When he checked the bread, it was done, so he took out the pan and set the loaf to cool, then he headed out onto the porch just as the occupants of the helicopter began to climb out.

First, Rod climbed down and then Jack, but a moment later a third figure emerged holding a cane. Both Rod and Jack reached up to help what Jason now realized was a man stepping down. He was tall, taller than both of them, tanned, and he was muscular with short, dirty blond hair. Then he smiled and waved.

"It can't be!"

"It is!"

Jason jumped off the porch at a run. When he got to the gate, he pulled it open and ran for all he was worth as he headed down the hill shouting all the way. When he reached the bottom of the second hill that led up to the helipad, he stopped. There were so many tears in his eyes, he couldn't see. Then he couldn't stand. He dropped to his knees and buried his face in his lap while he grasped at the remnants of stems from last summer's wildflowers and balled them in his fists.

****

Then there was a touch.

A hand caressed his back.

A voice murmured his name, murmured familiar words, murmured his name again.

Then two brown boots appeared in front of his knees.

Then there was a cane.

Jason looked up to see the two most beautiful gold-flecked, blue eyes he'd ever seen set in the most beautiful, smiling face he had ever known.

"Aaron! Aaron, what are you doing here? How? Why? What happened to you? I couldn't find out anything about you! It's like you disappeared from the face of the earth."

Aaron laughed, as tears were forming in his eyes. He pulled Jason into his arms and hugged him close. "Oh, Jason! Jason! How I've missed the smell of your hair and the touch of your hands. That's your heart..." Aaron began to weep. "Your heart beating ... beating against my chest, your breath ... your breath on my cheek, your tears on my ... my face, your beard ... your beautiful beard against my neck."

Aaron held him as his memories from what seemed like a lifetime ago replayed in his mind. When he pulled away, he lifted Jason off the ground as if to carry him over a threshold. "These are your blue eyes," Aaron kissed them, "with their hazel lines and flecks of green. Oh, Jason, my Jason, these are your lips," Aaron whispered as he drew Jason's mouth to his.

****

Rod and Jack stood at the crest of the hill and watched the two lovers reunite. During their long conversation in his office the week before, Aaron confirmed the relationship he'd had with Jason, and the future he hoped they could build together. Rod had always held out that at some point in time, he and Jack would be able to resume their weekend visits with Jason, but his conversation with Aaron extinguished that.

The truth of the matter was, Rod was a big boy, and it wasn't the first time in his life that he'd had to move on. In the end, he couldn't have been happier for the two of them. They had accomplished something that most gay men only dreamed of, finding true love. As he thought about it, tears began to stream down his face for Jason had found love. Finally, he'd be happy.

When Jack noticed Rod's tears, he patted him on the back.

****

"So tell me! What? When? Where? Why? How?" Jason asked impatiently.

"What am I doing here? I'm here for you, silly. When did it happen? Well, I'll tell you. It happened December eleventh. I'm no longer on the team, but we'll talk about that in detail later. Where? It happened over the phone, but it doesn't matter, and I'm really not that upset. Why? Well, the truth of the matter is that I'd rather be where I hope I'm still wanted, here with you, and oh yeah, I'm dying to find out what happens to Charlie and Peter. How? I hired Mr. Livingston to fly me up here. Now, are you ready for all of this? Us? Our future? Was I right to come back?" Aaron asked with a big smile.

"Oh, Aaron, you don't know how much!"

"Good, coz I'm starving, and I can't wait for a tall glass of Heather's milk."

"I love you, Aaron," Jason said with his arms around Aaron's neck.

"I love you too, Jason. Now come on," Aaron lowered him to the ground. "I can't wait to meet Heather and Jasper and Nellie and Sarah and Big John and ..."

When Jason stood next to him, he was startled. "Aaron, I've never seen you standing up. Good God, you're tall! How tall are you?"

"Ha! Ha! That's so funny. I'm six foot two."

"Oh, I can't believe it's really you." Jason hugged Aaron tight to his chest.

****

"You done a real good thing, Papa Bear. A real good thing," Jack said after a minute. "You think we'll be invited to the wedding?"

"Wedding?"

"Someday, Rod. Someday."

"Okay, enough of that talk," Rod said wiping his

eyes. "Now let's get this chopper unloaded."

"Boy oh boy," Jack said, rubbing his hands together, "is Jason ever gonna be surprised!"

****

As they began to walk towards the stockade, Jason stopped suddenly. "Wait a minute. Charlie and Peter? Charlie and Peter who?"

"You remember. Charlie and Peter, from Gordon Merrick's books. Do they live happily ever after? Is our story going to turn out like theirs?"

"Oh, Aaron. We've got our whole lives ahead of us. We'll write our own story."

To be continued...

FROM LIGHTNING TO LOVE

EVERNIGHT PUBLISHING ®

www.evernightpublishing.com